I0723159

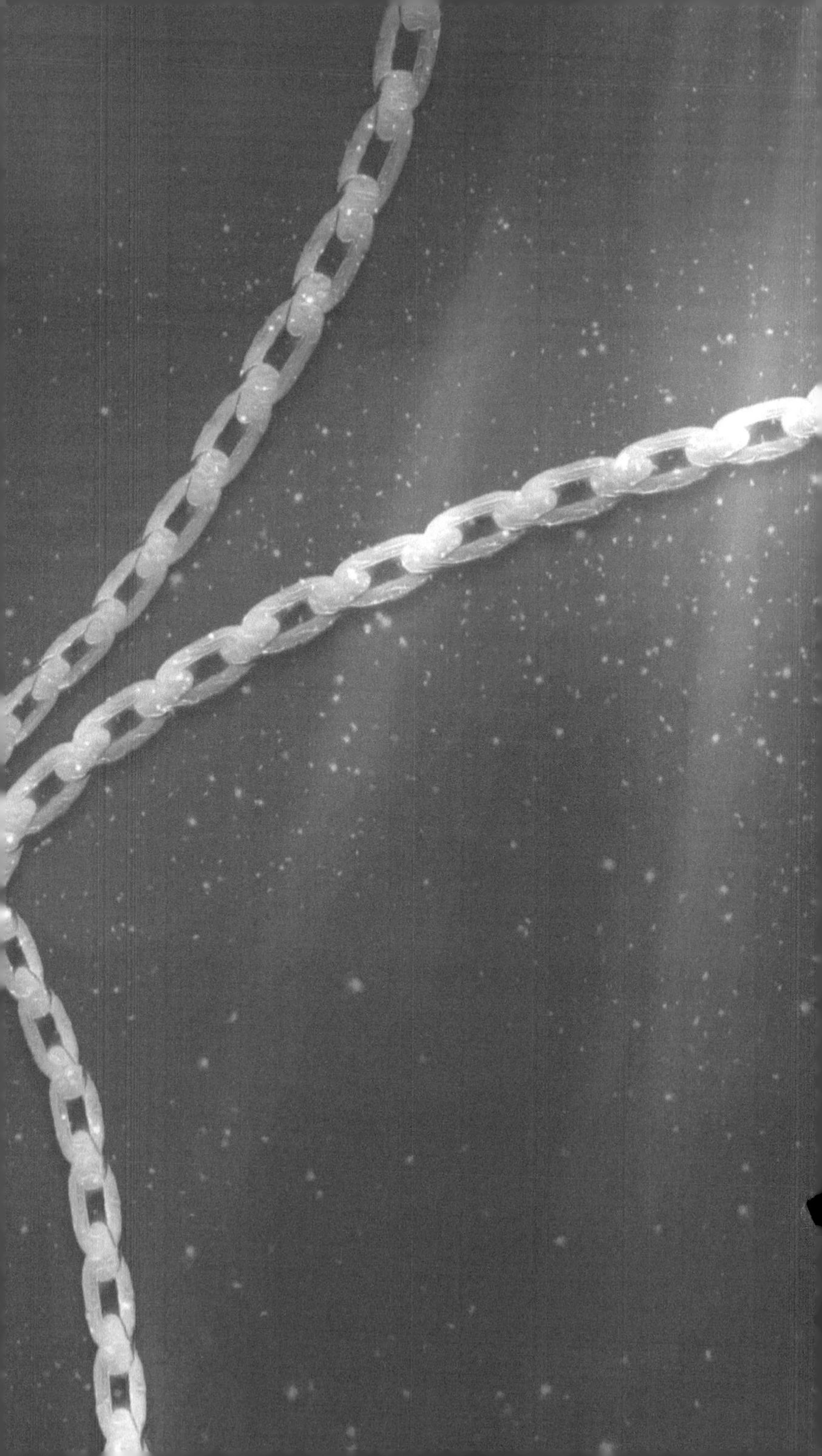

CORRUPTED

SPARROW AND THE MAFIA KINGS

BOOK 3

MAGGIE ALABASTER

TRIGGER WARNINGS

Blood play
   Torture
   Mentions of rape
   Mentions of child death

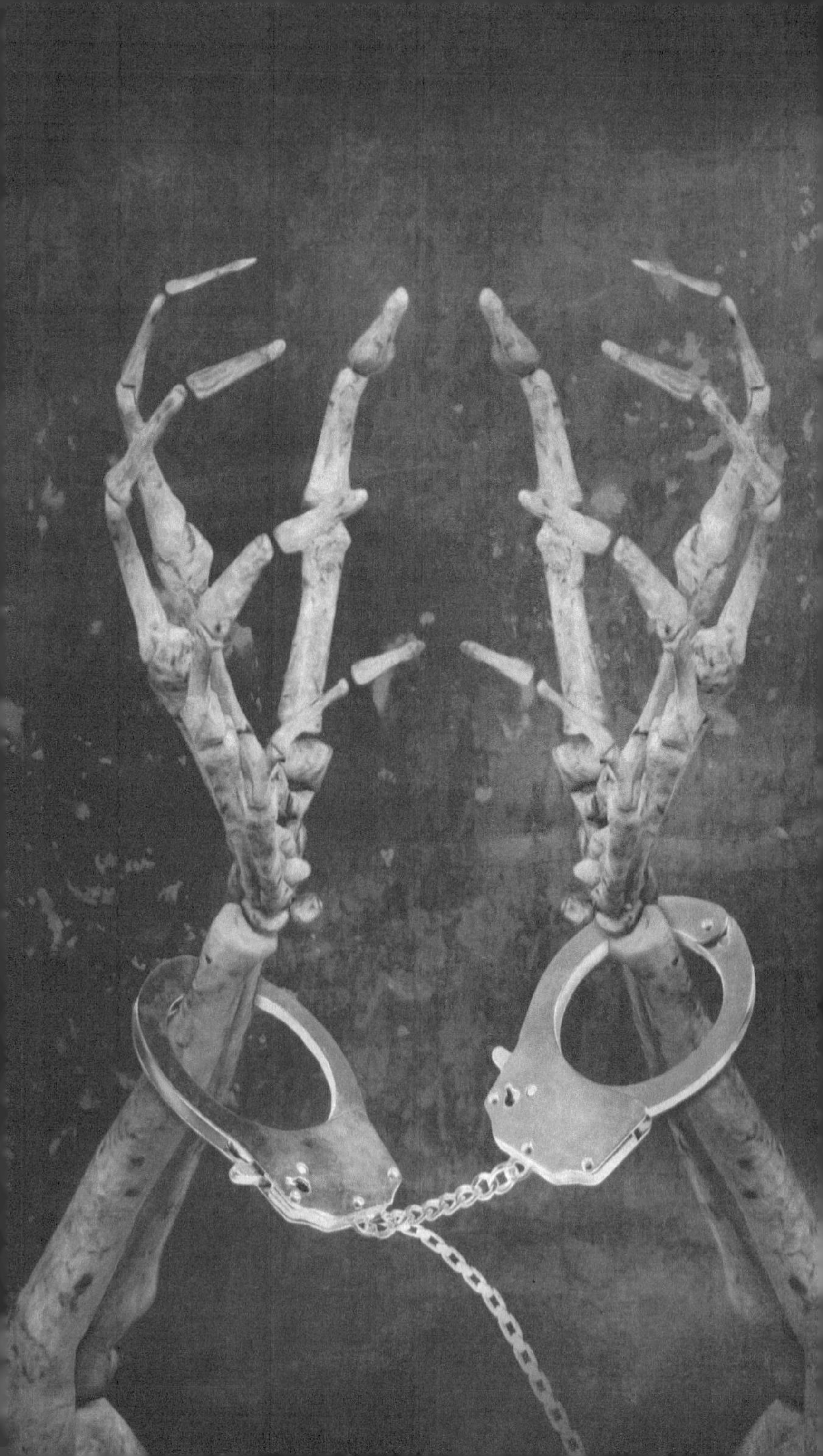

CHAPTER 1

MINA

The door that led down to the basement of the house in Dusk Bay swung open.

I snapped my attention from the view and looked over the back of the couch.

Typically, Gianni's expression was jovial, while Damon's was guarded. The two of them were like night and day. An open book and a closed one.

I adored them both.

"Did you learn anything?" Reuben asked before I could. He was seated at the head of the large dining table, laptop in front of him. He looked every part the successful businessman he was. As well as being a successful mob boss.

"You could say that." Damon leaned against the door frame, crossed his arms and closed his eyes. He looked weary. We all were. The hunt for Kurt Lasalle was taking a toll on all of us.

"Bitch ass prick sung like a bird," Gianni said. He flopped down beside me and put an arm around me. With only a moment of hesitation, he leaned over and kissed my mouth.

I was getting better at not flinching when anyone went to touch me. I'd even let Damon fuck me while the other two watched.

I was still getting my head around that. It was wonderful, special. Especially given I wasn't sure I'd ever be comfortably intimate with anyone. It was gratifying to know I wasn't as broken as I'd thought I was. Healing.

"What did he say?" I leaned against Gianni, inhaling his warm scent, drawing comfort from his closeness.

"He said that Kurt prick-of-the-year Lasalle is right here in Dusk Bay. Apparently," he drawled the word, "he's been here all along." Gianni gestured behind him, roughly in the direction of the city.

My heart skipped several beats. "He's right here?"

What the absolute, ever loving fuck?

"According to Leon Graves, he left Sydney after we found you in the cage and came here." Damon's tone was dark, laced with both thought and irritation. "He's been laying low ever since. He was waiting for his people to grab Mina and take her to him."

He opened his eyes and settled his gaze on me. Even for someone as guarded as he was, rage burned just below the surface. Fury at the idea of Kurt, or anyone else, touching me.

"Of course he is," I said absently, the possibilities tumbling around in my brain.

"No," Reuben said as though reading my mind. "There's no way in the world we would have let him take you, even if it meant leading us to him." He turned to Damon. "Did he say exactly where Kurt is?"

It was Gianni who answered.

"He passed out right before he got to that. Something about a knife in his calf being painful or something." He grinned and shrugged.

"He says he doesn't know," Damon supplied. "He was 'following orders'. Going where he was told to be."

Gianni made a sound of disbelief. "That's what they all say. I'll give him a few minutes, then try again. Otherwise we'll be searching for a needle in a haystack."

"It's a much smaller haystack than the one we had," Reuben observed. His gaze slid to me. "I don't suppose he ever said anything about having a house here?"

"He wasn't particularly forthcoming about his life," I said dryly. He was too busy taunting me, torturing me and forcing himself on me. Conversation wasn't part of the equation most of the time. Not unless he was telling me lies, like my siblings were all dead.

"I know we don't want to consider the possibility…" Damon said slowly.

"We have to," Reuben said. "If there's any chance Daisy Lasalle knew her brother was here in Dusk Bay, we have no choice but to find out."

I shook my head. "If she knew he was here, she would have dealt with him, or at least told us."

I trusted her almost as much as I trusted anyone not already in this room. She was as angry about what her brother did to me as my men were.

Unless she was an incredible actor.

"While it's even a possibility, we need to consider it," Reuben said. "Gianni, persist with Graves. Damon, tell the twins to go and collect Daze. Have them bring her here for a talk. Mina, you will *not* go off by yourself again. What we do, we do together."

His expression was firm. Set in granite. He'd take no arguments from any of us, not even from me.

"I was trying to protect you." I raised my chin, just as stony, even though I had no intention of going off alone. Not right now anyway.

"I was hoping it was Kurt who was going to turn up at Clarissa's. If it was him and only him, we'd be having a very different conversation." And Kurt would be dead.

"It wasn't." Reuben's expression was unchanged. "It was an ambush, designed to trap you. If it wasn't for Gianni following you, and Damon working out where you both went, we *would* be having a very different conversation. The three of us would be trying to figure out how to get you back."

"Which we totally would," Gianni said.

"Only if she was still alive." Reuben's expression

softened. "I can't tie you down or lock you up, but I can insist you don't risk yourself like that again."

The love in his tone was obvious, even if he didn't say the words. He didn't need to. We both knew the way we felt about each other.

"You're right," I said reluctantly. "I'm so used to being alone. Before that, I was doing things by myself and *for* myself. For a long time, I was the only one I could rely on. The only one that was keeping me sane." Or close to it.

"You can rely on us, sweetheart," Gianni said softly. "We can be clowns sometimes, but we love you. We'd do anything to protect and help you. That's what relationships are for. We take care of each other."

"What Gianni said," Damon grunted. "Except the part about being clowns. He can keep that description to himself."

Gianni flashed him a grin. "You know it fits. We just express it differently."

Reuben smirked. "Speak for yourself."

I flinched slightly at the sound of the door that led to the garage opening. It was all the way down the back of the house, but it got me every time. Someday, I'd grow used to it.

I hoped.

My shoulders relaxed when the twins stepped through the door. Both looked exhausted, but cheerful. Nothing seemed to hold either of them down for long. I envied them that.

"Cleanup is done," Hunter reported.

"Speaking of clowns," Damon said under his breath.

"We didn't see any of those," Parker said. "Thank fuck, because I hate clowns." He gave a full body shudder.

Damon snorted. "You're just in time, Reuben has a job for you."

They both groaned when he told them what it was.

"I was hoping for a nap," Hunter said. He exhaled, loud and dramatic. "Just for Mina, we'll do this one thing first. But we expect overtime for it." He clapped his twin on the shoulder and they turned to head back to the garage.

"They usually complain more," Reuben said. He arched an eyebrow at me. "This was exactly what I was saying. We look after each other. Including those two."

I raised my hands in surrender. "I promise I won't go off by myself again, unless I have to."

He arched the other brow.

"I can't promise more than that," I said. "I don't know what might happen in the future. I might have to work alone to save your ass. Or Gianni's, or Damon's. Or even the twins'. But I'll only do it if it's absolutely necessary."

Honestly, part of me was tired of working alone. Not in my job as an assassin, but when it came to the hunt for Kurt. This whole situation was easier, more tolerable, with them to support me.

"We'll make sure any circumstances that would force

you to work alone, don't happen." Reuben was nothing if not stubborn. He very much liked things done his way. Or else.

"Yes, we will," Gianni agreed. "We're a team and you know what they say about teams."

"You're not going to say 'teamwork makes the dream work,' are you?" Damon groaned.

Gianni chuckled. "I wasn't going to, but it's not wrong." He snuggled in closer to me.

Silence fell for a few moments, broken by Damon's frustrated sigh. "Fine, what were you going to say?"

"I don't know," Gianni admitted. "I was going to say something off-the-cuff. Like, teams get shit done."

"I should have known better than to ask," Damon said. He scrubbed his face.

"You really should," Gianni agreed. "I think we've left our guest alone for long enough already. I should go and check on him, see if he's enjoying my music."

"I'll come with you," I said. "I want to see what this asshole has to say for himself."

I didn't need Reuben's permission, but I glanced over at him anyway.

"Keep me informed," was all he said.

He stayed out of the torturing of people as much as he could. Especially, from what I could gather, if Gianni had his music playing down in the basement.

Reuben was a badass in his own right, but he didn't deal well with loud noises like music and screaming. He was a complicated man, but I loved that about him.

"Will do, boss," Gianni said.

"Gianni can keep you informed too," Reuben said before I stood. "You don't have to face Graves if you don't want to."

"I want to," I insisted. "Ever since I heard him speak, bits and pieces of the past keep coming back to me. He mentioned Jase and Hammer. I can almost picture their faces. If Leon Graves knows where they are, I want him to tell me." I wanted to find Kurt more than I wanted to find them, but they were still a priority. Which reminded me.

"Do either of you know someone named Prior?"

"It rings a bell." Gianni cocked his head at me. "Why's that, sweetheart?"

"Leon mentioned someone by that name," I said, playing the scene back in my head. "Apparently he tried to stop Kurt from caging and hurting me. He said... Prior told Kurt he was fucked up. Kurt shot Prior for it. It was one of the reasons Leon did nothing to stop Kurt from doing what he did. He figured Kurt would shoot him too."

Which was no excuse, but he was paying for that decision now.

All three men frowned in thought.

"I'll look him up," Damon said. "If he's someone who used to work for us, there should be a record. We tend to keep those for a long time. Bear in mind though, we may never be able to find him to give him a decent burial."

Trust him to understand why I wanted to know what happened to the one person who stuck their neck out for me. He deserved better than a shallow grave, or to have been tossed in the harbour for the sharks to eat. Or incinerated, which was more likely.

I nodded. "I appreciate that." We could at least try.

"If we can't find him, we can do a nice memorial in the garden," Gianni said.

"I'll go and see to it, and a few other things," Damon said. He pushed himself off the door frame and disappeared in the direction of the stairs that led to the upper level.

"I don't know about you, but I'm ready to have some more fun with our friend." Gianni offered me his hand.

I took it and rose. "He's no friend of mine." Gianni's hand was warm in mine, large and reassuring. He got off on the fact I was an assassin and enjoyed killing, but he could be surprisingly gentle when he wanted to.

"To be completely fair, people like him rarely have friends," Gianni said. "So, he's not mine either. That's what makes it funny. It's ironic."

"It certainly is that," Reuben said. "I don't think anyone will miss him when you're finished with him." He rubbed a hand over his eyes and turned his attention back to his laptop screen.

"I will," Gianni said. "He's been a ton of fun already." He smiled happily and we walked to the door that led down to the basement.

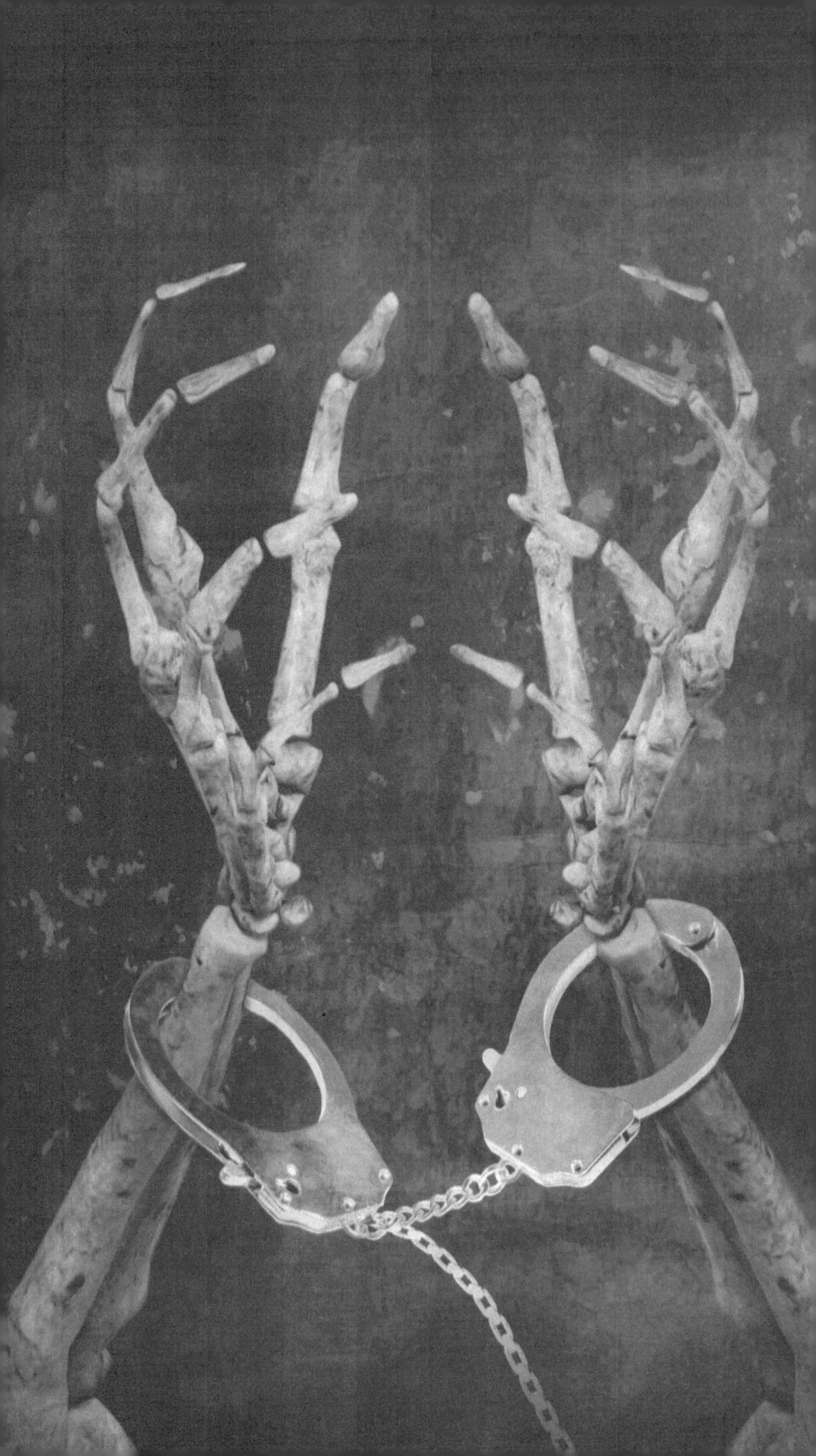

CHAPTER 2

MINA

The volume of the music made me wince the moment I stepped through the door at the bottom of the stairs. The room below was soundproofed, so until now, I hadn't heard a hint of the pounding drums or ear-splitting vocals.

Gianni grooved to the sound for a few moments before pulling out his phone and tapping the screen. The music stopped immediately.

The ringing in my ears would last longer.

Leon Graves was chained to the ceiling, his arms above his head. He lolled to one side, the chain holding up all of his weight.

"Thank fuck," he groaned. He raised his face to look up at us. His eyes were bloodshot, the exhaustion obvious. Apart from the knife sticking out of his calf, he seemed physically unhurt.

I wrinkled my nose at the smell. He knelt in what

looked like a combination of piss and vomit, mixed in with a bit of blood. Not enough blood, if you asked me.

"People often say that when they see me," Gianni remarked. "It must be my charm."

Leon snorted. Apparently some of his sense of humour was still intact.

"I think he misses your music," I said. "Don't worry, Leon, he'll turn it back on when we leave."

He looked at me like he was considering begging me to kill him so he didn't have to listen to it anymore. Noise that loud would grate on anyone's nerves after a while.

Which, of course, was the point. This wasn't a pleasure dungeon. Well, not for him.

Pleasure came in a variety forms, including seeing someone who had a hand in your personal hell chained to the ceiling.

Leon managed a venomous look before dropping his head back to the side. "I told you everything I know. Kurt is somewhere here in Dusk Bay. If I had more to give you, I would. Anything to get out of here."

I stepped closer to him. "You know you're not getting out of here alive, right?"

"Don't care," he groaned. "Get it over with." He raised his face until his stubbled throat was exposed, begging to be sliced open.

"Tempting," I admitted. "But too easy. Do you think Kurt would have killed me if I begged him to?" I had, but never when he was around. I'd managed to cling on to that much dignity.

"Kurt is an asshole," Leon said. "You can be better than him."

Gianni crouched beside him, gripped the hilt of the knife and twisted it until Leon screamed.

"We *are* better than him, *dickhead*," Gianni snarled. "We don't plan to keep you down here for five years. Not that you'd last." He twisted the knife again. "You'll die of cowardice long before that."

Tears poured down Leon's cheeks. "I will, but you could make it quicker. Please, for fuck's sake."

Gianni pulled the blade from Leon's leg and stood. "You haven't even been here for five hours yet and you're already begging to die. That must be a record. Most people last at least…" He held out his other hand, palm up. "Six or seven hours. The best last two or three days."

"He's far from the best," I said. "But maybe we can make this easier on him."

Leon looked up, suddenly hopeful. "Please…"

"You mentioned Jase and Hammer," I said slowly. "Where are they?"

His hope faded. "I don't know. I haven't seen Jase since that night. He might be dead. Hammer, I don't even know his real name. He could be anywhere. He might be dead too."

"You know where to find them," I said. "You have contacts. Tell us who we can ask."

"You're so hot when you're assertive like that," Gianni told me.

I glanced over at him and smiled before returning my attention back to Leon. "It's that simple."

"There's a woman named Martina," Leon confessed. "She deals in information like that. I can give you her number. You have my phone, it's in there." He nodded, then winced as though his head hurt. It probably did. Gianni's music would have given him a killer headache.

"We'll track her down," Gianni said. "With any luck, she'll tell us where they are. Hopefully they're still alive so we can kill them."

"If anyone will know, it's her," Leon agreed. He looked from me to Gianni and back again.

"When we have them, we'll deal with you," I said.

"But... But," he stammered, "I told you what you wanted to know."

"You gave us something for a start," I agreed. "But that's all it is, a start. For all we know, you might be lying through your teeth."

He wasn't. He was desperate enough to say anything, to get us to kill him or let him go. I suspected he was still clinging to some shred of hope we'd remove him from the chain and kick him out the door. Or better yet, help him disappear before Kurt caught up with him. I had to give him some credit for clinging to hope while there wasn't much of it to cling to. The moment he helped Kurt chain me up, he signed his own death warrant.

"I swear," he groaned, "if I knew anything else, I'd tell you." He swallowed hard. "Martina might be able to tell you where Kurt is. Or Clarissa. She works with him too, you know."

"Nice attempt to throw her under the bus," Gianni said. "You know she drugged you, right? She's the reason you're here."

His eyes flashed with anger, although he must have known what she'd done. One minute he was having a conversation with me, the next he was tumbling to the floor. Any bruises on the back of his head were from her dragging him down a set of stairs.

She was definitely not on his side.

"That won't go unpunished," he said.

Gianni laughed. "By you? Good luck with that, asshole. In case you forgot, you're chained up in here, kneeling in a puddle of your own vomit, and she's out there, living her best life." He jerked his thumb towards the door. "And she's going to go on living, because she works for us, not the prick who pulls your strings. That was your first mistake, Leon. You chose the wrong fucking side. What did you think working for Kurt would get you, anyway? It was only a matter of time before we figured out what he was up to and put a stop to it. And put a stop to *him* and anyone who works for him."

"I can give you details of his business dealings," Leon said, his voice strained. "They go way back before…" He glanced at me, obviously unsure as to how to word what happened to me. It was best he didn't articulate that. I didn't need a reminder and neither did Gianni.

"He was screwing Reuben over even before then?" Gianni asked. His apparent interest seemed to have given Leon an extra spike of hope.

"He was trying to screw the Brantley family over, yes," Leon said. "Indirectly." He exhaled painfully. "He stumbled upon a plan of old man DiMarco's. He was going to dispose of Reuben's father and take over his empire and assets. Kurt was going to go to Brantley and tell him everything. DiMarco begged him not to. He knew if he did, he'd be worse than dead."

My blood went cold. "So to stop Kurt from going to Reuben's father, he gave me to him. To keep him quiet." I glanced at Gianni. "That was the debt. Kurt was bribing my father. He gave me to him to save his own ass."

Gianni's lips pressed together in sympathy and anger. "That's fucked up."

That was one way to describe it. I was nothing but a pawn in my father's game. A game he ultimately lost after killing Reuben's parents. Reuben, in turn, had him and my mother killed. An act I didn't blame him for. Especially now.

"Shit," Gianni said. "So Kurt's business interests and influence go further than we thought. Who knows how much of DiMarco's he gained."

"A lot of it," Leon said. "DiMarco built an empire

almost big enough to rival Brantley's. He'd spend years building up all of that, ready to make his move. When Kurt found out, he panicked and brought his plans forward. Then everything went to hell. And Kurt stood back and reaped the benefits."

"He's an opportunistic prick," Gianni said. "But this explains a lot. Why it's been so hard to find him, and how he has the funds to finance everything he's been doing. And why Leon here is shit scared of him."

"His reach is further than you might think," Leon said. "Not as much as the Brantley family, but significant. He's arrogant and thinks he's smarter and better than everyone else. Between you and me, I don't think he's all there."

"Some of the best people aren't all there," Gianni said. "But he's not one of the best people."

"He's the worst," I said. My brain was still turning over with what Leon said. Why my father drugged me and handed me to the devil.

I'd always thought he was brave and strong, if somewhat harsh, ambitious and distant. Now I knew he was a coward. As big a wimp as Leon. He had to be, to hand over his eighteen-year-old daughter to save his own neck. He'd preferred that, than owning up to what he was doing, and wearing the punishment for the betrayal.

Better yet, he could have been loyal to the people he worked for. He got everything he deserved, and more, for the things he'd done. I hope he suffered when he died, knowing what I was going through.

He was a monster like Kurt.

"One of the worst," I amended. "Reuben doesn't know any of this?"

"If he does, he never shared it with me," Gianni said. "All I know is that your father killed his parents and he acted in retribution. He may have his suspicions as to what went down, but no one was alive to confirm it. At least, not that we knew of."

"That explains why Reuben doesn't trust Dane," I said. I had my own reasons for not trusting my brother too much, but our father's betrayal would have reflected on him. The son of a betrayer might prove to be one himself.

"Dane is a snake," Gianni said. "That's why Reuben doesn't trust him. He trusts Rose and tolerates Asher. And he loves you. He doesn't hold your blood against you."

For that, I was grateful. When he found me in the basement, I thought he'd kill me. After what Kurt said about the relationship between our families having soured, I expected nothing less. At the time, I didn't care. I wanted to die.

Now, all I wanted to do was live.

"We should tell him all of this," I said.

"So, I've been helpful?" Leon looked hopeful once more. "I don't know what more there is to tell you."

"You'll think of something," Gianni said. He pulled out his phone and smiled.

"No, please, I swear I'll—" Leon's pleas were drowned out by the sound of the music flooding the room again.

"Enjoy!" Gianni shouted. He took my hand and we stepped out of the room before the sound became over-whelming.

I sighed in relief as the door closed behind us, blocking off the noise.

"You're not feeling sorry for him?" Gianni asked.

I snorted. "Fuck no. I'm just glad it's not me."

"Would you prefer to kill him?" Gianni waved back toward the door.

"I think I'll savour the idea for a few days," I said. "I've waited this long to feel his blood on my hands. I can wait a little while longer."

He groaned. "Fuck, that's hot. Probably for the best too. I suspect he'll remember some more important information if he tries hard enough."

"Can I ask you something?" I asked, suddenly shy. "You mentioned you like… Knives?"

———

Gianni's hand in mine, we slipped upstairs to the room designated as mine. I hadn't actually slept in it, but my things were here, rather than cluttering Reuben's space.

"So, knives, you say?" Gianni stepped inside and let

me close the door behind us. He was letting me take the lead in this, every step of the way.

"I do say." I stopped short of engaging the lock. Closed doors were one thing, as was locking the world out of the house. Being inside a locked room was another. Even if it was locked from the inside.

"I don't want to—" I stopped a metre or so from the door, uncertainty seeping in.

"Whatever you want to do, sweetheart. I'm here for it. If you've changed your mind, and just want to talk, that's okay. Or if you'd prefer me to leave?" He stepped toward the door, but I put out a hand to stop him.

"No, don't leave. Please. I want…this. Us. You." So eloquent, but it was all I could manage right now.

I crouched down in front of my suitcase and pulled out a jumper. The black garment was wrapped around one of my favourite knives. The one I'd used the most often to kill.

If blades absorbed blood, it would have been soaked.

"She's beautiful." Gianni crouched beside me and looked admiringly at the cold steel. "Beautiful and deadly, just like you." He leaned over and kissed me.

I kissed him back before finding myself placing a hand on his chest and pushing him back onto the cool, hardwood floor. I straddled him and pressed the knife to his throat.

His eyes widened, but he smiled. "Hello there."

I smiled back. I could have taken his life then and

there, but he knew I wouldn't. He trusted me completely to hold a sharp blade to his throat and not drive it into his vein, or slice him open.

Would I trust anyone else to do the same? Didn't know, but this was both gratifying and arousing.

With my spare hand, I pushed up his t-shirt, only lifting the knife to push the fabric up over his head.

His upper body bare, I was free to run the tip of the knife over his rock hard skin. Light, so I didn't break it, not yet.

He half closed his eyes and smiled. "Fuck, that feels good."

I licked my lips and undid the button of his jeans before sliding down the zipper. I pushed them down far enough for his erection to spring free. He was already hard and ready.

I glanced at his face before carefully sliding the side of the knife down his length and back up again.

"Holy shit." He swallowed audibly. "Sweetheart, that is…" His hips rolled, equally careful, obviously mindful of the damage I could do to him right now.

I replaced the knife with my tongue, licking him from tip to balls and back again.

He quivered. "Mina…"

I set the knife aside and pulled my singlet off over my head and onto the floor. He gripped the waistband of my leggings and tugged. I half stood to pull them off, before lowering myself back onto him, dressed only in a bra and panties.

I picked the knife back up, and once again brought it to his throat. While I pressed lightly, he snuck a hand between us, over the gusset of my panties.

It was my turn to quiver.

Taking that as his cue, he tugged my panties aside and rubbed the pad of his thumb over my clit.

I swallowed down a ball of nerves and positioned my pussy over his cock. Blade poised in one hand, I slowly lowered myself onto him.

Until now, I was acting on instinct, and having read a lot of smutty romance books. I'd never imagined doing this myself, much less taking the lead. But the knife in my grip gave me confidence like nothing else could. It made me feel both safe and powerful.

Nothing and no one could touch me, unless I chose to let them.

"Don't be scared to draw blood," he said, rubbing more firmly on my clit.

My tongue slid over my lips. I nodded. I pressed down until a bead of blood formed on his throat. The sight was almost enough to make me come on the spot.

"Mmm, yeah," he groaned. He thrust up slowly, taking his time to enjoy every moment.

I moved to a different spot, a centimetre from the first, and pressed down until blood sprang from the small incision. It trickled over the tattoo on the side of his neck, and onto the floor.

Once, twice more, I cut into him, always gentle,

always shallow, my desire rising with every stroke of his thumb.

"I'm going to come," he said, sounding pained with the effort from holding back. "Come for me first."

With one last incision, I came, bucking slowly, holding my hand steady so the blade only went exactly as deep as I wanted it to.

He came a few moments later, eyes shut, expression one of total bliss as he spilled himself inside me. Cum flooding warm and wet like the blood that dripped onto the hardwood.

I sagged down over him and pulled the knife away. I breathed in heavily, inhaling the scent of sweat, blood and him. The most heady combination I ever remembered smelling in my life.

"See, I like knives," he said finally.

I laughed, deep and husky in the back of my throat. "So do I."

He chuckled. "I thought you might. That's why we fit so well together. We both like blood, death and sharp objects."

"Three of my favourite things," I said.

He wrapped his arms around me. "Mine too. After you. You're on top of me and my top four."

I rested my head against his chest and exhaled softly. Content to lie there for a while and be alive.

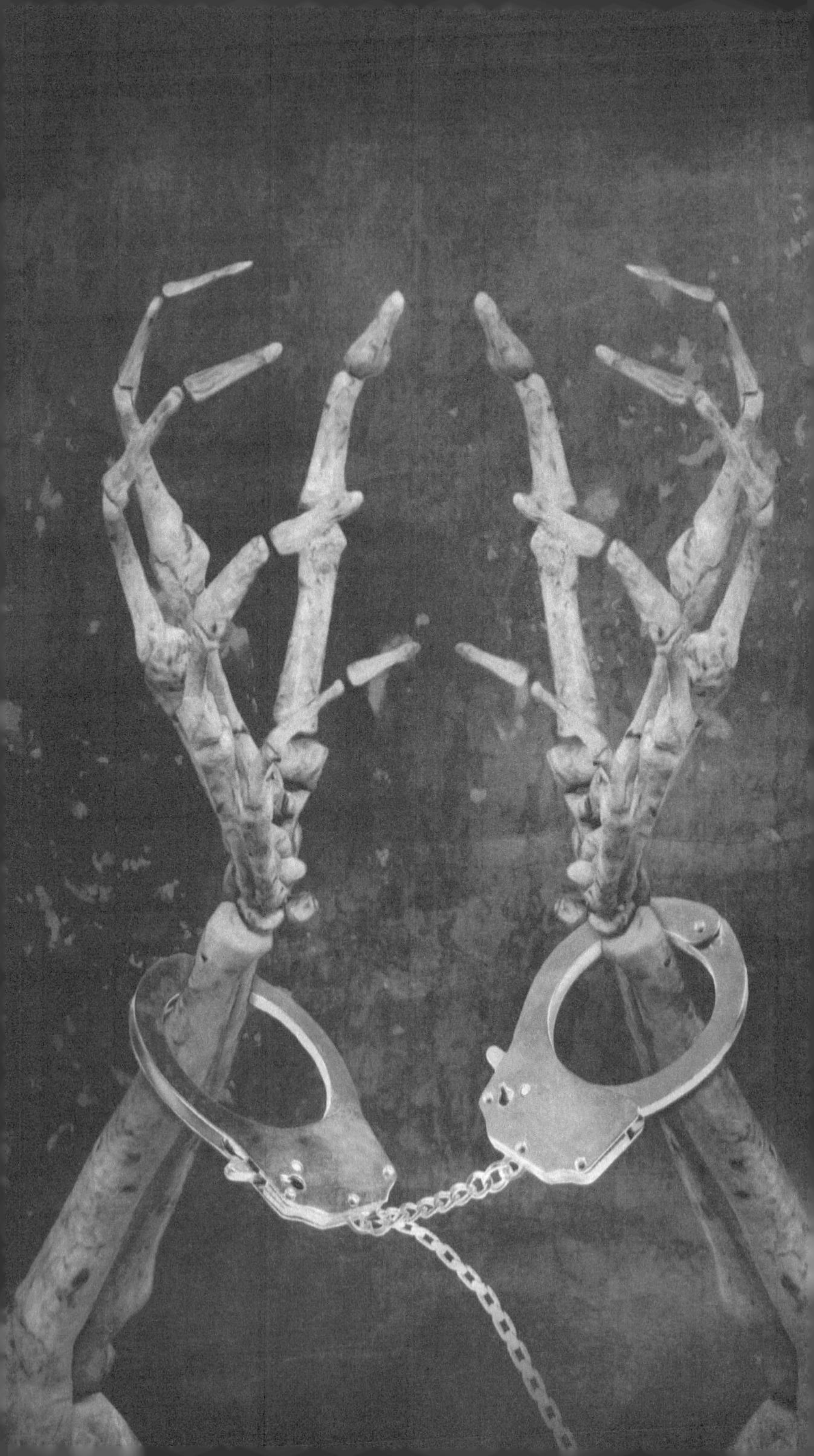

CHAPTER 3

MINA

Reuben sat behind his desk, hands in front of him, fingers laced together. To anyone who didn't know him, he'd appear calm and composed.

To those who did, he was filled with barely contained rage. His knuckles turned white. The vein in his forehead throbbed. He didn't say a word while Gianni and I told him what Leon said.

Everyone else in the room was equally silent, apart from the occasional mutter from the twins and gasps of surprise from Daze.

Damon and Caleb both sat in chairs, each as stony-faced as the other.

"That's horrendous," Daze said when we finished. She leaned against Ric, who insisted on coming with her, and closed her eyes. "If my father tried anything like that with me…" She shook her head.

Ric wrapped his arms around her and held her as if he could protect her from what she just heard. "This explains a lot. Including why we didn't know any of this. He had the funds to keep us from finding out." He glanced at me apologetically. Just because it made sense didn't make it right.

"He shouldn't have," Caleb snapped. "This shouldn't have gotten past our father. It shouldn't have gotten past *us*."

He looked at Reuben with an expression laced with accusation, but also with a touch of annoyance and fear. If anyone should have known what was going on after their father died, it was Caleb. If their father hadn't told Reuben anything, that was unfortunate. Caleb had five years to figure it out. He wasn't alone in that, but he clearly took it on his own shoulders. Or at least suspected he'd be blamed.

"It shouldn't, but it did," Reuben said simply. "Now we know. We can take steps to ensure it doesn't happen again. That isn't the most pressing concern at the moment." His gaze went to Daze and Ric.

"You didn't bring us here to fill us in on that, did you?" Daze asked. She glanced over to the twins who clearly hadn't given her or Ric a choice. That made her visibly nervous as hell.

"According to Leon Graves, Kurt is in Dusk Bay," Reuben said. "Do you know of his whereabouts?" He wasn't pulling any punches today.

Daze stared at him, then at me. "Of course not. You can't really think I'd… *We'd* keep that from you?"

"We don't want to think that," I said. I hated this. We were supposed to be on the same side, not accusing each other. I wanted to believe her and my cousin. I needed to, if only for my own sanity.

"Then don't," Daze replied. "We don't."

"But your concerns aren't with us," Ric said slowly. "You think someone who works for us might have some idea."

"Has anyone been behaving particularly twitchy lately?" Gianni asked.

"Apart from Caleb?" Hunter said. "But then, he's always twitchy."

Caleb gave him a dark look.

"Not that I can think of," Ric said. "That is to say, everyone's been on edge since we started digging into what Kurt was up to. We all feel responsible for everything. Me, Daze, Gunnar and Hilton, in particular."

Daze nodded her agreement. "We haven't been able to tell our people much, just that we're looking for him. Our concern might be somewhat contagious."

"Keep an eye out," Damon told her. "Someone knows something."

"Do you know anyone named Jase or Hammer?" I asked.

Ric looked contemplative, but ultimately shook his head. "I can't say either name rings a bell. That doesn't mean we don't know them."

"Did they..." Daze started carefully.

"They were there," I said simply. I didn't need or want to explain any further. Nor did I feel the need to explain that we got Martina's number from Leon's phone. We'd deal with her on our own.

Silence hung heavy in the air, finally broken by Caleb clearing his throat.

"From what I've been able to ascertain, Kurt either hasn't noticed, or doesn't care, that the account balance of most of his accounts is approximately sixty-nine cents each."

Parker grinned at having done that, transferring the money into different accounts Kurt couldn't access.

"Yes!" Gianni pumped the air. "Maserati, here I come."

"Can I have one too?" Hunter asked. "Parker and I would look good in matching Maseratis."

"If you can afford to buy them out of your own pocket," Reuben said.

All three of them sagged with playful disappointment.

"Spoilsport," Parker muttered.

Caleb cleared his throat again, clearly becoming impatient. "There's the matter of the information Kurt has, that he might decide to sell." He carefully avoided looking at me.

Everyone else did instead, including Ric, who looked confused.

I sighed. "He might as well know too."

"Know what?" Ric asked. He looked around the room, then at Daze.

She shrugged, then looked over to me.

"I'm the Sparrow," I said.

He stared at me in disbelief for a few moments before my words sunk in. "I see." To Daze, he said, "You knew?"

"I guessed," she said. "We're all sworn to secrecy. That includes you now."

"Yes, it does," Reuben said, his tone a thinly veiled threat.

"No one will hear it from me," Ric assured me. "Does—"

"Rose doesn't know," I said. "Neither do Dane or Asher, as far as I know. I'd like to keep it that way. For now."

"Because we need to sell the information," Caleb said. "To keep Kurt from doing the same thing."

"We talked about this," Reuben said.

"And we came to no conclusions," Caleb reminded him. "If I recall, Mina was in favour of this plan."

"As opposed to giving any more power to Kurt," I said. "We also talked about spreading the information that a woman was kept in his basement. Without naming me."

"We're happy to do that," Hunter offered. "Parker and I have many skills. Spreading gossip is one of them. We can make it sound as bad as you want, but keep your name out of it."

Reuben glanced at me before nodding. "Do it. But Caleb is right, we need to address the issue of the Sparrow. We need to take that information out of his hands and stop him from capitalising on it."

"By capitalising on it ourselves," Caleb said.

"Is it really necessary to mention Mina?" Ric asked.

Silence fell again while everyone processed his words.

"How difficult would it be to convince everyone Kurt is the Sparrow?" I asked finally. "We give out that information and he'll have people going after him, right along with us."

Hunter burst out laughing. "That's fucking awesome. Like throwing him in the centre of a shark-feeding frenzy."

"Right where he belongs," Parker agreed.

"Easier if we can find Kurt," Damon said. "Or better yet, have him turn up at a location where the Sparrow is expected. The second part will be easier than the first."

"We need to draw him out," I said. "We need to offer him something he won't be able to resist."

"No," Reuben said. "You're not putting yourself out there as bait. We've had that discussion."

I shook my head. "We already know that won't work. He didn't come for me in person when he used Leon as bait for us. There has to be something else."

"Like what?" Hunter asked.

"I have no idea," I admitted. "What does he care about more than me or his money?"

"Power," Ric said. "The same thing that drives most of us. If we can whittle down his power, he'll have no choice but to show himself. If we tell everyone he's the Sparrow, who...abducted a woman he met while he was working, people will start to turn on him."

"Definitely," I said. "That goes against the assassin code of conduct. But we can go one further. We can tell everyone he murdered an innocent child. They only need to look into it to learn the truth. We give them the place and the dates and they can confirm it."

Her face flashed in my memory, small and perfectly innocent. Another pawn in Kurt's fucked up game, like I was.

"I can provide the logs of my movements that night."

Reuben rolled his lips before he said, "Do it."

"Are you sure, sweetheart?" Gianni rose and came to put his arms around me.

The nicks in his neck had stopped bleeding, but my pulse ratcheted up at the sight of them. Each one of them. I had to push the thoughts aside before my panties ended up drenched again.

"Once the name of the Sparrow is tarnished, it's going to be hard to clear that," Gianni said. "Once people believe it's really Kurt, that's what they're going to keep believing. They're not going to want to hire the Sparrow when the rest of it comes out. You may never work under that name again." His brow creased, dark eyes worried for me, and the implications of the idea.

I appreciated his concern for me and the reputation I'd worked so hard to build. He was always first to think of me, and make sure I was all right, no matter what was happening.

I leaned into him and inhaled his masculine scent. Today he smelled like cinnamon and leather, and satisfaction. Maybe with a tiny hint of blood.

"I'm starting to think that persona is my past," I said. "I can build a new one. If this is the only way we can get him, I'll gladly give it up. It was a part of me, but not all of me. Not my entire identity."

"No, you're Mina fucking DiMarco," Gianni said. "My badass woman."

"Our badass woman," Reuben growled.

Damon grunted his agreement.

"Our badass woman," Gianni corrected himself. He kissed my forehead.

"I'll start to put out hints that we have this information to sell," Caleb said. "I doubt it'll take more than a day or two to get a few bites."

He looked satisfied at this compromise. That was fortunate, because I'd wondered if his intention was to throw me to the wolves. Evidently, he was more interested in the same agenda as the rest of us. Putting an end to Kurt Lasalle.

"I found references to a Gage Prior," Damon said, his blue eyes on me. "Apparently he worked for Reuben's father. As far as I can tell, he was investigating something, but there's no mention of what. If I had to guess, I'd suspect there were suspicions about Kurt and he was trying to uncover what he was doing. He disappeared around the same time as Mina. They never found his body." He looked regretful.

Caleb, on the other hand, looked shaken. "Gage Prior was investigating Kurt?"

"You knew him?" Reuben asked. There was more concern in his tone than I'd ever heard from him when he addressed his younger brother. He appeared genuinely concerned at Caleb's response. Even the twins were staring at Caleb like they might actually be worried about him.

"He… We were…" Caleb swallowed. "Yes, we knew each other. I was aware he disappeared, but never knew why. I always thought…" He looked rocked to his core.

"We only have Leon's word for it that he's dead," I said. "It's possible he's…somewhere else. I was." I briefly explained what Leon said.

Caleb swallowed, his skin slightly green. "That sounds like Gage. He was always trying to be a fucking hero. Like he could save everyone. He never understood some people couldn't be saved." He seemed to be talking about himself.

"Everyone can be saved," I said softly. "They just have to want to be."

He gave me a sharp look, and a curt nod. "I should get to work. The sooner this is dealt with, the better."

I got the feeling the matter had become personal to

him. I also got the impression I'd never get the truth out of Caleb, but at least he had answers about his... Friend.

Although, maybe it gave him more questions than answers. That might be cold comfort.

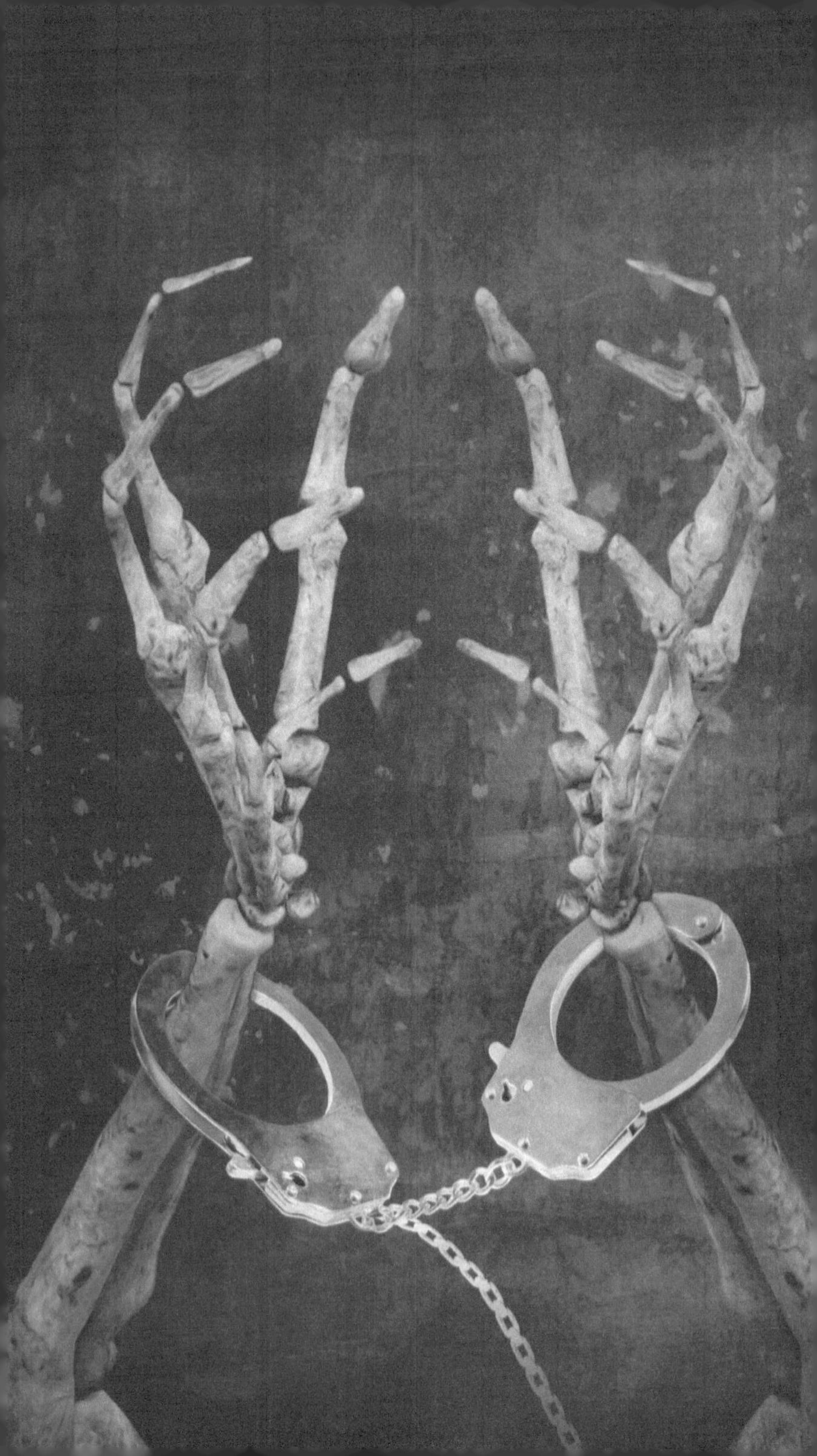

CHAPTER 4

GIANNI

"Are you sure this is the place?" I peered through the front windscreen at the small cottage.

"This is the address my contact gave us," Damon replied. "He's always been reliable before. No reason to think any different now." He didn't look as convinced as he sounded.

"No offence, but we have every reason to think other people might not be reliable right now," I said. "Including your contacts."

I thought about adding, 'especially your contacts,' but didn't. Judging by the expression on his face, he knew what I was thinking. That was enough to get a rise out of him. Or at least a scowl.

I grinned at him. He was adorable when he scowled.

"This is the place," Damon said with more certainty. There was nothing like having his professionalism questioned, to make him double down. "Do you really think I'd bring Mina here if I hadn't sent people ahead to check it out?"

"Of course not," I said. I glanced over to where she sat in the front passenger seat, beside him. She was even more adorable. In a deadly, kick ass kind of way.

The moment I saw her in that cage, I was head over heels for her. Seeing her change from a frightened, malnourished bird, into the confident woman she was becoming, was a delight. She was a bud then. Now she was a flower. The kind that thrived in the face of chaos and death. Not unlike me.

"What do you know about her?" Mina directed the question to Damon.

"Not a lot," Damon admitted. "I guess we're going to find out." He placed his hand on the door handle. "You can stay here if you want to." He knew he had as much chance of her staying behind as night becoming day, but he wouldn't be him if he didn't say the words.

His love language was reminding people they didn't need to throw themselves into the fire. He'd wade in for them.

She rolled her eyes at him, then got out of the car.

I followed right behind her. I wasn't going to let her out of my sight if I could help it. If this went south, I'd put myself between her and any shit that arose.

Yes, I'm fully aware she didn't need me to do that, but it's who I am. I protect the people I love, as much as Damon and Reuben do.

"We could have sent the twins to do this," I remarked. "It is basically their job to be lackeys."

If they were here, they'd give me shit for saying something like that. Lucky for me, they weren't. Although, it was nothing I couldn't handle if they were. The pair were like younger brothers to me. In fact, they were better younger brothers than my actual brothers. Which I'd never tell them, because they'd get huge heads. Given their already healthy egos, they didn't need the boost.

"I want to talk to her in person," Mina said. "If she knows anything, I want to hear it."

"Fair enough, sweetheart." I took her hand and tucked her in to my side, where she fit like we were made to go together. Two pieces in a complicated and sometimes crazy puzzle. "Damon and I understand that, right Damon?"

He pressed his kissable lips together in a line and gave half a shrug, but didn't disagree. He didn't agree either, because he was Damon. He never could, or would make things that easy.

Including our relationship.

I would happily have kissed him again by now, but I was giving him time to process how wonderful the last time was. The electricity that sparked between us was unexpected, in spite of the attraction we'd had bubbling between us for a long time. He'd deny it, but we both knew it was there.

Just like our attraction to Mina was there. And

Damon's attraction to Reuben. I can't deny I admired the man, but Reuben was like a brother to me. He was the one person who saw what I could be, when my family turned their backs on me, and no one else gave a shit. I owed him for that, but Mina and Damon held my heart.

Also, watching Damon fuck Mina, and the idea of him and Reuben together was the stuff of fantasies.

I touched my neck, where she'd drawn blood while riding me, my cock deep inside her. Seeing her surrender to the woman she always wanted to be was indescribable. Incredible.

Mina and I followed Damon up to the front door of the cottage and waited while he tapped.

"I can't help remembering the last time we approached a house like this," I remarked.

Mina gave me a look. "If this one explodes, I'm going to be really pissed off."

"Be pissed off at Damon, he's the one who sent people ahead of us. If we die, it—"

"Won't be my fault," Damon interrupted. "They checked the place out thoroughly. There are no bombs here."

"There are guns though," I said as the cottage door opened and a hand emerged, finger on the trigger, barrel pointed at Damon's temple.

"What do you want?" a female voice came from behind the door.

"Just some information," Damon said as though not

even slightly concerned she might be about to blow his brains out. "We're willing to pay for it."

"Information about what?" The gun didn't move.

"Just the whereabouts of a couple of people," Mina said.

"We have cash," I said.

The gun dropped and the door opened to reveal a woman in her mid thirties, with bright pink hair. "Why didn't you say so? Come in." She stepped back to let us enter the cottage.

Like her, the cottage was brightly coloured, with an array of mismatched furniture, rainbow coloured rugs and cushions everywhere. On one wall hung a huge painting of what looked like a cow skull on a bright blue background. On another wall was a similar one with a purple background.

"She must really have a thing for dead cows," I said in Mina's ear.

She choked back a laugh and gave me a pointed look that suggested she prefer I didn't make fun of our hostess's decor. And that I shouldn't say anything that might end with one of us shot.

Damon gave me a similar look before turning back and saying, "You're Martina?"

"That's what they call me," she agreed. "You're Damon Rivello and Gianni Covino. And…" She looked at Mina.

"Yes we are," Damon said before Mina could introduce herself. "We're looking for people named Jase and

Hammer. They both used to work for a man named Kurt Lasalle."

The moment Damon said his name, Martina looked disgusted. If we were outside, she probably would have spat on the ground.

"If you're friends of Kurt..."

"We're not," I said quickly. Ewww. We had better taste than that.

"Far from it. If you happen to know where he is, we'd appreciate that too. Obviously we'd pay for it."

"Obviously," she agreed. "I have no idea where that son of a motherfucking prick is. If I did, he'd be running for the hills. Backstabbing, two-faced piece of crap he is."

"I see you've met him," I said. "That's a very accurate description."

"I heard some disturbing as fuck rumours about him." She sat down on the middle of a bright orange couch, which happened to be the only place in the room to sit. "Something about keeping a woman chained in a basement?"

I squeezed Mina's hand, but glanced at Damon, deliberately not looking at her. I could tell what he was thinking. Caleb and the twins' gossip had started to spread already. Quicker than I thought it would.

"We heard something to that effect," Damon said. "It seems as though Jase and Hammer had a hand in that too. Which is another reason why we'd like to get our hands on them."

"What's the main reason?" She squinted and looked at us with suspicious, hazel eyes.

"The usual," I said. "Double-crossing the men they're supposed to be working for. And, believe it or not, Jase might have knocked up my sister and run."

Martina again looked like she was going to spit. "Cowardly piece of shit. I hate men like that. Did you know one hundred percent of babies are caused by cum? That only comes from one place. Men need to take responsibility for where they nut." She shook a finger at me and Damon.

I held up my hands to either side. "I would never get a girl pregnant and run." The first bit, yes, not the second. Like she said, every baby was caused by a man ejaculating. I'd always take responsibility for it, if it happened.

"She looks like she knows how to hunt you down." Martina looked over to Mina and nodded approvingly.

Mina smiled. "That I do," she agreed. "But like he said, he wouldn't run." She glanced over to Damon meaningfully.

He sighed. "Neither would I. Can we get back to the reason we're here? I realise it's not much to go on, but if you know anyone by those names, and where they might be, we'd be grateful."

"How grateful?" She held out her hand, palm up.

I pulled out my wallet and peeled out a pile of hundred dollar notes. I handed half of them to her and kept the other half. "Very grateful."

"I'll see what I can find out," she said. "Anyone named Jase is going to be difficult, obviously. But most men don't have the level of insecurity you need to refer to themselves as Hammer."

I grinned at her assumption, which was probably correct. Why would you use a nickname like that unless you were trying to compensate?

"I doubt too many people with that nickname worked with Kurt," Damon said.

"Probably not," Martina agreed. "It sounds like a match made in heaven to me. A pair of gutless men."

"They are also associated with Leon Graves," Mina said.

"Sounds like the Triad of Tiny Dicks to me," Martina said. "Leon is as gutless as a jellyfish. Not as smart though. He does like to throw his cash around, I'll give him that."

"Can I ask what Kurt did to you?" Mina asked. "You seem to hate him as much as we do."

"Before or after I found out about the woman in the basement?" Martina asked. She exhaled loudly. "He's the kind of man who uses people until he doesn't find them useful anymore, then he'll give out our identity to people who shouldn't have it."

She pointed a finger at us again. "I know what you're thinking. A woman with bright pink hair isn't trying to hide. I don't mean that he told people about what I do for a living. I have people in my past I don't want in my present. Or my future. He thought it was wise to swap my whereabouts for money. Or favours, or… Whatever. They came after me and I had to deal with them. Because of him. He thinks he's above the rest of us. The truth is, he has his own agenda and he doesn't give a fuck who he steps on to get there."

"What agenda is that?" I asked.

"Fucked if I know." She shrugged. "He'll do anything to get ahead. Fuck over anyone. Apparently he was fixated on some woman who rejected him. He seemed to lose it after that. If he ever had it."

I looked sideways to Mina, whose gaze seemed to be locked on a spot on the floor.

This couldn't have been easy for her, listening to us talk about him. I wished I could erase every memory of him that resided in her head, to take away all the pain he'd inflicted on her. And, preferably, give it all to him.

"That sounds like Kurt," Damon agreed. "So, you'll get back to us on finding Jase and Hammer?"

"Oh, I already know where, or rather, who Hammer is," she said. She cocked her head at Damon. "And so do you."

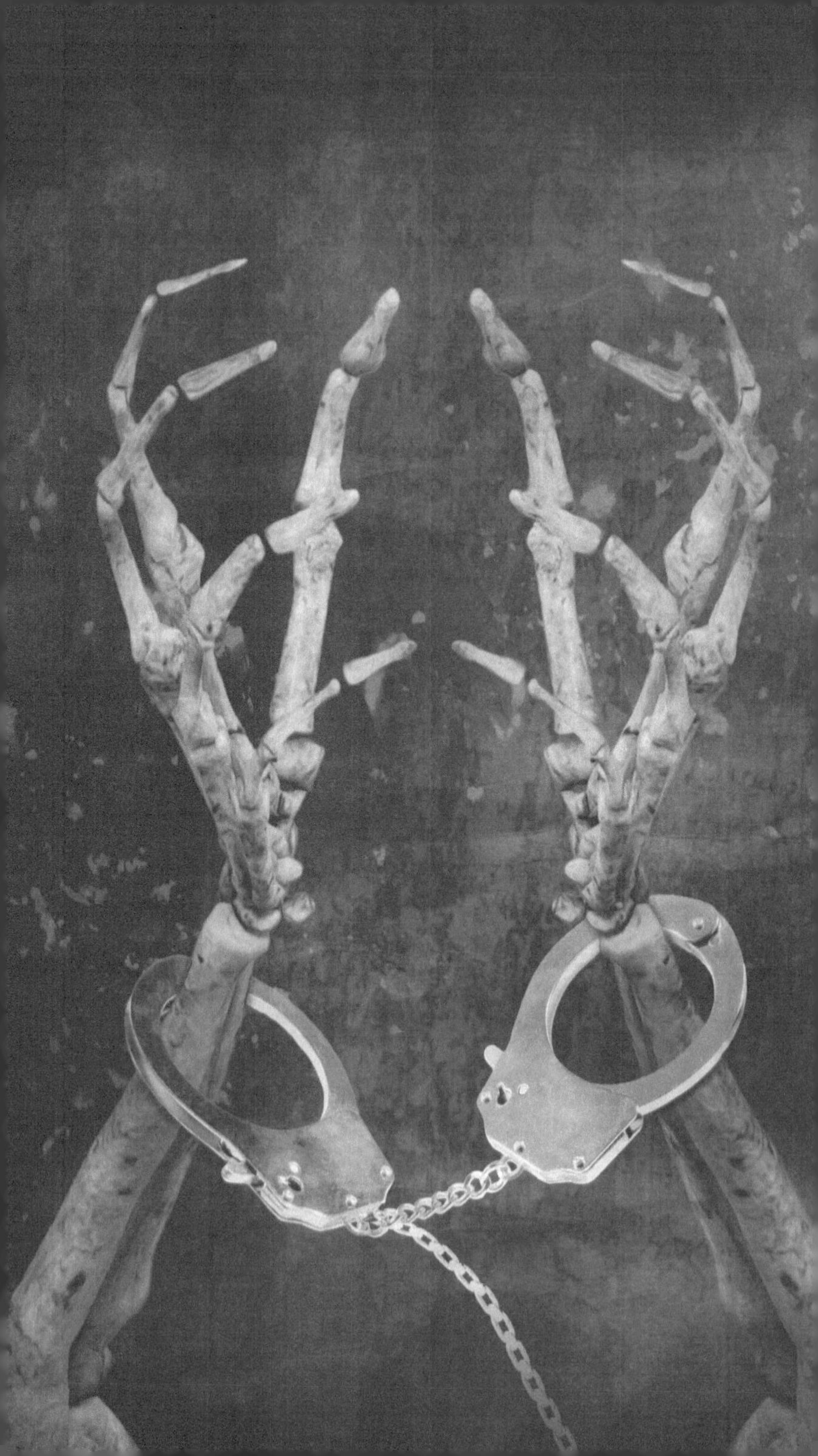

CHAPTER 5

MINA

I stepped out the back door of Reuben's house and headed toward the cliff. The breeze whipped my hair around my face. I pushed it back and turned my face into the wind.

Damon stood at the edge of the cliff, arms crossed, staring out at the ocean. His back was dead straight, eyes glazed like he saw nothing.

"What he did wasn't your fault," I said once I was close enough for him to hear. "You know that, right? You're not responsible for the actions of anyone else."

Damon spoke without turning towards me, his expression unchanged. "He's my brother. I should have been keeping track of him better. Enzo was always a hothead. Always the one getting into trouble. I'm his older brother, I should have…" He trailed off.

"Do you blame my older brothers for not knowing what happened to me?" I asked.

He was determined to take responsibility, but as far as I was concerned, it wasn't his to take. From what I remembered of Hammer, or Enzo, he knew what he was doing.

"Honestly?" Damon said. "Yes I do. Dane in particular. He was the oldest son. He's ambitious. If anyone should have known what your father was up to, he should. And if he didn't know, then he shouldn't have believed what your father said about you running off and getting married. Fuck, Rose should have known. *I* should have known."

I put a hand on his shoulder. "Is that what this is about? If you happened to be keeping track of your brother's whereabouts on one particular day, you might have stopped them from caging me?"

"I could have," he agreed.

"You could have tried," I said. "But it didn't get Gage Prior anything but dead."

I thought back to Caleb's reaction. I wouldn't have thought he was capable of being rattled until then. He must have had a close relationship with the other man.

Damon grunted. "I'm harder to kill. And I wouldn't have been alone."

"You might have gotten Gianni killed too," I said lightly.

"I'll deny ever having said this, but he's harder to kill than I am," Damon said grudgingly.

"Why do I think you know that because you tried?" I teased.

That drew a faint smile from him, which was about as much smile as anyone ever saw on him or Reuben. Gianni seemed to have enough for the three of them.

"I'll deny that too," Damon said before exhaling softly and turning back towards the view. "Enzo was the wild one in the family. He was always getting into trouble. He got suspended from school and thought it was hilarious. More time to run around with his friends and get up to shit. He was back for two days before he got expelled. He lasted a week or two at a new school before they kicked him out too. He was sixteen when Dad threw him out of the house. I let him live with me, but I couldn't control him either. In the end, I gave him two choices. Work for Reuben, or go to jail."

I slipped an arm around his waist. "I guess he chose to work for Reuben?"

"He did, and for a while he was...better. He seemed to enjoy what he was doing. He got paid to break the law, and beat the shit out of people. He always struggled when it came to taking orders, but I tried to be sure he was doing things that fit with his—for want of a better word—skillset."

"It sounds like you did everything you could," I said. "If he was determined to be an asshole, that's on him. That's his choice. There's only so much you can do for people who don't give a shit."

"Yeah, but I should have tried harder. I could have kicked his ass more often. I could have done more to make sure he didn't end up working for Kurt instead."

He dug the tips of his fingers under his opposite armpits.

"Correct me if I'm wrong, but Reuben would only have put up with so much bullshit before he lost patience with Enzo. His father seemed to have even less than he does."

From what I remembered of Reuben's father, he had a short temper and a world class scowl. Reuben was a pussycat in comparison.

"That's right," Damon said grudgingly. "Enzo wouldn't have lasted unless someone got him under control. I should have been able to do that. He's my fucking brother."

"You're right," I said. "It's totally your fault. You should have fit him with a shock collar and an ankle monitor. Then, the moment he put a toe out of line, you would have known. Hell, you should have kept him on a leash. Maybe one of those backpack ones people use with kids who like to run off."

Damon glanced at me, blue eyes narrowed.

"There's nothing you could have done that would have stopped him from doing what he did," I insisted. "He made the choice. He woke up that morning and decided to work with Kurt. He went along with everything he was told to go along with. Him, not you. Just because you're related doesn't mean you have any control over him, or any obligation to blame yourself for his decisions. Even if you did, it's in the past. Nothing that happened back then can be changed now.

The only thing we have any control over is ourselves and the future."

He regarded me, his expression softened. "You're going to want to kill him, aren't you?"

"For his part in that day, yes," I said simply. "Leon could have come to you and told you about me, and so could Enzo. But he didn't. That was another choice he made." I exhaled through my nose. "When was the last time you saw him?"

For a moment, I thought he might not tell me. Damon might have a brotherly need to protect his younger sibling. Even if that came between us.

"A few months ago," he said finally. "At our father's funeral. I didn't think he'd come, because they hated each other, but he turned up and stood at the edge of the crowd. He was only there for a few minutes, then he left. I think he just wanted to make sure Dad was gone."

"Were you close?" I asked gently.

Damon grunt-laughed, the closest to a sound of amusement I'd heard from him.

"No, he was an absolute prick. His idea of raising boys was to belt the shit out of us when he decided we did something wrong. That's also the kind of husband he was. It took years for me to ask Reuben to have him killed. He was dead the next day."

"Sounds like the world is a better place without him," I said.

"Accurate," he replied. "Enzo got his temper. I got his charm."

I leaned my head against his shoulder. "You're an asshole, but you're not as big an asshole as him."

"You sure about that?" He wrapped an arm around me. "Gianni might disagree with that."

"Gianni adores you and, as far as I can tell, he's a good judge of character," I said firmly. "But don't let that go to your head or anything."

"Not a chance," Damon said.

We stood in silence for a while, staring at the ocean as the wind whipped past us.

Finally, reluctantly I asked, "Do you know where he is now? Or his friend Jase? Would either of them know where to find Kurt?"

"I have no idea who Jase is," Damon said. "As for Enzo, I can think of a couple of places he might be. Places I prefer you not go."

"Because I might accidentally kill him?" I asked coolly. There'd be nothing accidental about it, but we both knew that.

"No, because I don't want to take you into the snakes' den. There are far worse people out there than us. If he's where I think he is—The Vipers are a ruthless cartel. They receive drug and weapon shipments from us. Other things too, from time to time." He didn't elaborate on that and I didn't ask.

He continued, brow lightly creased. "They're just as likely to kill you on sight as to welcome you in the door."

"But they won't shoot *you* on sight?" I asked. "Surely they won't shoot anyone in your company?"

Okay, I wasn't that naïve. People like that always had their own reasons for doing the things they did. They may kill me just to remind Damon not to bring anyone next time. Or for a lesser reason.

"I wouldn't take that bet. Their only allegiance is to themselves. They wouldn't kill me because we have an established network. If I was dead, that would inconvenience them. So much so, they'd probably kill whoever killed me. Like I said, they're ruthless."

"They don't sound like anything I can't handle," I said easily. "I'm also not easy to kill, remember?"

"I'm aware," he said softly. "I'll think about it. Reuben will also have an opinion. If he orders me not to take you anywhere near them, then I won't." The set of his jaw said that would be an end to the matter.

I nodded. That was as far as I'd get right now. Arguing the matter wouldn't change it.

Until now, I'd managed to stay clear of most of the known cartels, unless I was doing a job for them. Which was rare. They tended to do their own killing. The only time they needed an assassin was when they wanted to eradicate competition within their own cartel, and wanted to avoid all-out war.

In those circumstances, I had to make the hit look like an accident. That way, those who wanted to could pretend they didn't know anything. If anyone objected, they'd have a hard time proving who was actually behind it.

If I was honest with myself, proving it would be more than difficult. It would be impossible. I was good at what I did. Too good to make a mess with those jobs, or leave evidence. They were always a challenge, but I enjoyed them for exactly that reason. They gave me the chance to push myself to try new things.

"So, how brave are you?" he asked. He unwound his arm from around me, took my hand and stepped closer to the edge of the cliff.

I followed him carefully and peered down into the water below. "Depends. How deep is it?" I couldn't see sand or rocks, just relentless waves that struck the rocks over and over, wearing it down bit by bit.

"Deep enough." He dropped my hand and pulled his shirt off over his head. He tossed it aside on the grass. His shoes and pants followed, until he was down to his boxer briefs.

"You've jumped off here before?" It was a long way down, and if he was wrong about the depth of the water, the landing would suck. Only for a moment, because it would probably kill us.

Caleb hadn't threatened to throw the twins over for nothing.

"Nope," he said easily. "Never."

"You're not just an asshole, you're a crazy asshole," I told him. In spite of that, I stripped down to my underwear and walked right to the edge, until there was nothing under the tips of my toes.

"You know what they say. What doesn't kill us makes us stronger." He actually seemed to be enjoying this.

"If I die, I will haunt you." I grabbed his hand and pulled him close to me. If I was going, he was definitely going with me.

"Deal." He actually smiled right before we both jumped off the cliff, plunged down and landed with a splash in the ocean.

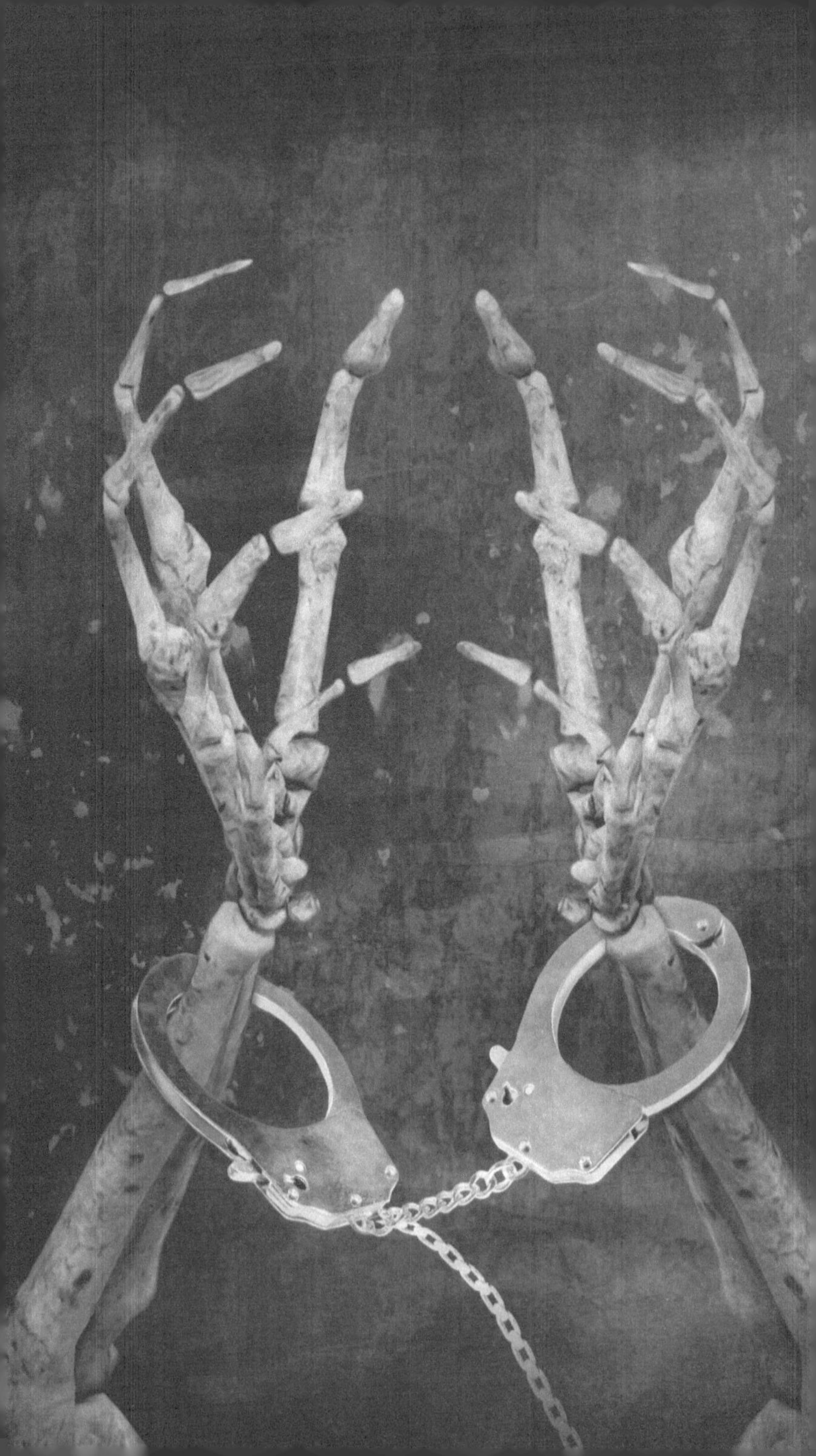

CHAPTER 6

MINA

"That was exhilarating," I said as we walked up the track that led to the house.

After a moment of terror that we might actually die after all, the water was more than deep enough. I'd plunged in hard before swimming back to the surface and popping out between the waves.

My heart was still racing. I couldn't remember the last time I did something like that. Something that wasn't planned, that had my adrenaline spiking like crazy. The pure rush made me want to do it over and over.

That faded when we reached the top of the track and saw Reuben was waiting, his expression a cross between stone and thunder.

"What the fuck were you doing?" He didn't snap or snarl, he didn't need to. His icy tone was enough to chase the smile from my face.

"Just jumping off the cliff, boss." Damon draped an arm over my shoulder, as though he needed to protect me from Reuben's anger. He was more likely to need protection from it himself. The majority of Reuben's fury was directed at him. Especially when he added, "You should try it."

Reuben's jaw twitched. He looked as though he was trying to form the correct response, but there wasn't one for this situation. We hadn't died, but we'd obviously given him a nasty shock.

Finally, he started to relax.

"When I saw you jump, I thought..." Apparently not caring that I was wet, he stepped towards me and placed his hands on my shoulders.

"We're fine," I assured him. "The water was deep and the tide's in. We wouldn't have jumped otherwise."

Did he really think we wanted to take our own lives? Evidently, he did. Or at least, assumed, when we disappeared over the side.

He wrapped his arms around me and held me tight, like he might keep me from jumping again.

I pressed my head against his chest and listened to his heart beat rapidly. Gradually, it began to slow to a normal pace. Strong, like everything about him.

"Don't do that again," he whispered. That was as close as he'd ever come to admitting he was scared of anything. "I lost you once. I'm not losing you because you jump off a fucking cliff."

"We didn't mean to worry you," I whispered back.

"It was spontaneous." I tilted my head back and looked up at him. "We'll warn you next time."

Instead of answering with words, he brushed his lips over mine. Feather light, with a hint of stubble.

In that moment, I realised I was standing outside the house in the fading light, dressed only in my under-wear. Rather than feeling vulnerable, I was aroused. My nipples, already hard from the cold, became harder still.

I deepened the kiss and wound my arms around his neck.

I sensed movement behind me before Damon placed his hands on my waist and stepped up to let his erec-tion graze the side of my hip. I found myself pressed between both of them.

My pulse ratcheted up. If my panties weren't already wet, they'd be dripping now. I was surrounded by so much hot muscle. At the same time, I knew if I stepped away, they'd let me go. If I felt uncomfortable, they'd stop.

I didn't want them to stop.

One by one, I started to slide the buttons on Reuben's shirt out of their holes.

"Mina…" he said softly.

"I want this," I said. "Please."

It was Damon who unhooked my bra. I dropped my arms from Reuben long enough for the straps to slip down my arms, onto the ground.

Damon pressed the palms of his hand to my belly,

then up to cup my breasts. He palmed my nipples until I groaned softly.

I pushed off Reuben's shirt and ran my hands up and down his rock hard abs and chest.

"We shouldn't do this here," Reuben said, his voice as strained as the front of his pants.

He swallowed audibly and led us over to a covered patio, surrounded on three sides by lattice and vines. The fourth was open to the ocean. In the centre of the patio, was a plush outdoor rug and a massive daybed.

He laid me back on the daybed, him on one side, Damon on the other.

Damon placed his thumb and forefinger on my chin and turned my face to him so he could kiss me.

Reuben hooked his fingers on the top of my panties and pulled them down my legs and off my feet. He scooted down, parted my legs gently and, eyes on mine, dipped his face down between them. Gripping my thighs with gentle hands, he started to explore and tease my pussy with his tongue.

Damon used his own tongue to taste mine, my lips, my throat, my neck, down to my breasts. He traced circles around my ruined nipple with the tip of one finger, while gently suckling the other.

I moaned, long and low with the sensations of plea-sure already washing over me deeper than the waves. Pushing me to heights bigger than the cliff.

"You like that?" Damon asked, around a mouthful of my sensitive flesh.

Reuben chose that moment to graze his teeth over my clit. My response was another moan and a full body shiver of delight.

"I asked you a question," Damon said more firmly. He lifted his face from me and looked at me like he expected a coherent response.

"Yes," I gasped. "Yes, I like all of it."

"Good girl." He went back to sucking, like my nipple was the most delicious thing he ever had in his mouth.

Any time any of the guys called me that, it got me going like crazy. I couldn't remember anyone having ever said that to me before and I loved it.

"Are you close?" Damon asked after a couple of minutes of spoiling my sensitive nipple, while not ignoring the other one. He seemed to like both of them equally, like Reuben did. Like Gianni did, too.

"So close," I panted. "So… Close… So…ahhh…" I arched my back as I came against Reuben's mouth.

I came so hard I might have caught a glimpse of stars in some distant universe. A universe where nothing existed but orgasms, and the stroke of his tongue on my clit.

I didn't ever want to leave that paradisiacal universe, but gradually, I floated back down to this one.

"You're so fucking perfect when you come," Reuben said. "Good girl."

I blinked a couple of times to clear my vision. "I want you," I said. "Please."

"She asks so nicely," Damon said.

"She does," Reuben agreed. He shed his pants and black silk boxers and tossed them aside. Eyes on me, he crawled up the daybed and kissed my mouth, so I could taste my release on his lips.

He gripped my hips and rolled us over so I was straddling him, his erection nestled between my thighs.

"Be a good girl and ride the boss," Damon said.

I glanced over at him and kept my eyes on his as I lowered myself onto Reuben's cock. "Be a good boy and take your pants off. Let me taste you."

Damon's eyes widened, but he hurried to do what I told him to. He knelt beside me and stroked his hand up and down his cock a couple of times before I opened my mouth to let him slide inside.

In the corner of my eye, I was aware of Reuben watching us both. I wasn't sure if I imagined him getting harder inside me. I was certainly aroused again.

I placed my hands on Reuben's chest and pushed myself up, sliding almost all the way off his cock, then down again.

He gripped my hips with his large hands and helped to guide me up and down, while he thrust up into me at the same time.

"You feel like heaven," he whispered. "I knew you would. I've waited so long… You're more than I imagined."

He had. He'd waited patiently for years for this.

I couldn't think of a more perfect place for our first time together. The waves crashed against the cliff, in time with his thrusts. The breeze blew off the ocean, cooling the sweat on my skin as it rose. The setting sun turned the water and the sky pink and orange, like it was celebrating with us.

I could only smile in response and massage Damon's balls while I sucked and teased him with my tongue. His cock was warm, smooth but hard, throbbing between my lips. Salty and sweet at the same time.

Reuben's cock was thick in my pussy, filling me like he too was made to fit inside me.

"Good girl," Damon soothed. "You take both of our cocks so well. You suck so beautifully. So fucking perfect."

Reuben hummed his agreement. "So fucking ours."

So fucking yours, I agreed silently.

I closed my eyes and focused on keeping the rhythm of sucks and thrusts, my breasts bouncing each time I rolled my hips.

"Do you want to taste Damon's cum?" Reuben asked.

Without stopping, I nodded.

I opened my eyes and locked them on Damon as his crossed and he started to pound harder into my mouth.

Finally, he grunted and his body went still. He squirted a mouthful of salty cum so hard and fast, I had to swallow before it went down my throat too quickly.

Puffing lightly, he slid his cock out of my mouth and flopped down beside us, his head right beside Reuben's.

They were both aware of that fact. They kept side eyeing each other without quite looking.

Would they act on their attraction? Did I dare to ask them to? I didn't want to push them into anything they weren't ready for, but I was aching to see them touch.

"If you wanted to…" I started tentatively.

"Tell us what you want," Reuben said, his voice low and husky.

Fuck yes, but I was still tentative. Still not wanting to press too hard.

"I want you to kiss each other," I whispered.

They turned and locked eyes. As if some kind of dam broke, they moved their faces until their lips met. Their first kiss was light, barely more than a brush of lips.

Then Damon cupped the back of Reuben's head and kissed him like he'd been aching to do it for his entire life. Like he was scared he'd never get another chance, so he might as well make this count.

But then, Reuben was kissing him back with lips and tongue. The only sound apart from the waves was the wetness of their kisses. They went on kissing as Reuben came inside my body, thrusting hard, and moaning against Damon's mouth.

I felt the warmth of his cum flooding inside me, like Damon's had in my mouth. I savoured every drop, knowing I did that to him. My body gave him pleasure, the way he gave it to me. The friction we created together, gave him an orgasm, moments of bliss he'd waited so long to experience.

That drew another orgasm from me, more intense than the first. I tipped my head back and cried out with pure pleasure, every sense tingling throughout my entire body. This time, it lasted and lasted, until I could almost reach out and grab that other universe.

With a gasp, I finally plummeted back down to reality, which was almost as incredible as a pleasure universe.

Only then did they pull apart and sag against the mattress of the daybed.

I slumped over Reuben, one hand his chest and the other on Damon's. They were both panting slightly, their hearts racing, skin damp with sweat in spite of the breeze. At the same time, rock hard and mine.

"That was...wonderful," I said between breaths. "Thank you."

"We should be thanking you," Damon said. He looked like he couldn't quite believe what had happened. Any of it.

Reuben had a similar expression on his face. Not regret, but something else. Relief, but with a hint of concern that this might change everything forever.

It probably would, but we'd figure that out together.

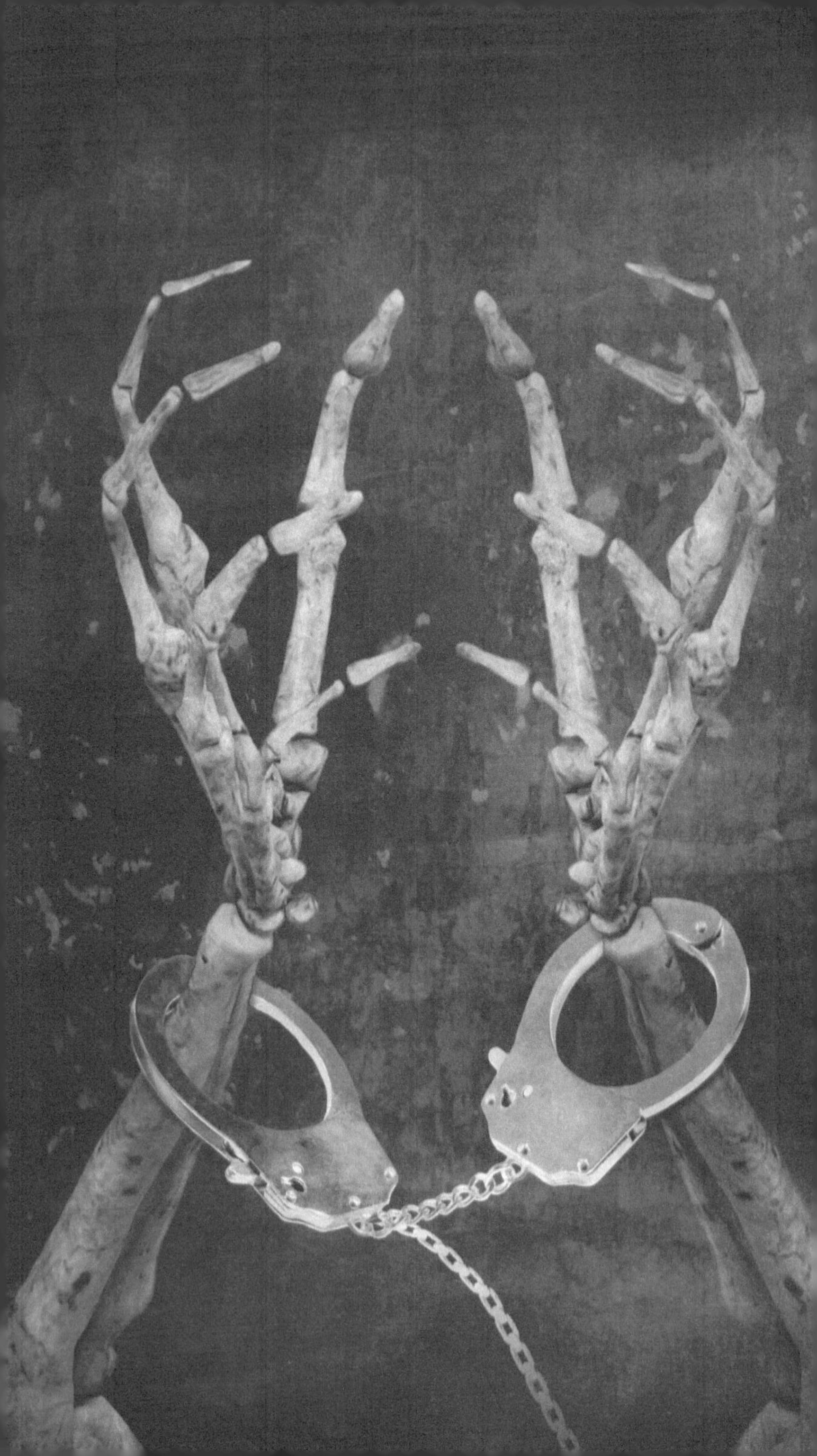

CHAPTER 7

GIANNI

Terry moved around the large kitchen, grumbling to himself under his breath. Every so often, he'd glance at us, Reuben in particular, with disapproval in his eyes. Not at anything we were doing, or talking about, but at him being uprooted from Sydney to come to Dusk Bay. He knew, as well as we did, that we couldn't function without him, but he was very much a creature of habit. That included knowing where everything was. Every time he came here, he had to rearrange everything in the kitchen to suit himself.

Ultimately, that was the prime source of his annoyance. The staff who worked here in our absence didn't leave things where he put them.

I patted him on the shoulder on the way to grab a fresh cup of coffee. "Maybe we should lock the cabinets when we leave."

He grunted his agreement and trudged off with a stack of plates.

I smiled to myself, picked up my coffee and carried it into the office. The air between everyone inside had changed since we were here last.

Reuben and Damon kept glancing at each other awkwardly. In between that, Reuben looked at Mina like he'd won the lottery. Considering he didn't need to play, because he had plenty of money, I assumed they'd fucked.

Good for them. It was about time.

I slipped into a chair just as Damon said something about the Vipers.

"If he's there, we need to speak to them," Damon was saying.

It took a moment for my brain to catch up to what he was saying. "You think Enzo is working with them?"

When it came to Damon's brother, I was as conflicted as everyone else in the room. I wanted to kill him on Mina's behalf, or at least hold him down while she did it. I also didn't want to cause a rift between either of us, and Damon by killing his brother.

"He has in the past," Damon said. "They'll know where he is, if anyone does. They're his kind of people."

"Riffraff?" I suggested.

Not that I was perfect, but the Vipers were a special breed of asshole. The kind that left their morals at the door. I was aware that we took part in human traf-ficking from time to time, but the Vipers put in orders for the kinds of people—usually women—they wanted to receive. I tried not to think too much about what happened to them after that, but I knew they had a lot more freedom than Mina was afforded.

Usually.

"Exactly," Reuben remarked. He rubbed his chin. For the first time in a long time, he actually looked relaxed. For him, that meant slightly less wound up than usual. Definitely the look of a man who got laid.

I glanced over to Mina, who sat on the couch near the window which was usually occupied by the twins. Her legs were crossed at her knees, eyes half closed as if she wasn't paying attention.

I knew better. She was listening to everything we said and everything we didn't say. Taking in every nuance and every movement. If things went to hell, she'd move in a heartbeat. Faster than a heartbeat.

I let my gaze linger on her, appreciating the sight. She was so fucking gorgeous, she sucked the breath out of my body.

I raised my hand to my neck and brushed the pad of my thumb across the healing wounds around my throat. Picturing her with the knife while she rode me made me harder than diamonds in a heartbeat. Just when I thought she couldn't surprise me, she went and did something like that. I had a feeling I'd still be uncovering layers of her until the day I died. She was fascinating and complex. I loved that about her.

My attention returned to Reuben as he spoke.

"We'll all go," he said finally. "They won't kill me, that would be too messy."

"If they know Mina is looking to kill Enzo, they might—" Damon started to push himself up from his chair.

"Then we don't tell them," Reuben interrupted. "You're looking for your brother. That's all they need to know."

Damon sank back down with a gusty exhale. "I don't trust them with her."

"That's why we're all going," Reuben said. "They won't get past us."

"Let them try," I said. I wasn't afraid of a bunch of street thugs. "I don't mind handing them their asses."

"This would be better if I went by myself," Damon said. One last attempt to change Reuben's mind, albeit a weak one. He was defeated and he knew it, but he wasn't going down without a final swing. "I can talk to them."

"They won't say no to me," Reuben said, effectively ending the conversation.

"No." Carlos Jones looked Reuben right in the eyes, arms crossed over his burly chest, chin jutting out like a dare. "I cannot give out the whereabouts of anyone who works for me."

"You mean, you will not," I said.

Carlos' eyes barely moved. "Same thing."

We'd been given a cool welcome to the Vipers' headquarters, which was little more than a warehouse beside the Dusk Bay docks. Several members of the cartel gave us dubious looks and a wide berth, as a young man led us to the cartel's leader.

A short, stocky man in his mid-forties, the only place he had no visible ink was his face. He didn't need it; the scars across his forehead and cheeks were enough decoration. They made him look exactly like what he was. The kind of man women should cross the street to avoid.

Like me, but with less class.

"Enzo is my brother," Damon said. His tone was as icy as Carlos. "I know the cartel rules."

"Don't quote my own rules to me," Carlos snapped. "I wrote them."

I decided that vocalising my surprise at his ability to write was low-lying fruit, even for me. I also strongly suspected that Carlos wouldn't care whose company I was in, if I insulted his intelligence.

Unless he was really, really big, then that was a gun in his pocket. If it wasn't a gun, I was impressed.

"So you're going to ignore them?" Damon asked. "The cartel is supposed to protect brothers. That's what I'm trying to do here."

Beside me, Mina stiffened slightly. I could almost feel her thinking, wondering if that was Damon's agenda. If anyone else was aware of a response, I saw no sign. They were too busy trying to out testosterone each other.

"In the cartel, brother doesn't mean blood," Carlos said. "It means we protect the brothers of our allegiance. Our brother Vipers. Blood means shit." He spat on the concrete floor beside Reuben's shoe.

"Name your price," Reuben said. He seemed completely unruffled.

Carlos' jaw moved in irritation. Of course, this was just part of the game. The harder he made it look like we wouldn't get what we wanted, the higher the price.

I doubted there was anything in the world that wasn't for sale if we offered enough. Men like this would sell their own mother if it benefited them and their bank account.

Finally, Carlos jerked his head towards a room to the side of the headquarters that he used for his office. The space was makeshift at best. Trestle tables and folding chairs, a locker to one side that probably contained guns and knives. None of the finesse of our lifestyle.

Which begged the question, why would Enzo prefer to work here than for Reuben? Each to their own.

Carlos sat on one of the tables. It groaned under his weight, but held.

"How much do you want to know where Enzo is? It seems to me you want that a lot. The question is, why?" His gaze slid to Mina, taking her in like she was a piece of meat.

To men like him, women were nothing more than a

commodity. A place to put his cock when he needed release.

He jerked his chin toward her. "That's why you brought her? You want to exchange her for him?"

We all anticipated the question, so none of us reacted. None of us even killed him.

Yet.

"That wouldn't be a fair exchange," I said easily. "She's worth more than six or seven of him."

That got Carlos' attention. He looked at her more intently. "You think so?"

"I know so," I said. If he looked at her like that for much longer, I was going to have to relieve him of his eyeballs. Didn't he know it was rude to stare?

"She's not for sale," Reuben growled softly. "We can double your next shipment in return for Enzo."

Carlos failed to contain his surprise at the generous offer. "You really do want him, don't you? If he's worth that much, maybe I should hold out for more."

"Maybe we should kill you and deal with whoever takes your place," Damon said mildly.

Carlos barked a laugh. "You think you'd walk out of here in one piece? I fucking dare you to try." He raised his hands to either side. He was beyond smug.

I would be too if I knew no one would kill me, even if I provoked them. Not openly, anyway. He wasn't stupid enough to turn his back on us, or anyone we might send to kill him later. Which we wouldn't do. Probably.

As long as he served our needs, he could keep breathing. He should be careful not to get too self-important though. That was when people started to make wrong moves.

"Do we have a deal?" Reuben said, clearly impatient.

"I'll take triple," Carlos said. "For four times that, I'll throw in my sister." He chuckled. "You look like you could handle a wildcat like her."

"Triple," Reuben said. "Keep your sister. I have no interest in buying women."

Carlos smirked. He was smart enough not to point out that Reuben didn't seem to have too much trouble selling them. A comment like that would see the price drop back to double. Or the regular price of shipments Carlos bought from us, would suddenly skyrocket. He couldn't afford that and we all knew it.

"Enzo first," Damon said. "Then I'll make the arrangements for the next shipment."

Carlos nodded. He jumped down off the table and sauntered over to the door. "Hades! Get your fucking ass over here."

I couldn't see who he was speaking to, but a male voice responded, followed by the sound of heavy footsteps heading out of the headquarters.

Damon's expression was tense. The muscles in his face were going to hurt later if he kept them as tight as they were.

I gave him a smile, which he responded to with a

nod. That was as much comfort as he was going to accept right now.

Mina appeared less apprehensive, but she was getting better at containing her emotions.

Having only been around Kurt for so long, she'd had to relearn how to interact with other people. Including not flinching when the instinct told her to.

Honestly, I wished I had half of her self-control. Whenever she was in assassin mode, she was as closed a book as Damon or Reuben. Only the slightest twitch of her right hand gave away any hint of what she was feeling. Poised, ready to pull out a knife and use it.

I couldn't see one, but I knew she'd have several on her, within easy reach. Reuben would have insisted before bringing her here, but he wouldn't have needed to. She would have stashed them on her with as little thought as pulling on clothes.

The Vipers weren't given to being welcoming towards women.

I was tempted to suggest we take Carlos' sister, to save her from whatever might happen to her. Chances were, he'd sell her to a rival cartel to make an alliance. If she was the wildcat he suggested she was, she'd be pissed off at him for doing that.

Mina must have sensed my scrutiny. She looked over at me and offered a small smile. I gave her a bigger one in return.

Carlos stepped back into the room. "Seems you're

out of luck. Enzo met with the wrong end of a bullet last night. He's dead."

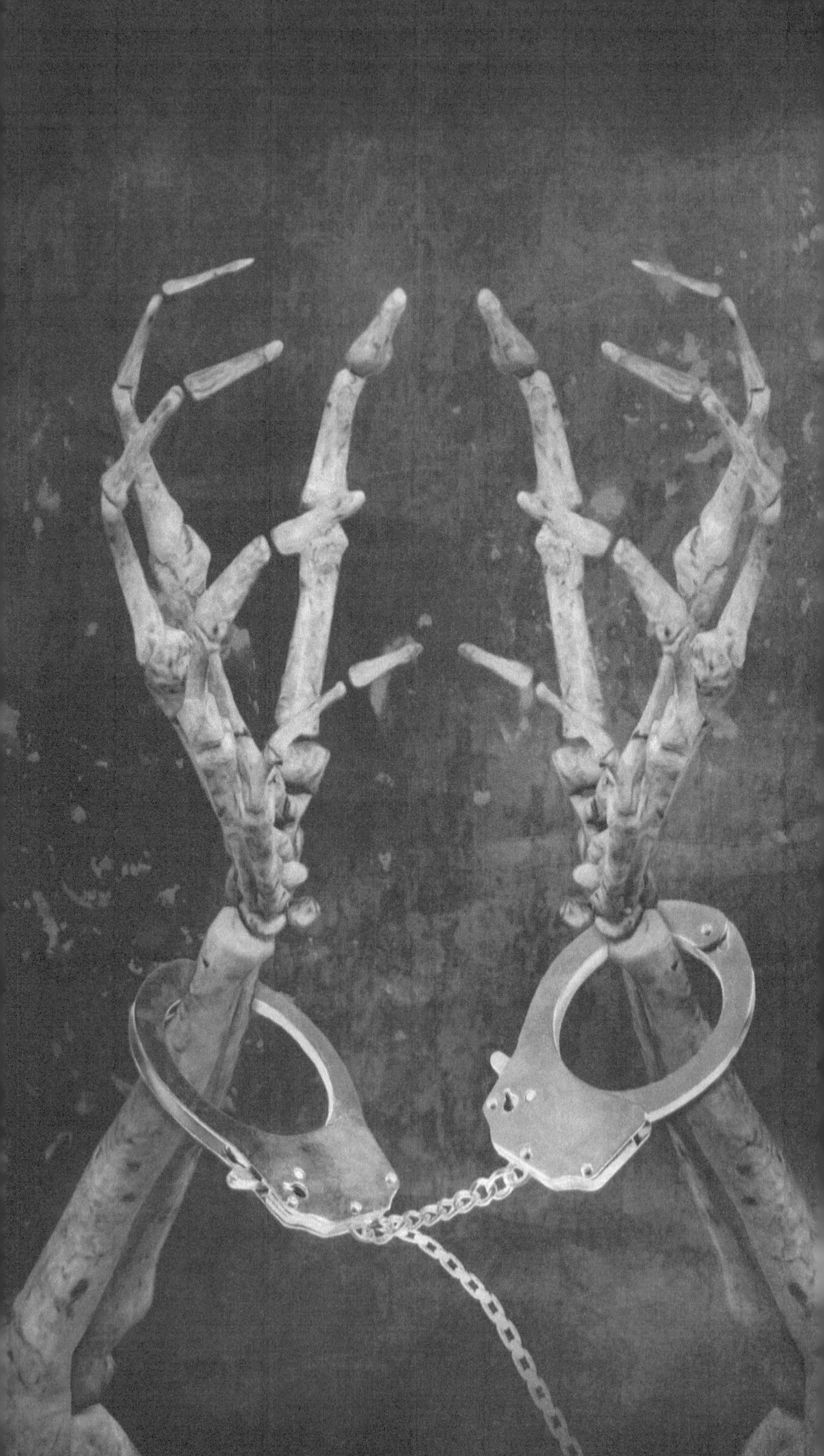

CHAPTER 8

MINA

"Do you believe him?" I asked Damon as we stepped out of the warehouse and toward the ocean. Reuben and Gianni walked ahead of us, both quietly furious on my behalf. How did I feel about being robbed of my revenge? In some ways, this was easier. If Enzo was already dead, Damon couldn't blame me for killing him.

If he was dead.

"Not for a minute," Damon said. "Either he doesn't know where Enzo is and doesn't want to admit it, or he's expecting a bigger payday than we can offer." He looked ready to chew rocks.

"Who from?" Gianni asked over his shoulder. "You don't think Kurt would bother, do you?"

"I don't know," Damon admitted. "It might be that he doesn't know, but I can't see him giving up triple the shipment unless the stakes were really high."

"Maybe Enzo ran off with his sister," I said dryly.

Damon snorted. "She might be better off away from Carlos, but with Enzo..."

"Do you know her?" I asked. I was in no way jealous, but I was curious.

"Angelina Jones? Yeah, I've met her a couple of times," he said. "Wildcat is accurate. She doesn't take shit from him or anyone. If he'd suggested he'd sell her, she probably would run off. If he survived the night. She's as headstrong as they come."

"It sounds like you admire her," I remarked. Maybe there was a little jealousy there, but they all had a life before me, I knew that. Relationships, lovers. That was the past. It couldn't hurt me now, except to remind me of everything I'd missed out on. That would always sting, no matter how much time passed.

"He's scared of her," Gianni said.

"Fuck off," Damon told him. "I'm not scared of Angie. She's more likely to get a man killed than kill them."

"Carlos would kill Enzo if he ran off with her," I said.

"Very likely," Damon agreed. "He's probably planning to have Enzo meet the wrong end of a bullet as we speak."

I put a hand on his bicep. "I know this isn't how you want things to go."

"He was going to end up dead either way." He shrugged. "At least, this way, I don't have to kill him. And neither do you."

"I would have killed him to save you from doing that," I said.

I'd hesitate, because he was Damon's brother, but when it came down to it, I'd spill his blood if necessary. If it helped me to put the worst of my demons to bed.

"Doesn't she say the sweetest things?" Gianni said. "For the record, I'd kill him for you too."

Damon nodded in response to his offer. "I thought you might."

"I'm sweet that way too," Gianni said. He dropped back to walk on the other side of me.

"You want to find him, don't you?" I asked softly. "You want to find Enzo."

Damon hesitated. "If I don't, I'll never know the truth of what happened. Why did he work for Kurt? Why didn't he try to stop him? He could have convinced Gage Prior, Leon Graves, and Jase to overpower him. Lasalle wasn't a match for four other people. Five if you were conscious." Regret flashed through his eyes. "He also might know where Kurt is."

"Is there any chance he ran because he was scared he'd be associated with Kurt after the rumours we spread?" I asked. "When people hear what Kurt did, they'll start pointing fingers at anyone who worked with him. Especially those who worked *for* him. Or, they might go after Enzo because they want to hunt down the Sparrow."

"Both are possible," Damon said. "That being the case—"

"Carlos is trying to put us off his trail so he can find Kurt himself," Reuben said. "He must know Enzo worked for Kurt and how to get to him. Once he has Kurt, he can make more money than triple the shipments."

"He's a crafty bastard," Gianni said. "Smarter than I gave him credit for."

"Never underestimate Carlos Jones," Damon advised him. "He didn't get where he was by being stupid and making mistakes. He got there by being smart and ruthless."

"We need to find Enzo before Carlos does," I concluded. "I know we're only guessing about Angelina Jones, but—"

"She'd be a good place to start," Damon said. "I have a feeling if we find her, we'll find him."

"I have the same feeling," Gianni said. "If you were a cartel princess, where would you be?"

"Probably as far away from the cartel as I could get," I said. "Before my brother could sell me."

What was it with men? When Carlos said that, I had to resist the strong urge to kick him in the balls. I didn't give a fuck if the cartel did things differently, there was nothing I hated more than men thinking women were possessions. Angelina could end up the same way I had.

"Neither of your brothers would have dared," Gianni said.

I raised my eyebrows at him. "You really think Dane would have hesitated if it was worth it to him?"

"I think you, Rose and Asher would have torn him a new one," Gianni said. "I would have helped them."

"So would I," Reuben said. He paused for a moment. "I would have outbid everyone else. I wouldn't have let anyone else buy you."

"If it was you, I would have gone along with it," I told him.

If only that was what happened. I would have preferred to be sold to him than given away like a used doll. I might even have insisted Dane take whatever offer he made. He would have had money and I would have had a completely different life.

"That might be the most romantic thing I've ever heard," Gianni said. "Would you buy me too, Reuben? Or Damon?"

"I pay you," Reuben pointed out. "I don't need to buy either of you."

"Good point," Gianni said. "I think I prefer that to being bought and sold. So, where do we find Angelina Jones?"

"We start by speaking to her mother," Damon said.

———

"What is my son up to now?" Bianca Ramirez looked unimpressed. She was even shorter than me, but very much the kind of woman you would never underestimate. Her side eye alone would make the average man think twice about fucking with her. Her full on glare almost intimidated me.

Almost.

"Probably a fuck ton," Damon said. "Including trying to sell Angie."

Bianca swore under her breath in Spanish.

I expected her to curse out her son, but instead she said, "That girl will be the death of us all. I said to her, if she doesn't behave, no man would want her and you know what she did? She laughed and said no man could handle her anyway." She threw her hands up in the air. "It would take an army to control her."

"Just like her mother," Gianni said, unflinching.

She said a few more words in Spanish. None of them sounded flattering.

Gianni grinned and replied in Spanish. Whatever he said had her cheeks turning red.

She waved a finger at him. "You, you're trouble. No sensible woman would let you near her daughter." She turned the waving finger on me. "Are you with this man?"

"Yes," I replied. "I'm with all of them."

"Madre dio!" she exclaimed. "Loco."

Now *that* I understood. Sometimes I agreed that I might be crazy. "Do you know where your daughter is, by any chance?"

Bianca grunted with annoyance. "Probably off with that boy. I told her, Angelina-Maria Marguerite-Rosa

Ramirez-Jones, you stay away from that boy! Did she do what I said? Of course not? I should have told her to go with him. She would have done the opposite, like she always does."

Bianca crossed her arms and rolled her eyes toward the ceiling.

"If I recall correctly," Reuben said slowly, "your father was trying to negotiate a marriage for you and you ran off with Anthony Jones instead."

Bianca sniffed. "That's right. Tony had more brains in his little finger than the man my father was trying to sell me to. He was bad. No bueno. We would have killed each other. No, let me correct myself. I would have killed him. Before I let him put his greasy fingers on me." She shuddered.

"So you think women should be free to choose who they're with," I stated.

As I expected, she saw right through what I was trying to imply. "Unless they are a no good, two-bit troublemaker like Enzo."

I grabbed Damon's wrist before he could respond too strongly.

"Where is he?" he asked, his voice barely contained. "When did you see him last?"

"This morning," she replied. "Climbing out the window of Angie's bedroom. As if I wouldn't notice." She scoffed.

"Carlos said he was shot last night," Reuben said.

"He might have been shot, but it wasn't last night,"

she said. "I chased him away and Angelina left maybe an hour later. Wherever they are, they're together."

"If Carlos tries to kill him, he might accidentally hurt her," I pointed out. "If you can tell us where you think they might be, we can stop that from happening."

I wasn't sure if Carlos wanted Enzo dead, but if Bianca thought that, she might help us. At this point, it was all we had to go on.

Bianca looked reluctant, but sighed. "I can give you an address. If they aren't there, then that's all I have." She grabbed a notepad from a side table beside an ancient couch and scribbled with a blunt pencil.

She tore off the paper and handed it to Reuben. "If you weren't with her, I'd insist you take me out. I've been lonely since Tony passed away."

Reuben carefully folded the page and tucked it into his pocket. "Thank you."

I suspected he was thanking her for the address, not the flirtation. I couldn't remember having seen him with another woman other than Daze and some of the staff, but he wasn't the flirtatious type. That was Gianni's wheelhouse.

"You could always ask Carlos to find you someone," Gianni said. "I bet a woman like you would go for a shit ton."

She gave him the stink eye. "If you don't get out of my house, I'm going to put a curse on you."

He grinned. "You wouldn't do that. You secretly like me. I can tell."

"So secret I don't even know," she said dryly. "Did you hit your head too many times?"

"Probably." Gianni chuckled. "That would explain a lot."

"Pretty much everything," Damon agreed. "I should have thought of it."

"You really should," Gianni agreed. "How did you miss something like that?"

Damon rolled his eyes at him.

"I'm starting to think you're all trouble," Bianca said. "Except Reuben. If she ditches your fine ass, you know where to find me." She winked at him.

He looked back at her, clearly uncomfortable.

"I don't plan to ditch his ass," I said. "Sorry, his *fine* ass." I put an arm around him. "But if I do, I'll remind him of your offer."

He gave me the same look he'd been giving her. If things didn't work out between us, he was not coming back here for her. He looked as though he'd prefer to swallow a whole echidna. Spines and all.

Lucky for everyone, I couldn't imagine life without him and I knew he wouldn't let me go without one hell of a fight. Unfortunately for Bianca, she was out of luck when it came to him. I doubted they'd be a good match anyway. Although, a woman her age might teach him a thing or two.

"If you find my daughter, tell her that if she takes off again, I'll let Carlos choose a husband for her," Bianca said. She led us to the door and opened it before hanging on to it as though she wanted to be certain we actually left.

"Will do," Gianni said. He made kissing faces at her before leading the way out the door.

My arm still around Reuben, I shook my head and followed him out.

If Angelina was anything like her mother, she'd marry Enzo today if we gave her that message. I had a feeling I'd like her, but she wouldn't like me if she knew I'd leave her a widow.

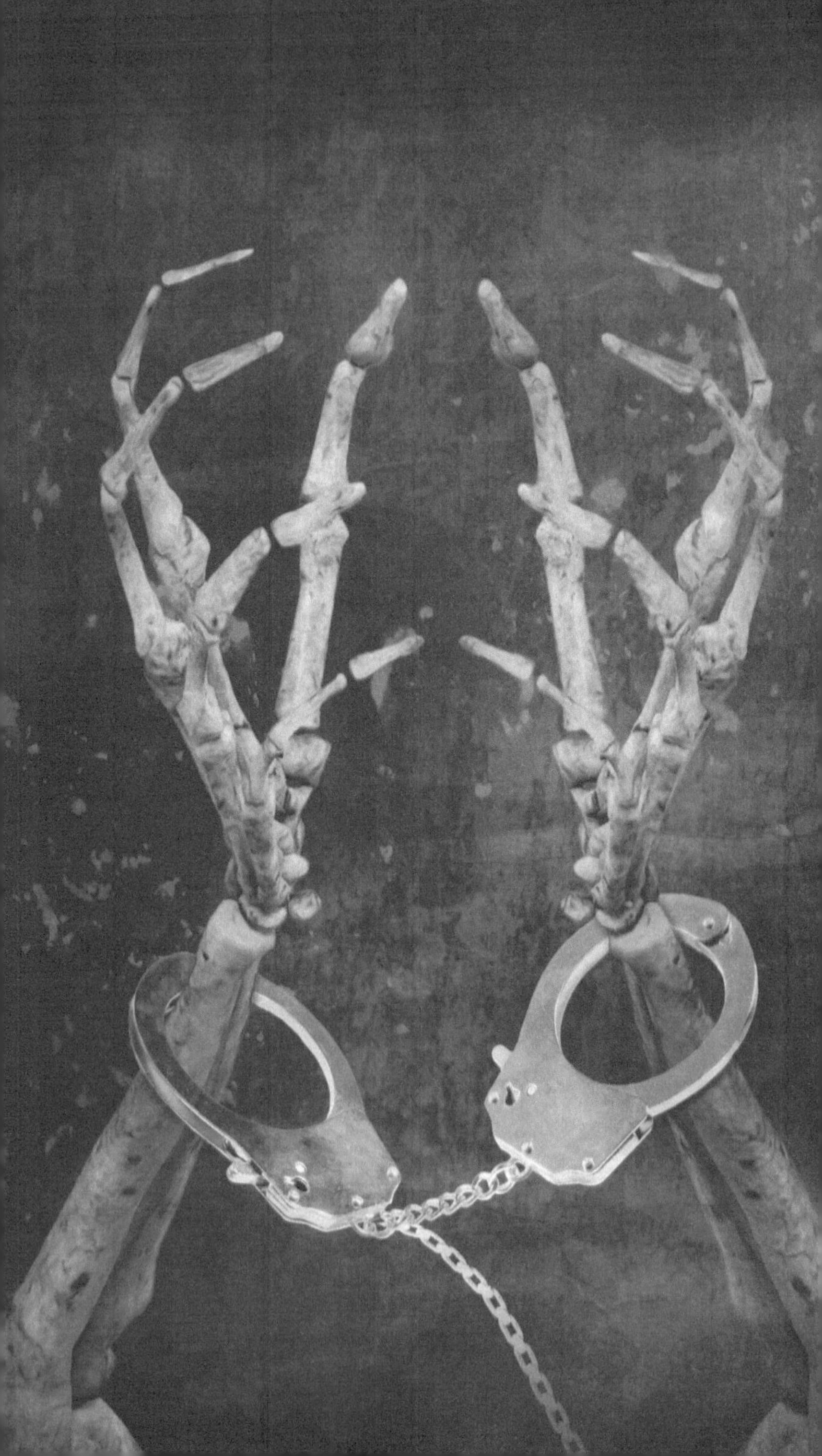

CHAPTER 9

MINA

"How many languages do you speak?" Gianni hooked his arm through mine and walked beside me to the car.

He shrugged. "Four or five. Italian, Spanish, French, English, and of course, bad."

I laughed. "I think we can all speak bad language."

"Fuck yeah we can." He grinned. "How about you?"

"I can definitely speak bad," I said. "Also, Italian and French, but I'm rusty. I learned French at school and Italian at home. And bad from Asher and Zeke."

Reuben grunt-laughed. "That sounds accurate."

"You learned all your naughty words from your younger brother?" Gianni teased.

"Who else?" Reuben asked. He shot us a playful look of mock innocence, but it only lasted a moment.

Those flashes fascinated me. The insight into the man under the stony exterior. I suspected we'd never see more than flashes, but those he displayed were endearing. Every time I saw them, I fell in love with him a little more. They made him seem more human, and reminded me that he also had vulnerabilities. None he'd admit to, but he had them.

"My guess would have been the twins," I said.

I glanced over at Damon, ready to tease, but the expression on his face made me hold my tongue.

He was clearly not listening to us, his mind elsewhere. On his brother, I presumed. In a mood like that, he might be inclined to shoot first and think about what he was doing later. Not that he was a hothead, usually, but he was wound up tighter than a spring, ready to burst. Now was the time to step lightly around him.

I wanted to reassure him we'd find Enzo, but I had no idea what would happen after that. Carlos might kill him or we might.

I considered suggesting we put my vendetta aside, but I sensed Damon wouldn't stop until he found his brother, regardless of what he'd done. Regardless of what I might do to him.

Damon unlocked the SUV and we all climbed inside without another word.

"Is it far?" I asked to fill the silence.

"Nope." Damon started the engine.

Gianni scooted over closer to me and fastened his seatbelt. He took my hand and squeezed.

"No one will blame you for what you have to do."

His tattooed fingers were warm around mine, reassuring.

I looked over at him and pressed my lips together. "I might. Damon will."

Nothing quite says 'I love you' like killing his brother. Even if he understood, some part of him would always resent what I did. He'd always wonder if maybe he could have found a way for Enzo to make up for the past.

But this wasn't a romance novel, and no amount of grovelling from Enzo could undo his part in everything. His death wouldn't take away the pain either, but it would help to give me some peace.

Was it worth the risk of starting a war with Damon? I didn't want to lose him, especially not like this.

I tried, but I couldn't remember a time when I was more conflicted than I was right now. I might have been about to rip us all apart, just for revenge.

What did that say about me? Was I as bad as Kurt for wanting to burn down everyone who burnt me? I reminded myself that if I didn't, and another person suffered because of it, that would be my fault. Their blood, their suffering, would be on my hands.

That, I couldn't, *wouldn't* tolerate. If I could help it, they wouldn't touch another person. I owed that little girl that. I owed younger Mina that. I owed it to Daze's daughter, to make her safer.

No matter the price.

"Damon understands what's at stake here," Gianni

assured me. "So does his brother. You can't be responsible for his actions. That would be like blaming Damon for them."

He raised his voice to make sure everyone in the car could hear. "And anything Enzo did is not Damon's fault."

Damon tensed, but didn't glance back or respond. He was clearly not finished blaming himself. What would it take?

I spent five years hating myself for something I didn't even do. I blamed myself for her death, but I was starting to accept that everything which happened was Kurt's fault. Not mine.

Someday I may forgive myself and hopefully, so would Damon. Otherwise, we'd spend the rest of our lives eating ourselves up from the inside out, with remorse for things we didn't do.

"Give him time," Gianni said. "He knows the score, even if he's busy beating himself up right now." His tone was soft, gentle with affection for Damon.

At some point, they'd gone from working together to being something more. At least, as far as Gianni was concerned. I was almost certain it was reciprocated. They weren't rushing into anything, but the feelings were there, like they were between Damon and Reuben.

I remembered the way they kissed and my blood suddenly became hot. Being fucked by two guys at the same time wasn't something I would have dreamt of, but it was incredible and I wanted to do it again. Next time, with Gianni present too, and taking part. What would it be like to be with all three of them at the same time?

Fuck, now my panties were wet. Good. I deserved to enjoy intimacy with my three incredible mafia kings. Sparrow and the mafia kings, who would have thought? Certainly not me, but here we were. If I didn't break us all apart, we could be together forever.

Plenty of time for us to explore each other and all the possibilities.

All I could do in response to Gianni's words, was nod and lean against him while we wound through the streets of Dusk Bay.

———

The address on the piece of paper Bianca gave to Reuben, led to a large house a block or so from Demons' Arena, where the ice hockey team played their home games.

"They're actually a front for a lot of Caleb's smuggling operations," Gianni said. "As a team, they kinda suck. In a loveable losers kind of way." He nodded towards the arena.

I'd watched a game or two on TV with Gianni and he wasn't wrong about that. I didn't know much about ice hockey, but they lost both times I watched. Their goalie was my cousin, Phoenix. As far as I could tell, he was good at what he did, saving more goals than letting them through, but the team still lost. What would Phoenix think if he knew I watched him play?

I hadn't seen Ric's brother since the guys found me, but I would eventually. He was on the list of people who weren't allowed to know about me yet. Although, he was lower on the list, because we were never close. Not in the past, anyway. In the future, I hoped we could form a bond of some kind. The frustration he showed every time the puck got past him was pure DiMarco. We hated losing. He must be irritated as hell at doing it all the time.

I couldn't imagine Caleb giving a shit about the team's performance on the ice, although he technically owned them. Honestly, I felt sorry for them. Professional athletes worked hard and deserved better than to be an afterthought in the life of Caleb Brantley. Just another part of the business.

I made a note to suggest to the twins that maybe they could take over the team. Between them, they'd run it better than he did. Without a doubt, if I suggested it to Caleb, he'd tell me it was none of my business. This was a handy sidestep, and the twins would, if nothing else, get a hoot out of it. Anything to get under Caleb's skin.

I turned my attention to the house, and shivered. It reminded me of the last job I did.

The house where the girl died. I tried not to think about her blood seeping into my clothes. Her eyes, staring at me…

Two stories, brick painted cream, black windows and a roof that slanted across the top of the structure. The look was too modern for my taste. Judging by the look on his face, it was too modern for Reuben's taste too.

"Who owns this place?" I asked.

Damon was on his phone, searching for exactly that information. "Not us, or the cartel. Or the brotherhood, as far as I can tell. It seems to be privately owned. Someone by the name of Karrie Levine." He shrugged.

"Hopefully we won't get too much blood on Ms Levine's house," Gianni remarked. "Although, if you rent houses to dubious people, you get dubious things happening."

"Gianni and Mina, you go around the back," Reuben said. "Damon and I will check out the front."

"On it, boss," Gianni said. He grabbed my hand and we slipped over to a side gate that led to the back of the house.

"How inconsiderate of them to lock it," Gianni remarked.

"How considerate of them to have such a simple lock." I pulled out my lock picking tools and had it open in about ten seconds flat.

"I've always said locks only keep honest people out." He grinned and pushed the gate open.

"Considering we could have climbed over it, yeah," I agreed. We might have been seen by the neighbours, so that would have been a last resort. Why risk what could be done with a turn of my hand?

We walked slowly across paved ground, past raised gardens with the kind of plants that didn't need any attention. The kind that were planted for decoration, not because the owner enjoyed getting their hands dirty.

Terry would have hated the place.

We walked past windows with curtains drawn over them, to the back door. Beside it, a keypad was attached to the wall, a light flashing at the top.

"I've been looking forward to this," Gianni whispered.

From my pocket, I drew out my device and placed it beside the keypad to turn off the security. The screen turned on, numbers tumbling over numbers, letters over letters until they hit on the combination and the light turned dark.

"That was fucking awesome," Gianni whispered. "I want one."

"If I can find out how to get one, I'll give you one for Christmas," I assured him.

"Fucking yes, please." He tried the door, but it was locked. With an elaborate gesture, he stepped aside for me to pick that too. "No wonder you could get in anywhere. Is there anything that could keep you out?"

"Not that I know of," I said. "But no job ever included a moat and crocodiles. Yet."

He laughed softly. "If anyone could get past those, it would be you."

I didn't know about that, but the vote of confidence didn't hurt my ego.

I eased the door open and listened carefully.

Grimaced.

Unless there was someone else in the house, Angelina and Enzo wouldn't hear us coming. By the sound of it, they were too busy coming themselves.

My hand in Gianni's, we moved slowly through the darkened house, towards the source of the sound.

I caught a hint of movement at the front of the house. Reuben and Damon must have entered when I turned off the security system. I estimated that the pair were between the four of us. With that in mind, I slowed slightly.

Let Damon find his brother first.

I caught a glimpse of them moving down the corridor towards us, illuminated in the light that came from a single room. It shone across the floor, glowing on pale hardwood.

Damon stepped into the doorway and stopped.

I moved to stand beside him.

Sure enough, a dark-haired woman around my age was riding a man who bore a striking resemblance to Damon. Her head was back, eyes closed, her hair long enough to brush her ass. Her breasts bounced with every roll of her hips.

"That's Enzo," Damon said.

They didn't realise we were there until he spoke. Angelina let out a squeak and threw her hands over her breasts.

Enzo turned to stare at us, squinting in confusion and disbelief.

I gave him the same look. "I've never seen him before."

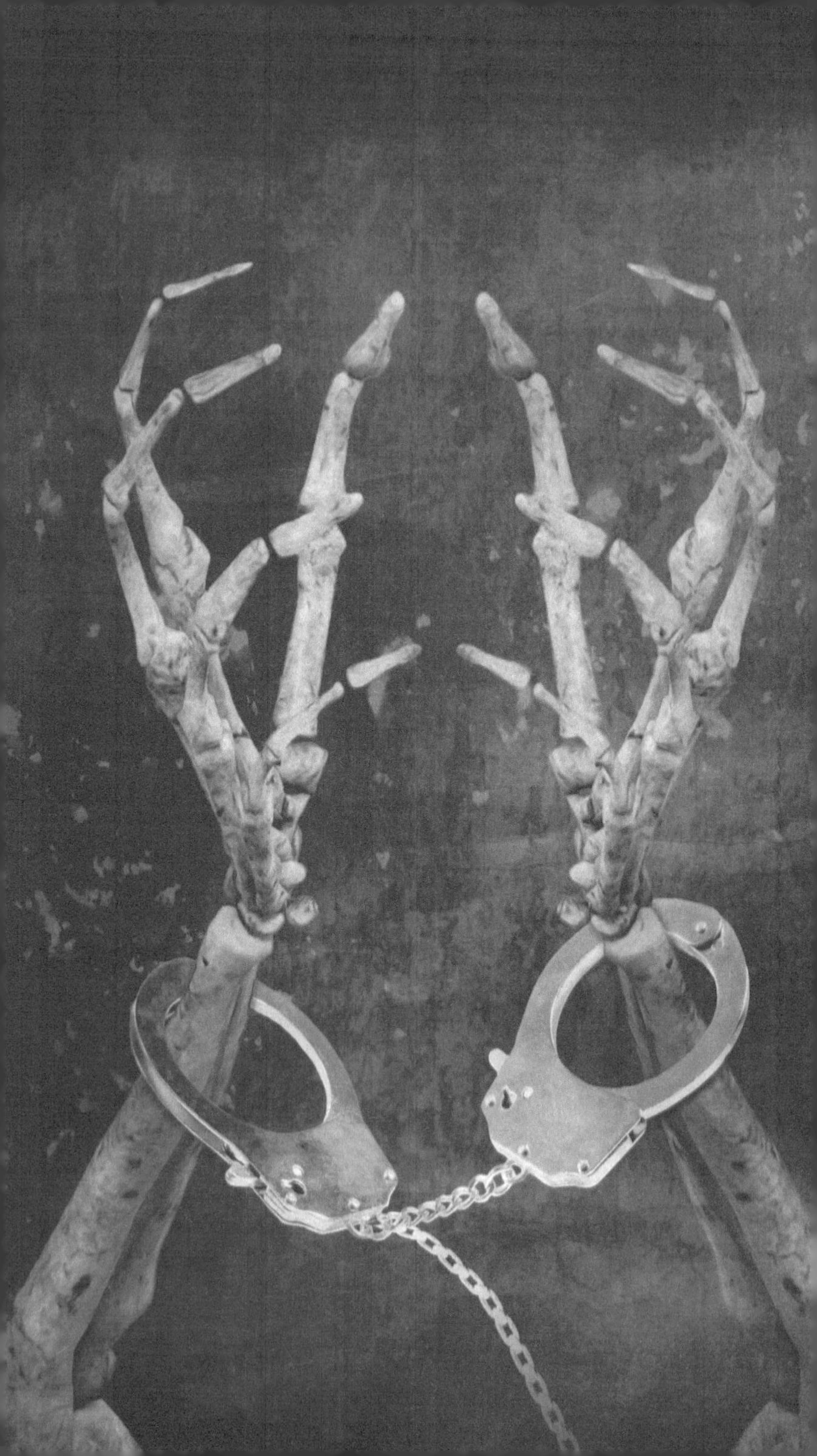

CHAPTER 10

MINA

Damon turned slowly to stare at me. "You've never—"

"I've never seen him before," I repeated. "Whoever Hammer is, it's not him."

"That's a matter of opinion." Enzo placed his hands behind his head and grinned at us, completely shameless. "I've been called very similar. Damon, what the fuck are you doing here?"

Angelina slid off him and onto the floor on the opposite side of the bed to scoop up a shirt and pull it over her head. Enzo's shirt, by the look of it. It fell to her knees, the sleeves down to her elbows.

"What the hell?" she demanded. She placed her fists on her ample hips and glared at us. She was a younger version of her mother. Dark hair, dark eyes and a pissed off expression on her face.

Damon ignored them for a moment. "You're absolutely certain? Think back carefully. You were drugged at the time."

I frowned and thought, but ultimately shook my head. "It's definitely not him."

For one thing, Hammer was blonde and Enzo had dark hair, like his brother. Hammer had a slim build and Enzo was muscular. Even if he'd dyed his hair and bulked up, Enzo looked nothing like Hammer. Even his face shape was different. His voice wasn't one of the ones that haunted my nightmares.

Thank fuck, because I really hadn't wanted to kill Damon's brother.

Damon closed his eyes in relief and turned back to the pair, arms crossed over his chest as he lounged against the door frame. "Do you want to put that away?" He nodded at Enzo's still erect cock, which was in full view.

"Nope," Enzo said easily. "How about you fuck off so we can finish what we started?"

"Nope," Damon repeated. "If we can find you, then Carlos can. He wants you killed for some reason." He nodded toward Angelina.

She groaned in frustration. "How many times do I have to tell my brother to fuck off? I am not marrying Salvador! I am not marrying any man my brother chooses for me. Especially Salvador. I'd rather marry Hades."

Enzo glanced over at her. "Hey!"

She rolled her eyes at him. "I don't want to marry

Hades either, fuckwit. I'm just saying he's better than Salvador." She shook her head at his apparent obtuseness.

"Everyone is better than Salvador," Gianni said, although he clearly had no idea who Salvador was.

Neither did I, but I could make some assumptions. Anyone who wanted to buy a woman, or marry her against her will, was immediately on my shit list. Even after a handful of minutes, I knew it would take a certain type of man to fulfil her needs. Someone with balls of steel.

Angelina turned to Gianni and raised her hands. "Right? Tell my asshole brother that. And tell him I'm not coming back. He and my mother can go right to hell. I'm staying with Enzo." She nodded like that settled the matter, once and for all, although she must have known it wouldn't make the situation go away. Nothing about her suggested she was naïve, just frustrated and determined to get her way.

Enzo finally rose from the bed and moved to stand beside her. His cock had finally softened enough to hang heavy between his thighs. "Exactly. Angie and I are getting married and there's not a fucking thing Carlos can do about it."

"He can have you killed, *fuckwit*," Damon said. "Do you really think someone like Carlos is going to let her go that easily? Because he won't. He'll keep coming after you until you're dead."

Enzo lifted his chin. "Then we'll go somewhere no one can find us."

"Like here?" Damon gestured around with one hand, without unfolding his arms. "It wasn't that difficult to find you."

Considering how easy it was, both of them should be more worried than they were. What must it be like to be so carefree and sure of yourself? It would be nice until it got them both killed. Or worse.

"My mother told you I was here, didn't she?" Angelina's eyes snapped with anger.

"Yes, and if she told us, then who knows who else she's told," Damon said. "There could be people right behind us." He jerked his thumb towards the road.

"We should get out of here," Angelina said. She started to gather up her clothes.

Enzo didn't move. He nodded towards me. "Who's she? Why was she supposed to know me? Who the fuck is Hammer?"

He didn't look worried, but he also looked as though he wouldn't move until he got some answers. In that, he reminded me of his brother. They also had the same firm jaw and blue eyes, the same fierce independence. No wonder they clashed, they were a lot alike.

"Mina DiMarco," I replied. "We were given the wrong information. We were told you were someone else. We came to kill him." I saw no reason to pull punches. People like this heard worse on an hourly basis, they wouldn't flinch.

"You're not going to kill him?" Angelina stopped, still crouched behind the bed.

I would have bet anything she had a gun. She'd use it, depending on what I said next. Assuming she could aim before I embedded a blade between her eyes. Which was unlikely, so I replied calmly and honestly.

"Not unless you gave us a reason to, then no. I think we can help you instead."

"With a threesome?" Enzo's gaze grazed up and down my body. "Sounds good to me."

Angelina threw a shoe at his head. It bounced off his cheek and fell back to the floor.

She swore at him in Spanish while he chuckled.

He spread his hands and shrugged. "Sorry, baby, another time maybe."

Reuben shot daggers at him with his eyes. For a moment I thought he may order one of us to kill Enzo after all.

I put a hand on his bicep to remind him I wouldn't have taken up the offer, and Enzo was joking around. I doubted Angelina would share anyway, even if I was interested.

"We can help by getting you out of here," Damon said. "We'll take you back to the house and sort something out from there. You'll be safe from Carlos, and Angelina's mother."

Enzo clenched his jaw. For a moment I thought he'd refuse. He glanced at Angelina who nodded.

He exhaled and nodded. "Fine. We'll go with you.

For now. Only for Angie's sake. I know what Salvador would do to her if he got his hands on her. He's a fucking slug."

"He's a fucking slug who'd get me pregnant and keep me that way," she said bitterly. "Then fuck around with whoever he could get his dick into."

"He sounds charming," Gianni said sarcastically.

I murmured my agreement. It sounded to me like Carlos was trying to kill the wrong man. "Maybe we should let them get dressed." I stepped away from the doorway.

"I don't mind who sees me naked," Enzo said pleasantly. "But if you keep looking at my woman, I'm going to have to shoot your eyes out."

As if any of my men were leering at her in any way. I knew all of them better than to even glance at them to check. They weren't interested in another woman. They wouldn't stare at one.

"Bro, none of us wants to see you naked," Gianni said. "No offence or anything."

Enzo grinned. "None taken, bro." He turned around and bent over, baring his ass to all of us.

I grimaced and stepped into the darker part of the corridor so I couldn't see him anymore.

"This all begs more questions than it answers," Reuben said. He slipped an arm around me.

"It does," I agreed. "Why did Martina think Enzo was Hammer? And if she knew he wasn't, why tell us he was?"

"Where is the real Hammer?" he added to the list of questions.

Gianni went one further with, "*Who* is the real Hammer? And can he sing 'Can't Touch This'?"

"And why send us after my brother?" Damon leaned against the wall, his hands in his pockets.

"To stop Carlos from getting to him?" I suggested. "Why would Martina give a shit?"

Damon shook his head. "I have no idea." He turned his head towards the bedroom. "Enzo, why would she?"

Enzo strutted out, fully dressed in torn jeans and the T-shirt Angelina was wearing a few moments before. He gave me a wink before turning to his brother. "Because I'm smoking hot and awesome?"

Damon snorted. "That's a matter of opinion and doesn't answer the question. Why would someone like Martina get involved? Stepping in between you and Carlos, I mean."

Enzo looked down at the floor and shuffled his feet. "I might have done her some favours in the past."

"Must have been some hell of a favour," Gianni said. "We might have shot you before checking that you were who we thought you were."

Enzo looked up and gave Gianni a lopsided smile. "The favours didn't always go the way they should have. I never said she was looking out for me."

"She set you up?" Angelina emerged from the bedroom, dressed in leggings and a crop top, her dark hair wound in a messy bun.

I envied the way she looked, comfortable in her own skin. I was getting more confident in myself, but some days I still wanted to peel off mine and step out of it.

She had an effortless beauty, and an attitude that gave absolutely no fucks. She was exactly the kind of person I wanted to keep away from men like Kurt. If Salvador was anything like him, the further away she was from him, the better.

Right now, Angelina looked ready to tear Martina apart, if she tried to get Enzo killed. It was easy to see why Carlos described her as a wildcat. She was all of that and more.

"Can you blame her?" Enzo shrugged. "If it wasn't for me, she wouldn't be on Carlos' radar. She was doing good at lying low and dealing out her information. Now…" He didn't elaborate on what he did to piss her off. He didn't need to. Revealing someone like that to anyone else was a good reason for that someone to want you dead. We'd be doing Martina a favour if we killed him, but we wouldn't. We owed her absolutely nothing. Less than nothing, since she'd given us information that was completely useless and self-serving. Clearly she had no idea who or where Jase or Hammer were.

"I see you haven't changed," Damon said dryly. "Still causing trouble."

Enzo rolled his eyes. "I see you haven't changed either, big brother. Still being a judgemental prick."

"We could always inform Carlos of your whereabouts," Reuben said. His gaze slid from Enzo to Angelina and back again. He wasn't bluffing. He had neither time nor patience for their bullshit.

Enzo looked like he was ready to lunge at Reuben, but Angelina grabbed his arm and held him back.

"Don't be a fucking idiot. Attacking Reuben Brantley will get you dead. Did you hear their offer to help us, or do you need your ears cleaned?" She let go of his arm and grabbed his earlobe to pull him closer to her. Speaking loudly she said, "*Don't. Do. Anything. To. Get. Killed.*"

He winced. "Okay, okay. I'll be nice. As long as they are."

"We're always nice," Gianni said. "But I think we should get out of here before someone else shows up."

Reuben nodded. "Let's go."

I slipped into the lead as we headed to the front of the house. No one said a word. No one complained when I held my hand to stop them.

"What is it?" Reuben whispered.

"Someone else has already shown up," I whispered back.

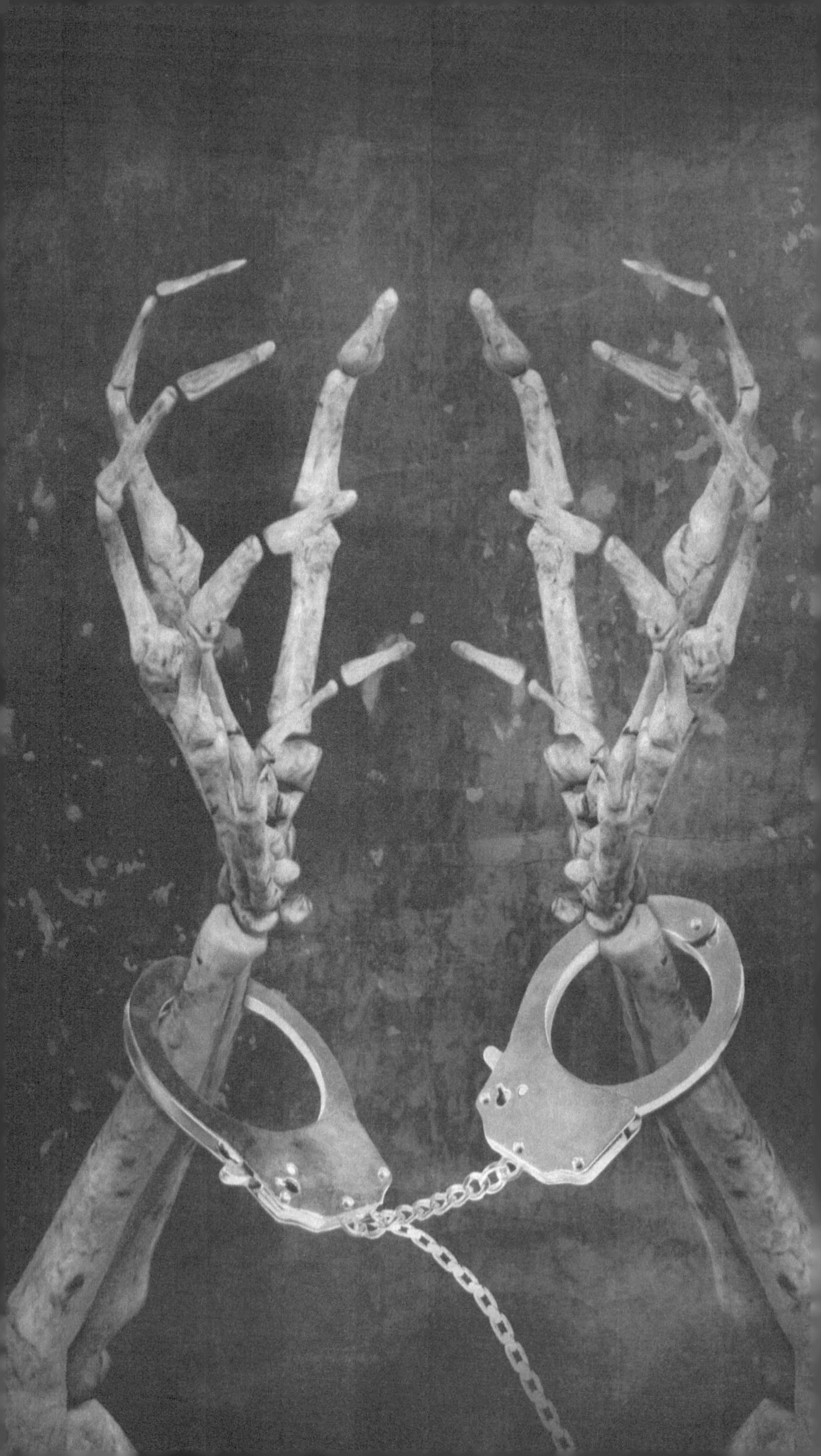

CHAPTER 11

GIANNI

"It's party time," I said under my breath.

Damon glanced at me like I lost my mind.

I grinned back. We both knew he enjoyed this shit as much as I did.

He shook his head and pushed past us all to the front of the house. He teased open the space between two curtains and peeked outside.

"Fuck," he said softly. "There's four cars out there. All facing the front of this place. They're not making any effort to hide. They want us to know they're there."

"I'm going to kill my mother." Angelina marched to another window and yanked open the curtains. She glared outside before unlocking and sliding the window open. "Fuck off, Carlos!" she shouted. "We don't want any of what you're selling."

Carlos stepped out of the vehicle and onto the front

lawn. He held his hands behind his back like they might just have a pleasant conversation.

"I'm not leaving without you, hermana," he called back. "I won't touch Enzo if you just get your ass out here."

"Bullshit, *hermano*," she spat. "The moment I'm inside that car, he's dead."

Damon pulled out his phone and started to tap on the screen, giving orders for our people to get themselves here for backup. As awesome as we were, we were boxed in here.

"I'll check the back," Mina said. She slipped away down the corridor to the back of the house, moving silently. If I couldn't see her silhouette in the light from the bedroom, I wouldn't have known she was there. She was beyond incredible. My heart swelled with love for my gorgeous little assassin.

She returned a couple of minutes later. "There's people waiting for us to sneak out that way. At least another eight of them."

"Nothing we can't take care of," I said. "Right, boss?" I glanced over to Reuben.

He seemed to be weighing up his options. I had a feeling fighting our way out was at the very bottom.

"Boss?" I pressed.

"If they want her that badly..." he said slowly.

"I won't let you hand her over." Enzo's hands were in fists, ready to take a swing.

"Don't do anything you'll regret," Damon warned.

"We're on your side. No one wants to give Angelina to Carlos." He turned his face toward Reuben, wanting agreement.

Reuben didn't agree, but he didn't disagree either. Top of his agenda was us getting out of here alive. Whether or not that included Enzo and Angelina was less important to him.

"We're going out the back." Enzo grabbed Angelina's hand and started to lead her that way.

"Last chance, Angelina," Carlos called out. "Otherwise, I might be forced to do something drastic." He gestured to the car behind his.

The door opened and one of his men pulled Bianca out onto the street.

Angelina stopped and stared in horror and disbelief. "You'd kill my mother?" she called out the window.

Carlos shrugged. "She's not my mother."

"She raised you," Angelina hissed. Her eyes shone with tears. "You're the devil himself."

Carlos raised a gun to Bianca's temple. "I'll count to ten. One."

"Angelina…" Enzo said softly.

"Two."

Angelina shook her head. "She's my mother."

"Three."

"I can't let you go," he pleaded.

"Four."

"I can't let him kill her." She wiped tears from her cheeks.

"Five."

"But I love you." He pulled her to him and held her tight.

"Six."

"I love you too." She squeezed him, but pulled away. "But she's my mother."

"Seven."

Angelina stepped over to the door, unlocked it and wrenched it open. "Stop!"

A shadow slipped past me. Past Angelina.

Mina pulled out a knife and aimed it. She threw with deadly precision, the knife slamming into the gun in Carlos' hand. It flew out of his grip and clattered onto the road.

Bianca dropped to the ground and rolled under one of the cars.

"Fucking hell." Carlos rubbed his hand.

"The next one goes into your brain," Mina said coldly. She already held another knife in her hand. I hadn't even seen her pull it out.

"This is none of your business," Carlos said, trying to pretend he wasn't rattled.

She could have killed him, but she hadn't. She was smart enough to know that would provoke a war between the Brantley family and the Vipers. That would get ugly and bloody very quickly.

Although, getting in the middle of a transaction like this also might. In my opinion, it was totally worth it. I was with Mina, women were not possessions.

"I'm making it my business," Mina said. "Enzo is family. That makes Angelina family. We take care of family. Tell Salvador to look elsewhere for a wife."

"There's a shit ton of dating apps out there," I said helpfully. "Or he could try one of those dating shows. Maybe— Asshole Wants a Wife. I'm sure that's a thing. If it isn't, it should be. The ratings would go through the roof."

"We aren't done," Carlos said, his tone icy. He nodded to his men and climbed back into the car.

Bianca rolled out from under the one she was hiding under, and bolted for the door.

Angelina grabbed her hand and pulled her inside. They both stepped back, growling at each other in Spanish. Something along the lines of, "How the fuck could you let him bring you here? You knew what he'd do. He's an ungrateful piece of crap." And so on.

We all waited until the cars pulled away before closing the door and collectively exhaling.

Enzo shoved his hands in his pockets and shuffled his feet. "Thank you," he said to Mina. "Those are some sick knife skills."

"I don't like bullies." She slipped her other knife away. "If I was you, I'd take his warning seriously. He will come for you again."

"They will," Damon said, stony faced. "The only reason he left now was that he doesn't want trouble with us. If we weren't here, this would have ended differently."

"We would have handled it," Enzo said. His voice held more confidence than his eyes did.

"Let's go," Reuben said. "We've wasted enough time here." He didn't bother to hide his irritation at Enzo and his continued stubbornness. He waited until Damon opened the door and stepped out again, before he followed him, leaving the rest of us to fall in behind.

"It's going to be a tight fit," I remarked as seven of us headed out to the SUV. "Mina, you can sit on my lap."

She leaned over to snatch up her knife from the road and tuck it away. "Better than being in the boot."

I caught her hand and pulled her to me. "First of all, we'd never put you in the boot. Second of all, the way you dealt with Carlos was hot as fuck." I whispered in her ear, "When we get home I'm going to fuck your pussy with my tongue until you scream."

"Is that a promise?" she asked. Her voice was husky, like throwing a knife at Carlos turned her on as much as it did me.

Death and violence were an addiction neither of us needed, or wanted, help for.

Lucky for us we had the jobs we did, or we'd get our rush by doing things which were more illegal than the things we already did.

"You can bet your cute little ass it is," I said. I cupped her ass cheeks and squeezed, while pulling her closer still. "I can't wait to have the taste of you on my tongue."

I pressed my quickly growing erection against her

leg. I wanted to push her up against the SUV and fuck her, here and now.

I kissed her mouth, thrusting my tongue between her lips as though it was my cock pounding into her pussy. Her mouth was warm, her plush lips tasting faintly of coffee and something sweet that was uniquely Mina.

"Get a room," Enzo called out.

My hands still on Mina's ass, I flipped him off with two fingers. "You can talk. We've all seen your cock, remember?" The guy had absolutely no shame. Not unlike me. Life was too short to care about shit like that.

"Only because you broke in for a look." Enzo grinned.

Damon shook his head at all of us and raised the seats in the third row of the SUV. He gestured for Enzo and Angelina to sit back there. "Don't fuck in the back of my SUV."

"That hadn't occurred to me until you suggested it." Enzo grabbed Angelina's hand and pulled her into the back of the vehicle.

"We'll make a stop at the Vipers' headquarters to leave you there if you do," Reuben said.

That was both a threat, and a promise. I suspected he wouldn't lose much sleep over it.

On the other hand, Mina was right. Damon's brother was family and we took care of each other. Reuben would tolerate Damon's brother, even if he, and Angelina, pushed him too far.

"Don't you fucking dare," Angelina hissed.

Apparently Reuben didn't intimidate her. Or maybe she knew Mina would never let him do that. Women's intuition and all that.

"Have some respect for the boss," Damon told her. "What happens to you now is up to him."

She gave him a look that suggested she didn't agree, but she flopped back against the seat and fell silent.

I followed Mina into the car, where she settled between me and Bianca.

Bianca looked weary and more than a little pissed off.

"I thought I raised Carlos better than that. He really would have shot me." She rubbed her temple where he'd had the barrel of the gun pressed.

I got the impression she might shoot him the next chance she got. That was her prerogative. If Vipers wanted to kill Vipers, that was up to them. As long as they left us out of it.

"I wouldn't have let that happen to you." Angelina leaned forward over the seat in front of her, and kissed her mother's cheek. "Even if I had to marry Salvador. But now, thanks to Mina, I can marry Enzo."

Bianca groaned. "Can't you find yourself a nice boy?"

"I'm nice," Enzo said. "You just need to get to know me."

She looked as though that was the last thing on

Earth she wanted. He was better than Salvador, whoever he was, but apparently not by much.

I had a sneaking suspicion she'd have to get used to him. He wasn't going anywhere if Angelina had anything to say about it.

I caught Mina's eye and grinned. The three of them made our lives look easy and peaceful. For a while, they'd taken my mind off Kurt Lasalle. Now, I wondered if he had a hand in all of this somehow. Like he'd set this up to distract us. I wasn't sure how, but if he had, it worked.

"You think Kurt paid Martina to do all of this, don't you?" Mina asked softly. "The fact she was pissed off with Enzo was an added bonus."

"The thought crossed my mind," I admitted. "If I had to bet, I'd say if we went back to her house, she'd be long gone by now."

"Without doubt," she agreed. She looked tired too. But something else. Satisfaction at keeping Angelina away from her brother and a life she didn't want. She seemed to have made it her mission to save women from a dark fate, even if she had to do it one woman at a time.

"I'll send the twins to check anyway," Damon said. "She might have left some sign behind."

We all knew that was unlikely. People like her knew how to disappear without a trace. At this point, she didn't matter all that much. What mattered was, what

was Kurt up to while we were looking in a different
direction?

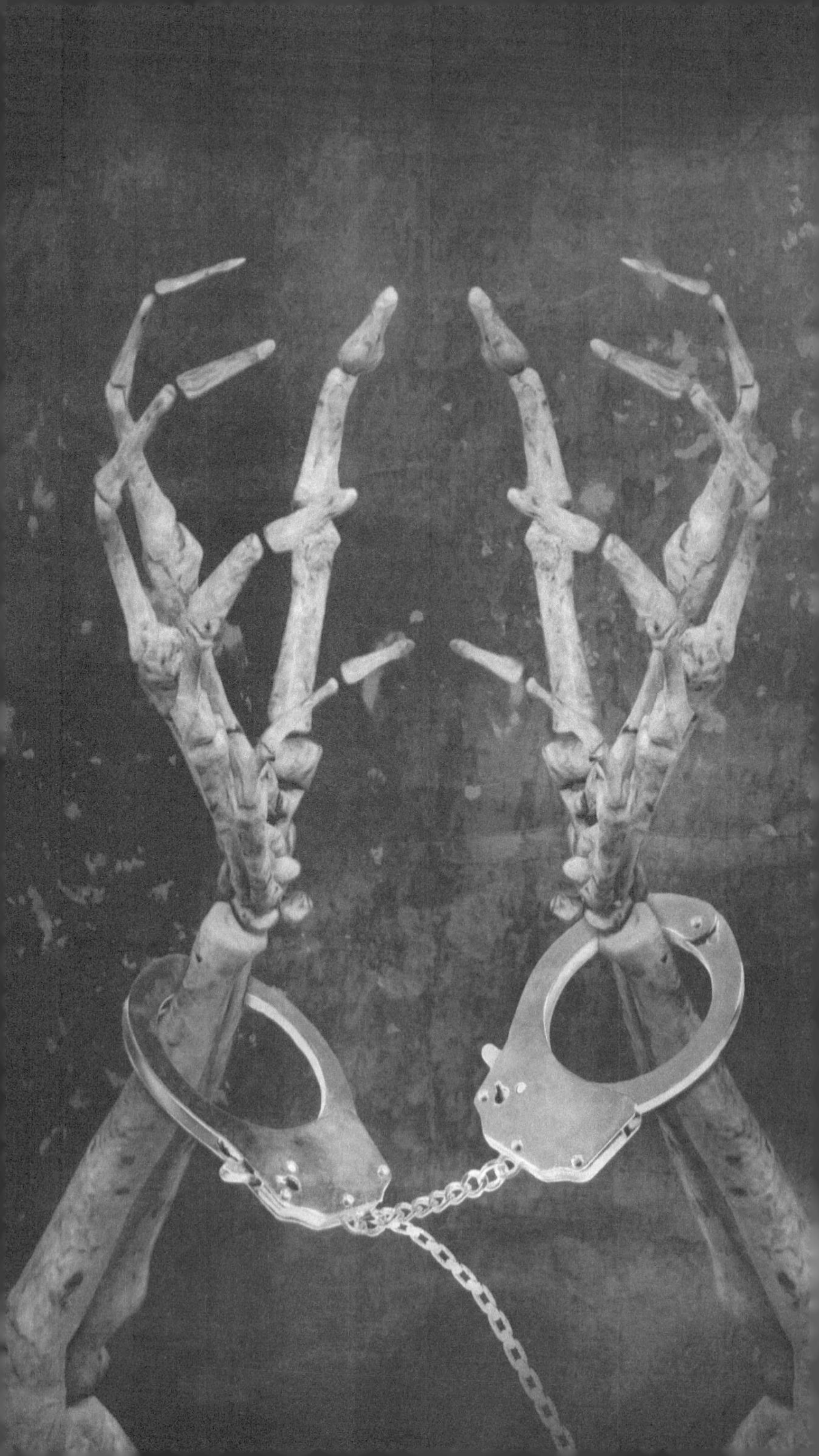

CHAPTER 12

MINA

Damon directed Enzo and Angelina to a room in the house, where they promptly disappeared, closing the door behind them. Bianca, with several rolls of her eyes, disappeared into a room on the other side of the corridor.

She muttered something that sounded like, "Far enough away that I don't have to listen to them fuck."

Damon grimaced and headed back down the stairs.

I followed him, watching the tension in his shoulder and back. He looked stiffer than a column of stone. Hard, but not brittle. Nothing about him was fragile, in spite of Enzo pushing his patience to its limits.

We reached the lower level as the twins returned.

"Just as you said, there's no sign of Martina," Hunter said. "The entire house was empty."

"Personally, I'm impressed at how quickly she

cleaned the place out," Parker said. "It couldn't have been more than a handful of hours."

"She had help." Reuben stood with his hip against the kitchen island, a glass of whiskey in his hand.

"Probably lots of it," Gianni agreed. "The question is, from whom?"

Reuben shook his head. "It doesn't matter now. I'll have Caleb keep an eye on the chatter about her. She'll turn up sooner or later."

"People like her always do," Hunter said. "Like a proverbial bad smell."

"Like you two?" Gianni teased.

"Exactly," Hunter said, not rising to the bait. "They can't keep people like us down. Right, Park?"

"Right," Parker agreed. "On a scale of one to a hundred, how much did you piss of the Vipers?"

"Nothing we can't handle." Reuben took a sip of his drink. "They know we could squash them if we wanted to. Or cut them off from our supply of goods."

The second one would hurt them worse than the first. They could fight off an attack, but not being able to get shipments would bring them to their knees within weeks, if not days.

Reuben could sell contraband elsewhere, but if no one would sell to the Vipers, they were fucked.

"I'm sorry I missed all the fun," Hunter said. "Did you really throw a knife at Carlos Jones?"

"Yes, I did," I said. "And I'd do it again. I will if he keeps trying to sell his sister."

"He's probably going to claim you tried to kill him, but missed," Gianni said.

"Of course he is." I shrugged. A man like him wasn't going to let the truth get in the way of his…manly reputation. He'd lie to save face.

No doubt everyone there, those who worked for him, would agree with his claim.

I didn't give a shit, we knew the truth. If his ego couldn't deal with that, that was his problem. I knew the extent of my abilities.

"If Mina wanted to kill him, he'd be dead," Reuben said. "If that needs to happen in the future, then it will. It might be a good idea to consider replacing him with someone we can continue to work with. I don't need anyone with an ego his size creating trouble for us."

"I'll look into who might potentially replace him," Damon said.

Reuben nodded. "Do it."

Hunter lounged against the island, on the opposite side from Reuben. "Parker and I have been talking to some people. Casually mentioning Kurt keeping a woman in his basement, like you asked us to."

One day, someone might mention that basement and I wouldn't shudder, but it wasn't tonight.

"And?" I prompted.

"And people believed it," Parker said. "Mostly, they're speculating on who it was. We also circulated the information that someone knows who the Sparrow is, and that the information was for sale."

"We might have also slipped in a rumour that the Sparrow kept a woman in their basement," Hunter said. "Sooner or later, people are going to start comparing notes and coming to conclusions. It won't be long before they realise that one and one equal three. Then, the shit will hit the proverbial fan."

"Good work," Reuben said. "Keep spreading those rumours. The sooner we can push this to a conclusion, the better. Any further information and the whereabouts of Kurt Lasalle?"

The moment the words passed his lips, my phone vibrated in my pocket.

I had the ringer turned off, because no one had any reason to call me. The number was new and the only people who had it were in this room.

That is, the only people who *should* have it were in this room.

"Let me guess, telemarketer?" Gianni asked.

I pulled out my phone. As expected, the screen said 'unknown number.'

I knew exactly who it was before I pressed on the screen to accept the call. I put the call on speakerphone and held the device on my palm.

We all waited in silence for the caller to speak.

"What fucking game are you playing, Mina?" Kurt's voice echoed through the kitchen. "You think people are going to believe I'm the Sparrow? Yes, I heard the rumour your little twin friends are trying to spread. "

"We're not little," Parker whispered.

"People will believe what they want to believe," I said coolly. "Although, most people who've met you don't need an excuse to want you dead. You seem to have that effect on people. Probably because you're a slimy prick."

He laughed. "Is that supposed to hurt my feelings, bitch? You need to work on your insults."

"It wasn't an insult, it was an observation," I said.

"An accurate one," Damon said.

"Sounds like the whole crew is there," Kurt said. "Hi guys. Long time no see. Don't worry, I'm working on rectifying that as soon as possible. Did you have fun on the side quest I sent you on? You knew that was me behind that, right? Martina was paid well to give you that false lead. Don't bother trying to find her, she's long gone. In the meantime, I put some plans into place. It's only a matter of time before you're back where you belong. On your back, under me."

Reuben, Damon and Gianni all growled softly.

The twins looked murderous.

I swallowed to keep from throwing up my last meal and said, "You're cocky for someone who won't be alive much longer."

He laughed again. "Threats? That's fucking adorable. You can't even find me. I could be right under your nose and you wouldn't have a clue. By the way, nice aim on that knife you threw at Carlos. I could tell you were aiming for his gun, not for him. Bravo." He clapped slowly.

My blood went cold. Kurt was watching? Of course he was. The question was, where was he watching from? Another house, or a camera? Would he have dared to get close enough to watch in person?

"You should have come out and said hello," Gianni said. "But you wouldn't, would you? You're too much of a fucking coward. I'm looking forward to seeing how tiny your cock is, right before I slice it off." He made a slicing gesture with his hand.

"More threats?" Kurt sneered. "I had no idea how pathetic you all were. Disappointing, really. Still, it'll be easier to replace the Brantleys when people realise how much more competent I am."

"You said 'fucked up in the head' wrong," Gianni said.

Kurt snorted. "Please, you're embarrassing yourself now."

"Did you actually want something?" Reuben asked. "It seems to me all you're doing is wasting our time. Making idle threats and pretending you have power and contacts you clearly lack. No one in this room is fooled by your bullshit."

"Reuben Brantley himself," Kurt said derisively. "Does Mina moan when you fuck her? She has the best moans. She has spread her legs for you, hasn't she? I'm sure she has, she loves nothing more than being fucked. Especially when she's restrained. I recommend chains, but rope would do too."

Reuben's fingers tightened around his glass, so tight

it shattered in his hand, sending a spray of whiskey onto his sleeve and the floor.

"You'll moan when we're done with you," Damon said darkly. "You'll beg us to kill you." Before Kurt could respond, he leaned over and ended the call.

"Have I mentioned recently how much I really, really hate him?" Gianni said. "He's such a shithead. Actually, that's an insult to shitheads. He's worse than a shithead."

"He really is," Hunter said. He looked like he wanted to live up to his name and hunt Kurt down personally and drag him here by his balls.

Parker looked similarly furious. "He must have missed the part where pissing off a member of the Brantley family was a really, really bad idea. People who do it tend to live to regret it."

"Yes, they do," Hunter agreed. "What else can we do? It's not fair for this oxygen thief to keep living any longer than necessary. Another hour is too much."

"Short of knocking on every door in Dusk Bay..." Damon rubbed his forehead with the heel of his hand. "We're doing everything we can think of."

No one suggested actually going door-to-door. That would be time-consuming and ultimately pointless.

Kurt was likely moving around, and wasn't dumb enough to open a knock on the door. He'd have someone to do that for him. Someone to take the bullet if one was aimed at him. No, we'd have to be smarter than that.

"Mina, can I have your phone?" Parker asked. "I can at least try to trace wherever he called from. I couldn't last time, but it's worth a try."

I nodded and handed him my phone. "Just don't go poking around in the apps in there."

He grinned. "I wouldn't dream of it. And I won't look at your photos either, just in case there's a dick pic from Reuben." He stuck out his tongue in playful disgust, his eyes shining with amusement.

Reuben gave him a look that was drier than a martini, before raising his hand in front of him. His palm was red with blood from the imploding glass. Indifferent, he walked over to the wet bar on the side of the room and poured himself another drink, this time a double.

"She's more likely to get a dick pic from me," Gianni said.

Parker grimaced. "That's just as good a reason not to look in her photos. No offence. You're almost as much a big brother to me as Reuben is."

"How am I supposed to take offence when you finish with something like that?" Gianni stepped over to give Parker a hug.

Parker hugged him back. "I know what to say to avoid getting shot."

"So far," Damon said. He smirked at Parker.

Parker grinned. "I'm going to fuck up at some point and I know that, but in the meantime, I'll keep trying to be smooth. It's gotten me this far. I might even live to be as old as Reuben."

"Not if you call me old." Reuben downed the contents of his glass in one gulp and poured another.

Both twins chuckled and fist bumped at the expense of their oldest brother. If they weren't giving him hell, they wouldn't be themselves. Even if it scored them dark looks from time to time.

"I'll get this back to you as soon as I can." Parker nodded towards the phone in his hand. "And I'll change the number to one that'll be harder for him to get a hold of."

I shook my head. "Don't bother. The cockier he gets, the better chance he'll make a mistake. He already did by reminding us he was watching tonight. We know he's still in Dusk Bay. We know to look out for something. Something big."

"He could be trying to convince us he's doing something when he's not," Damon said.

He didn't look like he believed that any more than I did. Something was coming and, whatever it was, we had to be ready.

If not, I might have to take a leaf from Angelina's book and step out the front of the house before someone else paid the price for me.

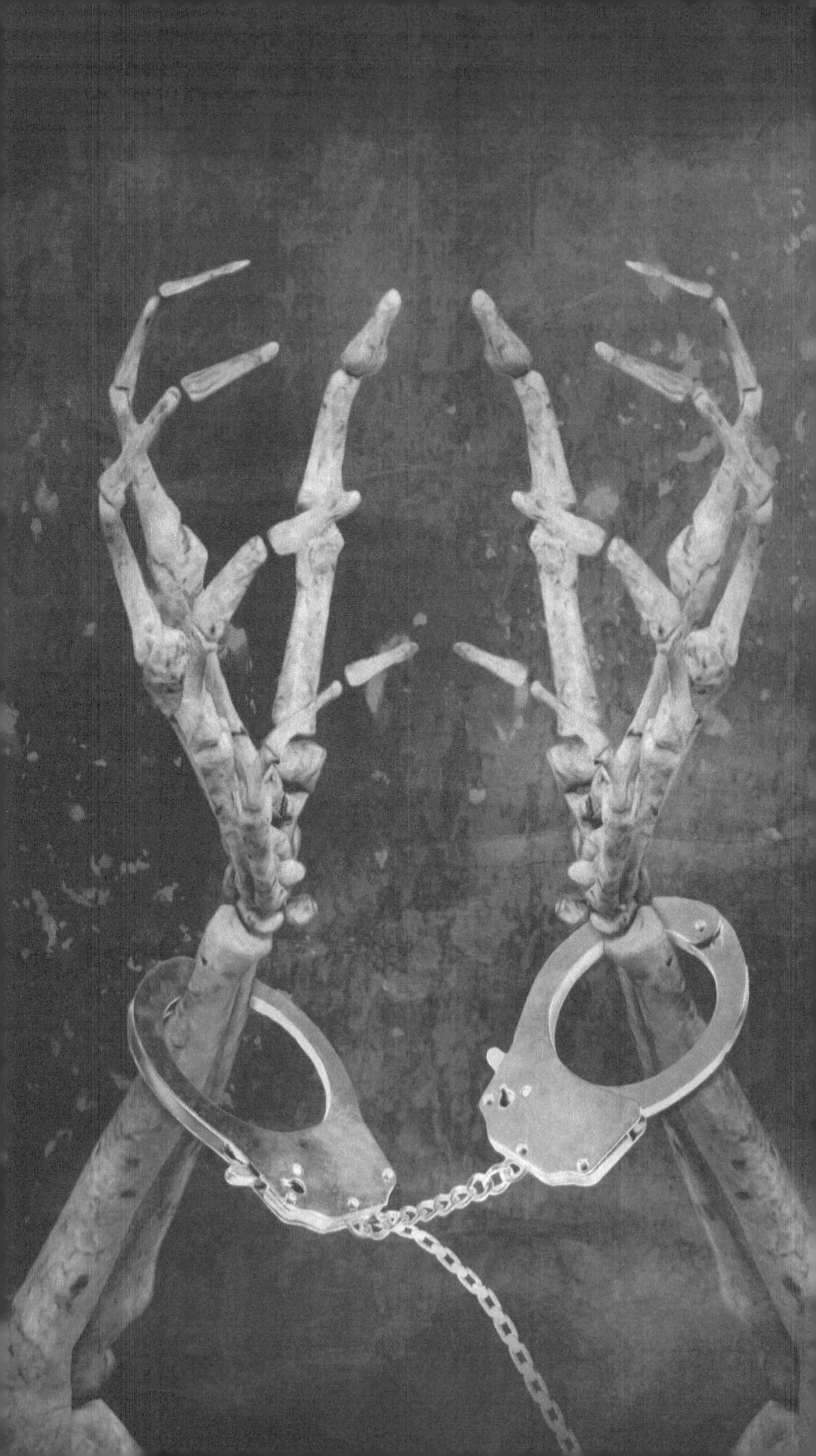

CHAPTER 13

MINA

My hair still damp from the shower, I stepped out of Reuben's ensuite and into his bedroom.

All three of my guys stood beside the window, talking in hushed tones. They stopped the minute they saw me and stared with open hunger in their eyes, like three lions sizing up a delicious deer. Trying to decide which bit they'd feast on first.

Not long ago, that deer's instinct would have been to flee into the forest. Now I stood my ground, letting them appraise me. Admire and want me.

Making me want them.

"Did I miss something?" I asked lightly.

I combed my fingers through my hair. Healthier than ever, dark waves hung down to my shoulders. Now I was eating properly and keeping clean, it was growing quickly. My scars would never disappear, but my skin was healthier too.

At some point, I might get past the urge to shower two or three times a day. After being filthy for so long, I loved being clean. I couldn't get enough of standing under, or soaking in, hot water. It was the ultimate luxury. Sometimes it really was the little things in life that mattered. I didn't care if we lived in a tiny house, as long as we had running hot water. I promised myself I'd never wash in cold again. Not if I could help it.

"No. You didn't miss anything important." Reuben's tone made it clear that whatever they were talking about, they wouldn't elaborate.

Not long ago, I would have been insecure about them keeping something from me, but now I trusted that if I needed to know, they'd fill me in. They might have been discussing nothing more important than the weather. Making small talk while they waited for me.

All right, I suspected it was something more than that, but still not vital. Not more important than us spending this time together.

Reuben moved towards me, took my hands to pull me to him. He kissed my mouth, softly at first, but quickly deepening.

Every time he touched me, he held back less and less. So did I. What used to be terrifying, was becoming as comfortable as it was natural. More and more, I could let go of my inhibitions. I could be myself around them, like I never could with anyone else.

In the corner of my eye, I watched Damon walk over to the door. I thought he was leaving, but he closed it and turned the lock, to give all four of us privacy from the rest of the house.

A shiver of excitement passed through me. In the back of my mind, I still struggled to get my head around the fact three incredible men wanted me, but I pushed the insecurity aside. They'd all made it abundantly clear how they felt. It was time for me to accept and embrace everything they wanted to give to me. Including themselves.

Gianni moved to stand behind me. His hands were firm on my shoulders before starting to massage them, his long fingers working out all the knots. Gradually, he moved his hands down my arms, down my sides, to my hips. He held them cupped in his palms while pressing his erection into my side.

"The things you do to me," he whispered. "Since I met you, I feel like I'm hard all the time. No one has ever made me feel like that. Not even Damon."

Damon grunt-laughed. "Same here."

I broke off my kiss with Reuben to grab Damon by the front of his shirt and tug him in for a kiss. I needed him to know he was very much wanted.

My feelings for all three of them were equal. I needed all of them as much as each other. When it came to intimacy, I wanted Damon to put his insecurities aside like I was trying to do. Put them aside and let go.

Surprised at first, Damon quickly rallied and kissed me back, his tongue probing into my mouth. Sliding against mine. He tasted of whiskey and spontaneity.

Like he understood my desire for him to let me in more. He wanted me to know he was trying.

I gave him that back with my kisses. I was also trying. Together, we could do this.

We explored each other's mouths for a minute or two before we were forced to come up for air.

I sucked in a breath and laughed at the headiness of being kissed so thoroughly. When Damon started to let go, he didn't hold back. He'd put everything into the kisses. Everything and then some.

"My turn." Gianni gripped my chin and turned my face so he could kiss me.

Beside us, Damon and Reuben looked at each other warily, before they came together, hands on each other's shoulders, mouths pressed against each other.

I moaned at the sight in the corner of my eye, and the feeling of Gianni's lips on mine.

The rest of the world evaporated, and all that was left was the four of us. Maybe the world burned down around us, because we were so hot we ignited it. I was that aroused, I wouldn't have been surprised. My panties were so drenched, it was about to trickle down the insides of my thighs.

I found myself lying back on Reuben's bed while all three of them jostled to help me out of my silky sleep shorts and singlet.

After hearing Kurt's voice again, I needed this. I needed to feel wanted and safe and loved. I needed to be touched and to touch. To remind myself I was Mina

DiMarco and I was stronger than anything he ever did to me.

All three of my incredible, sexy guys shed their clothes. Shirts, pants, socks and underwear flying. I was quickly surrounded by bare, hot muscle.

As he'd promised, Gianni scooted down until his face was between my legs. Dark eyes on me, he teased my clit with his tongue and fingers. He thrust his tongue inside, and tasted all around my pussy.

Reuben lay beside me running his hands and mouth up and down my body and lavishing attention on my breasts.

Damon watched us for a while, the smallest hint of uncertainty in his eyes.

I gave him a smile of encouragement as he looked at Reuben's cock, while trying not to look at it.

Reuben was also looking at him, speculatively. Not unwelcoming. Not insistent either.

Gianni's gaze swivelled over to Damon, watching intently as the other man lowered himself so Reuben's cock was right in front of his face. His tongue swiped over his lips before he tasted Reuben's head with the tip of his tongue.

Reuben shivered, but didn't pull away.

Encouraged, Damon swirled his tongue around Reuben's tip before taking him into his mouth and starting to suck.

"Good boy," Gianni said before lowering his face back to my pussy and lapping at me more firmly.

Damon managed an eye roll without losing his rhythm.

Reuben and I both rolled our hips in time with each other. He kept one hand on my breast and held my hand with the other, our fingers laced. His grip tightened the closer he came to coming.

"Be a good girl and come with me," he said breathlessly.

I moaned in response. "I'm so close."

"Me too." He forced the words out.

I squeezed his hand hard and came, grinding myself against Gianni's mouth while I saw stars. My ears were filled with the pounding of blood, and the sound of Reuben as he too orgasmed.

For the longest time, there was nothing but bliss and the pleasure of knowing he was feeling the same thing at the same time. That he was squirting his cum into Damon's mouth. That Damon was tasting the salty release that must have coated his tongue.

We sagged back, side-by-side on the mattress.

I lay puffing lightly, catching my breath.

Damon slid his mouth off Reuben's cock and swallowed.

"Just when I think you couldn't get hotter, you do," Gianni said to all of us. He snaked an arm around the back of Damon's head and slammed his mouth down onto the other man's. Letting Damon taste my release from his lips.

Damon groaned. He grabbed Gianni's arm and kissed him like the world was about to end.

They finally broke off and Damon scooted on the bed until his cock was in front of my face.

Gianni rolled me onto my side and gently parted my legs. He gripped my hips, positioned his cock and slid himself into my pussy.

I closed my eyes to savour the feeling of him inside me, his piercings already massaging me.

I opened my eyes again, and my mouth, to take in Damon's cock.

We let Gianni set the rhythm, as he thrusted into me with deep, even strokes.

Reuben moved around to the other side of me so he could slip his hand between my legs and tease my clit with the tips of his fingers.

I was right, the attention of three men at once was incredible and compelling. I'd never felt so full, spoilt or loved in my life. These three men, who would kill without a second thought, fucked me like I was a queen.

I felt like one.

Their queen.

"Good girl," Reuben said. "You take both of their cocks so well. You like being filled like this, don't you? You like it when we fuck you."

I could only respond to him by smiling with my eyes, my mouth was too busy sucking and teasing Damon's cock with my lips and tongue.

"You feel amazing," Gianni said, thrusting slowly.

"Fucking amazing," Damon agreed. "Fucking perfect."

"Fucking ours," Reuben said. "Always. I love you, Mina DiMarco."

I slipped my mouth off Damon's cock long enough to say, "I love you too, Reuben Brantley." I smiled and went back to sucking.

Between Gianni thrusting inside me and Reuben's fingers, I was pushed all the way to the edge and over again. This time, even more intense and all-encompassing than before.

Every single part of my body was on fire with pure heat and pleasure. Nothing existed but that, and a shower of fireworks in my otherwise darkened vision.

"Good girl." Reuben's voice was barely audible over the blood in my ears. "You come for us so beautifully. So fucking gorgeous."

I came back down to reality, quickly catching my breath without stopping sucking.

My whole body went on tingling, but I wanted Damon and Gianni to feel good like I just had. I wanted to give that to them.

"I want both of you to come inside her," Reuben said. "Show her you love her. Show her she's ours."

"Yes, boss," Gianni said, his voice strained. "Just about to... Come... Inside her..." He thrust more frantically before groaning and coming inside my body.

Damon was only a couple of moments behind,

thrusting into my mouth, all the way down to my throat.

I gagged, but went on sucking until he exploded in my mouth. A blast of warm cum shot into my throat before I swallowed it down.

"Good girl," Reuben said. "Take every drop. It's all for you. All for our beautiful woman."

Damon slipped out of my mouth and sagged down in a corner between Reuben and the wall.

Gianni, panting lightly, stayed buried inside me until his breath finally slowed.

"I could stay here forever." He sounded sleepy. "My cock doesn't want to leave your pussy. He might just live there forever."

In spite of that, he gradually slid out of me and held me close. "I love you."

"I love you too," I told him. I snuggled up to him and glanced over to Damon.

"You're still a distraction, but I also love you," he said with a grunt.

I smiled. "You're still an asshole, but I love you too." He wasn't that much of an asshole anymore, but I couldn't resist ribbing him. What were boyfriends for, after all?

"Let's get you cleaned up," Gianni said. "Then, maybe round two, in the shower."

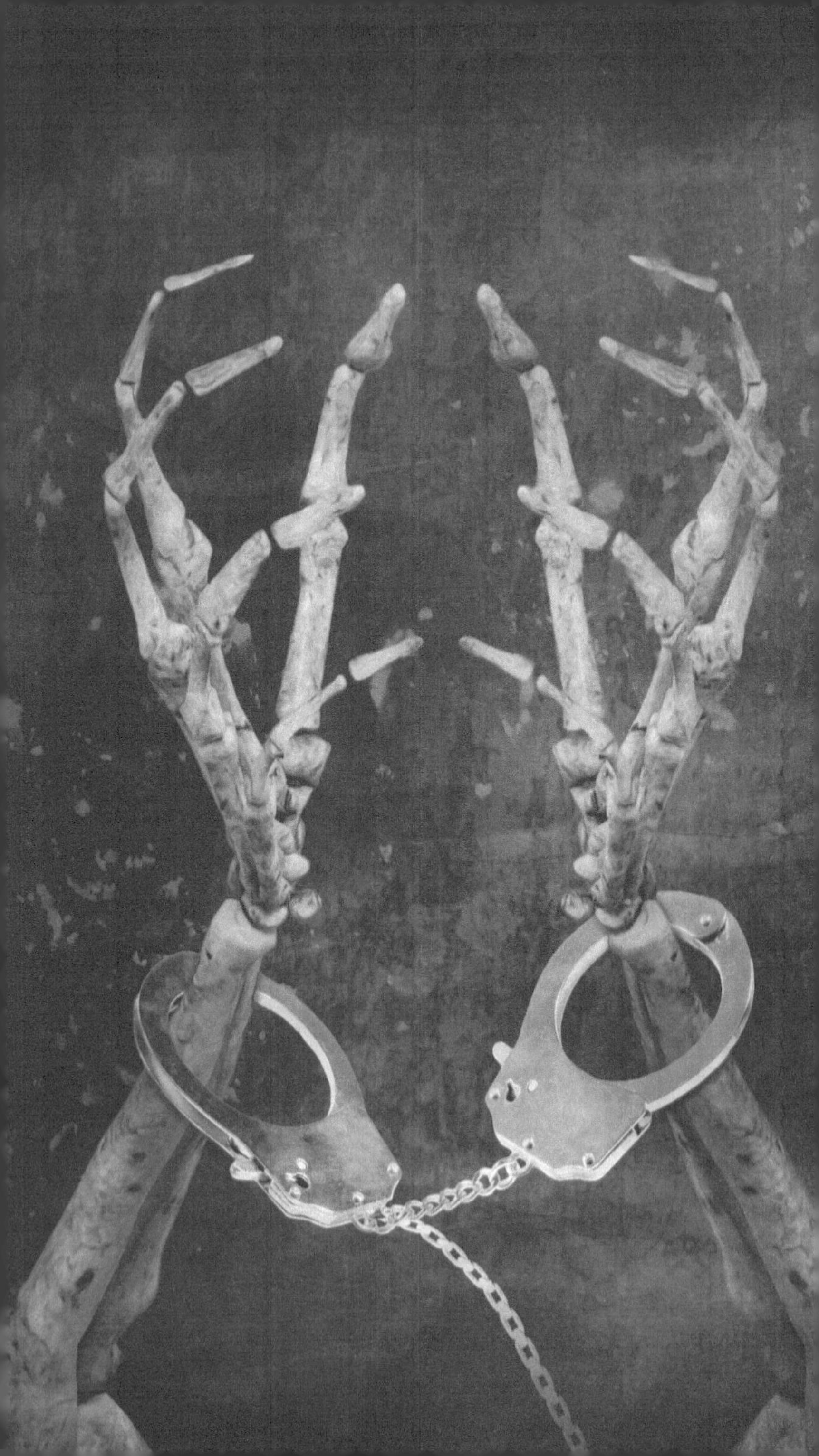

CHAPTER 14

MINA

"He's not looking so good." Gianni looked sideways at Leon Graves. "I guess hanging from a chain for a week will do that to a guy."

"I guess so," I agreed with no shred of remorse.

Leon was pale, and his wrists chafed from the cuffs around them. Heavy circles surrounded his eyes, and bags hung underneath. He couldn't have had much sleep between the position he was chained in, and the constant barrage of loud, metal music.

He looked all but broken, and the only place Gianni touched him was in his calf. As torture went, it was clearly effective.

"I told you everything I know," Leon said. "Please…" There was no hint of hope in his eyes anymore. Nothing but the desire for all of this to end.

"Martina was a bust." Gianni briefly told Leon about our meeting with her, and about Enzo and Angelina.

And the phone call from Kurt. "So you see, we're back at square one. Reuben doesn't like being at square one, Leon. Especially when you were the one who guided us there. We need more information. Better information. Who exactly is this Jase? Who is Hammer?"

"I don't know," Leon whined. "I swear. I've told you everything I can think of. Please…"

"Everything you can think of?" Gianni echoed. "I guess you better think about things you haven't thought of yet. Otherwise, I might have to find some different music to play for you. What about some kid's music?"

"That would be evil," I remarked. "I've heard some of it since… I came home. It would drive anyone crazy."

"Exactly." Gianni grinned. "Can you imagine hearing 'climbing goat, goat, goat,' over and over? Or the next chorus, 'fainting goat, goat, goat.' I guess whoever wrote that has a thing about goats."

"I think they have a thing about earworms," I remarked. "Excuse me if I stick to Bobby Sparkle."

Gianni snapped his fingers. "We could play that and pretend we're at a school disco."

Leon groaned. "You're both out of your fucking minds."

Gianni crouched down in front of him. "That's not a nice thing to say about my woman, Leon."

Leon raised his chin and almost managed to look defiant. "Why don't you go on and kill me then?"

He sucked in a ragged breath and spoke in a hoarse voice. "Kurt enjoyed raping her. I enjoyed watching it. I enjoyed every moment of it. I was hoping he'd let me do it too. I wanted to stick my cock in her mouth and make her suck it."

I pushed down the spike of anxiety at the memories his words evoked.

"I was just about to tell Gianni I thought you'd outlived your usefulness." I stepped closer. "But for that, you can live for a while longer." He deserved to suffer a little more for bringing all of that up. A lot more.

His head flopped back down and he groaned softly. Frustrated that his attempt to provoke us into killing him had failed miserably.

His next words came out in a pleading rush. "Jase's last name is Andrews. Jason Andrews. He was an old friend of Kurt. Hammer's real name is Wade. I heard Kurt call him that once. I don't know what his last name is, I swear. They might be brothers, I don't know."

Gianni glanced over to me questioningly, but I shrugged. Neither name was familiar. Leon might have made them up in the moment, to give us something.

I pulled out my phone and sent off a message to Damon to put his contacts onto finding anyone by those names.

"That wasn't so hard, was it?" Gianni asked. He gave Leon a shove, just enough to force him half a metre sideways, and put more pressure on his wrists.

Leon screamed. "Fucking hell. Please, for fuck's sake, I don't know anything else."

"What about Kurt's addresses in Dusk Bay?" I asked.

"You must have some idea. Where were his minions supposed to take me?"

"I don't know." He shook his head and winced.

"I don't believe you," I said. "I might reconsider letting you live for longer if you can give us more."

"On my laptop," he said finally.

"We got it from Clarissa, but haven't been able to get into it yet," Gianni said. "You can imagine what that did to the twins' egos. Especially Parker. He prides himself on that shit."

"I can tell you how to get in," Leon said eagerly. "There's more information on there. Most of it is encrypted. You'll need my help to access it. If you let me go, I can—"

Gianni said. "Tell us how to get in. If that works, we might decide to go easier on you."

Leon exhaled, long and ragged, but started to explain.

———

"I'd be impressed if he wasn't a toad," Parker said. He lounged over the kitchen island, Leon's laptop open front of him. "I've never seen encryption like this. He must have developed it himself."

"Is there anything useful on there?" I asked. As far as I could tell, computer code was another language. One the twins were apparently fluent in, but that made little sense to me.

"That depends on your definition of useful," Parker said. "There's a shit load of records of transactions. Money coming in and out, goods being moved around. That should help us find some of the shipments he stole from us. And from the Bell family." He glanced at Hunter, who didn't quite meet his eyes.

"What about addresses?" Damon asked. "In particular, in and around Dusk Bay?"

"Several," Parker replied. "Nothing that stands out."

"Anything near Demons' Arena?" I asked.

"A couple of them," Parker said. "By the way, no luck on tracing Kurt's phone number." He pulled my phone out of his pocket and handed it to me. "He's a slippery motherfucker."

"Yes, he is." That wasn't news to any of us.

I put my phone away and waved toward the laptop. "Any indication of a connection between Kurt and those addresses?"

"Those addresses being on here suggests there's a connection," Parker said. "There's nothing concrete. Nothing is labelled 'Kurt's main residence,' or 'Kurt's place of business.' You think they would have tried to be more helpful, but apparently not." He flipped the laptop off.

"Send them to me," Damon said. "I'll see what our people can find out."

"Tell them to be on their guard," Reuben said. "There's a good chance Kurt will expect us to check out each location for ourselves. Which is why we won't. We won't walk into any traps."

"Kurt probably gave those addresses to Leon, knowing we might find them," I said.

Reuben was right, that was a trap waiting to happen. And probably the exact reason why Kurt mentioned watching me throw the knife at Carlos. He was hoping to draw us to him. We needed to find a way to turn that back on him.

"He really screwed Leon over," Gianni remarked. He didn't look even slightly sympathetic. "He used him to try to lure Mina, knowing if we got to him first, he could turn it to his advantage. I'd be impressed, if he wasn't such a complete and utter prick."

"Kurt or Leon?" Hunter asked.

"Yes," Gianni replied with a smile.

Hunter grinned. "Both sounds about right."

While Parker continued to go through the laptop, I stepped over to Damon. "Any luck on finding Jason Andrews, or Wade?"

He rolled his lips. "We've discovered Jason Andrews is a very common name, as is Wade. I have my contacts looking for brothers called Jason and Wade, who might work for Kurt. Or be an old friend of his. If they even exist, they'll be found."

"They exist," I said. "Or, they used to."

I'd thought about them often, but I still couldn't clearly picture their faces. Just vague details about their build and hair colour. Their voices were more vivid than their appearances. But I knew if I met them again, I'd know them immediately.

"Either way, we'll find out." He put a reassuring arm around me, his large hand squeezing my shoulder. "We're closer than we were when we just had the nickname, Hammer."

"Yeah, I know we are," I said.

We weren't close enough, but Damon was doing the best he could.

I knew I wasn't alone in my frustration. Kurt had been playing games with us for weeks, and it was getting exhausting. Every time we seemed to be getting somewhere, we took a step back. Or several.

I pictured him laughing at us as he toyed with our strings, like we were his puppets. Tweaking and making us dance to his tunes.

Fuckhead.

I wanted to punch the smug smile off his smug, asshole face. Right before I sliced of his cock and balls and made him eat them. And then—

"Bingo, motherfucker," Parker said suddenly.

"What is it?" Reuben leaned over his shoulder.

"It's an encrypted conversation between Leon and Kurt," Parker said. "Kurt telling Leon when to arrive in Dusk Bay and where to go. It goes back a lot further than that. There are details of meetings between them, including addresses of the places they met up. Kurt telling Leon who to speak to. A number where he can be reached."

My heart started racing. "Any chance you can trace that number?"

"There's every chance I'm going to try," he agreed. "In the meantime, I'll send all of this to Damon. This could help narrow things down."

"Only if it's legit," Damon said.

"Considering the layers of encryption, we weren't meant to find this," Parker said. "I don't mean to toot my own horn, but someone less skilled than me wouldn't get in." He tapped the tip of his finger on the island, beside the laptop. "We definitely weren't meant to see this. I'd bet my trust fund on it."

"If you lose that bet, I'm not sharing," Hunter told him.

Parker flashed him a grin. "I won't lose." He turned back to the screen. "All of this goes back before Kurt took Mina." He squinted. "By the look of it, Kurt had all of that planned for weeks. Maybe even months." He frowned deeply.

"What is it?" I asked.

"It seems like Leon is the one who found out about your father's attempt to take down the Brantley family. There's messages in here of him telling Kurt all the details. He must have been pleased with himself, because he didn't delete what I'd consider to be fucking damning evidence. Smug prick. He was very sure no one was getting past his encryption. I love being underestimated. Especially when it helps to fuck people over. There's enough chain in here for him to hang himself."

"Yeah," I said vaguely.

I'd known Leon was a snake, but now I knew he was the one who gave Kurt the weapon to get to me. He was as much to blame as Kurt was. They were in all of it together. Right from the start.

"How did Leon find out?" I asked.

"It seems he stumbled upon some transactions that didn't add up. He looked into it and found evidence that pointed straight to Mina's father," Parker said. "I get the impression Leon and Kurt were pretty tight. Assholes of a feather and all that shit. He ran straight to his bestie to spill the tea. And Kurt used that information to his own advantage. Leon gave him an opportunity and he took it. Some close friend Kurt turned out to be. The first chance he got, he threw him right under the bus and into our basement. With friends like him, who needs enemies?" He turned to Hunter and they both shrugged.

"What do you want to do?" Gianni asked me.

I became aware of all of their eyes on me. My tongue slid across my lips. "I think we should let him go. Leon Graves, we should unchain him and let him out."

"Why would we do that?" Reuben asked.

"Because I think he can lead us to Kurt," I said.

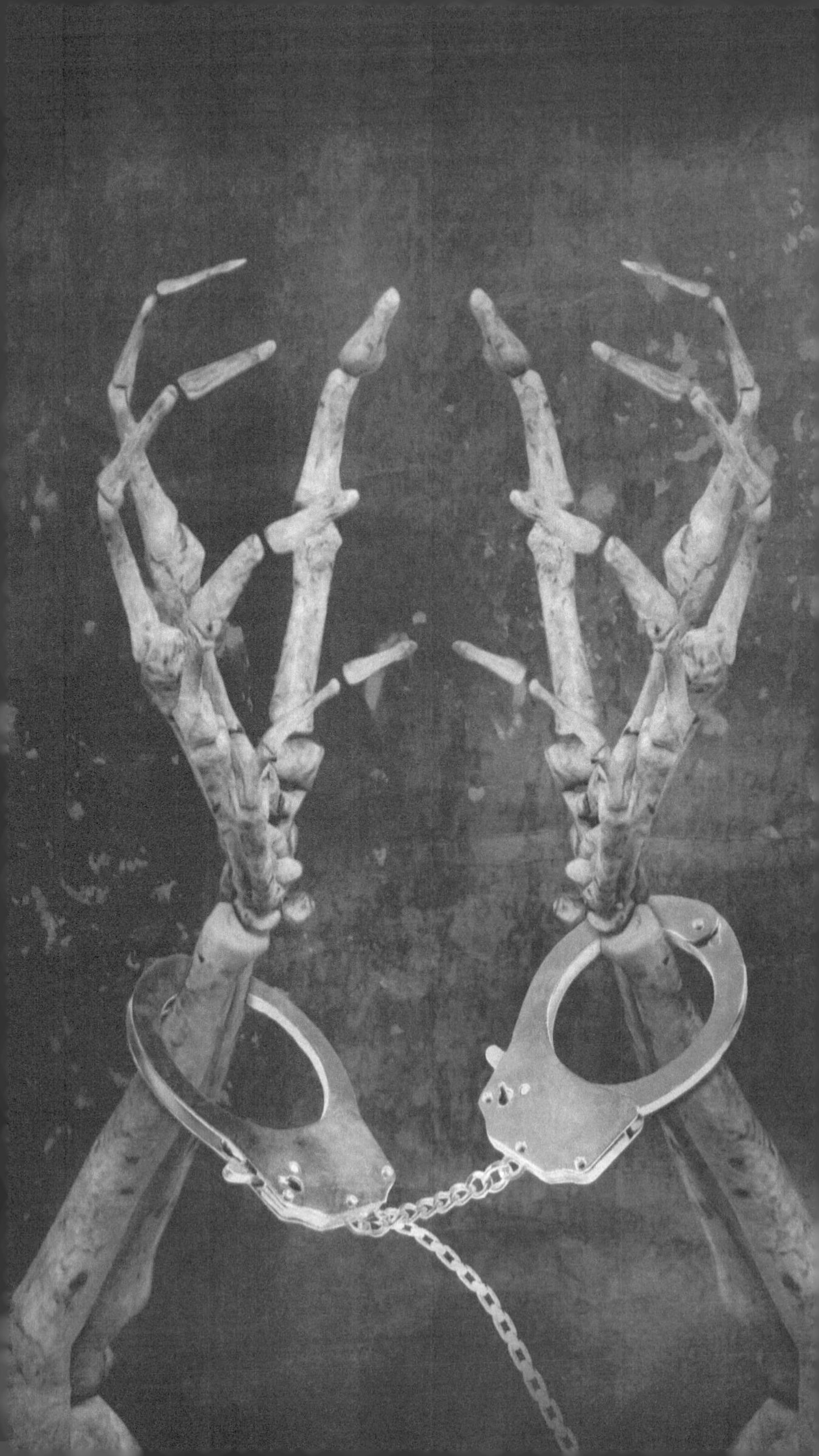

CHAPTER 15

GIANNI

I leaned my shoulder against the wall and watched Leon eat his bowl of soup.

He stopped every now and again to dip in a chunk of bread, before stuffing it into his mouth. The whole time, he kept half an eye on us.

Unfortunately, his food wasn't poisoned. Not even with a handy laxative. I suggested it, but no one seemed to like the idea apart from me. I put it aside for potential future use on Caleb instead. It might help to get the stick out of his ass. Or on the twins, just for shits and giggles.

We all ate from the same pot of soup made by Terry. And the same loaf of freshly made bread. Personally, I would have given Leon stale bread and maybe a glass of dirty water. Between Terry's pride and Mina's insistence we treat him well, I held my peace.

For now.

I wouldn't have minded if he choked on that bread. We'd been too nice to him as far as I was concerned. We'd even stopped to treat the knife wound in his leg. And of course, slip in a tracking chip. Asshole wasn't getting off that easy.

"How long have you known Damon?" Mina asked Angelina. She was chewing on a piece of bread covered in a thin layer of butter. She still half closed her eyes while she ate, as though everything was pure heaven. Granted, Terry's bread was that good, but when you're virtually starved for so long, even substandard food would taste amazing.

I made a mental note to let Terry have a night off and make her my family's special carbonara recipe. I prepare it with a secret ingredient I don't share with anyone. If I did, I'd have to kill them. That's how secret it is.

Angelina shrugged and slurped her soup. "A few years, I guess. Ever since Reuben took over as head of the Brantley family. I used to have the biggest crush on him." She slid a sly glance toward Enzo and Damon.

Enzo glared at Damon like he might carve out his brother's heart out with the spoon in his hand.

"Me too," I said to break the tension.

Damon wouldn't have been interested in Angelina in that way anyway. Especially given her relation to Carlos. Carlos would have come after him instead. Nothing Damon couldn't handle, but a complication he neither needed nor wanted.

I got the impression he thought of her as something of a little sister. To be honest, I was starting to think of her in the same way myself. She had more balls than most of the men I knew. Enzo would certainly have his hands full with her. And vice versa. Their lives together wouldn't be boring.

Hopefully it wouldn't also be short.

Damon shot me a glance before returning to his meal.

"Who is Salvador?" Mina asked.

I'd been wondering the same thing myself. Damon worked closer with the Vipers than I did, which wasn't saying much. They were secretive when it came to outsiders. Just like we were. Let people in on your secrets, and they tend to use them against you. Or mess up perfectly good carbonara. That was a crime if there ever was one.

"Salvador Briggs is my brother's right hand," Angelina said. "At least, that's what he's angling for. He's about fifteen years older than me." She made a face like that made him incredibly old.

The age difference in age between Mina and I was about the same. And that between her and Damon and Reuben. Although, Mina was mature for her age.

I wouldn't wish for Angelina to grow up quicker, as she had. She had plenty of time. I hoped.

Reuben slid her a glance, suggesting he wasn't as engrossed in his own meal as he looked. Of course not, he was always paying attention. Nothing got past him.

People were more likely to let down their guard when they thought someone wasn't listening, even when that someone was him. It was a good way to learn any number of things.

'Observe, listen and absorb,' might be his motto. Along with 'anyone who got in his way was dead.' Or wished they were. Sometimes, he liked to bide his time, but he always fucked back sooner or later. Usually way worse than anything inflicted on him.

"He needs to keep his hands to himself before someone cuts them off," Enzo said. "If he touches Angie…"

Once again, he gripped his spoon like he'd use it as a knife.

"You're so hot when you get angry and possessive." She leaned over to kiss his cheek.

He melted immediately.

"Just then?" he asked, the dimple in his cheek showing. That dimple would have gotten him into a lot of trouble over the years. And probably got him out of just as much.

No one could resist guys like him. Guys who were much prettier than me. Luckily, I could get by on my charm and personality. And lack of remorse when people who pissed me off ended up dead.

"No, not just then." She socked him on the arm teasingly. "Other times too, but don't let it go to your fucking head."

He grinned more broadly. Clearly, he was head over heels for the woman.

I hoped they'd find a way to get their happy ending.

In the meantime, my attention returned to Leon. Like Reuben, he was pretending not to listen. He was probably taking in every word, but he'd learn nothing important from us. All he got so far was a couple of crushes, and the weather forecast for the rest of the week.

"This soup is really good," Leon said. "Much nicer than the food in the basement." He glanced at Mina, as though maybe he wasn't referring to our basement.

To her credit, she didn't stab him in the neck with a butter knife, or even look angry. She was completely composed and calm. Ready for him to try to provoke her. Ready, also, to pretend she wasn't ready to slice him into pieces for his part in her imprisonment.

"We take good care of our guests," I said. "You've been helpful to us, so there's no reason to be anything but nice. Right, Damon?"

Damon grunted and went on eating.

"That's Damon for, 'you're absolutely right, like always, Gianni.' With a little bit of, 'how did you get so wise?' As a matter of fact, I wonder that myself some days. But here we are."

Damon and Leon both snorted. Then glared at each other.

"See how well we're getting along?" I asked.

I briefly wondered if I could change everybody's

mind and, instead, tie rocks to Leon's ankles and throw him off the cliff. The only person in the room who didn't want that was Leon. Frankly, if the rest of us did, then he didn't get a vote.

Unfortunately, right now, neither did I. I'd just inserted the tracking chip as ordered and hoped like hell the plan went the way it was supposed to.

"It's all rainbows and lollipops around here," Parker said from the other end of the table.

"And sunshine and bunny rabbits," Hunter agreed, sarcastically. "Are you almost finished?" He glanced at Leon's bowl. "Reuben wants us to drive you into the city. After that, you're on your own. If it was up to us, you'd walk there."

"True story," Parker said. "But thanks to you telling us how to get into your laptop, we're that much closer to pinning down Kurt."

Leon glanced at him, visibly worried we got into the heavily encrypted information he'd tried to hide.

Every single person sitting at this long dining table had perfected the art of the poker face a long time ago.

Parker had closed those files and assured us Leon would never know we were in there.

All we'd told Leon was that he was actually helpful, and we'd decided we got all we could from him, and couldn't be bothered to kill him.

We also all knew he wasn't that stupid. Of course we wouldn't just let him go and that was that. Leading us to Kurt was a faint hope at best. But with the tracking chip embedded in his leg, we could take him back anytime we wanted to. He'd get that one way trip off the cliff, soon enough.

"Yes, I'm finished," Leon said finally. "Let's go."

If I didn't know better, I'd think he was worried we'd change our minds. Okay, I'd be worried about that too, if I was him. People like us didn't show mercy. He knew we were up to something, if not what. He'd go to ground the second he could. And we'd be watching every move.

The twins leapt to their feet and Hunter hurried to grab the keys to the SUV.

"Drive safely," I called out behind them. "And Leon." I waited until he turned back to say, "Be good."

He looked as though he wanted to sneer, but instead he nodded and hurried after the twins.

"Is anyone counting down?" I asked.

"I am." Damon had his phone in his hand and was watching the app that tracked the SUV. "It won't be long."

Enzo and Angelina glanced at each other.

"Is there anything we can do?" Angelina asked. "I mean, you helped us, so it's only fair."

Enzo looked at her funny. "What the hell? We need to get the fuck out of here."

"You're not going anywhere," Damon said without looking up.

Enzo glared at him. "You can't—"

"Yes, we can," Reuben said. "You can help by staying here. We'll need you. And anyone else we can get."

"What are you expecting?" Enzo asked.

"It's time," Damon said without answering his question. He rose to his feet "Enzo, Angie, stay here and listen to Caleb's orders. He should be down soon." He nodded towards the stairs. "If all goes well, we won't be long."

"What the fuck?" Enzo insisted.

Angelina actually looked excited. "You have enough weapons for us?"

"We have plenty." I placed my hands on the table, to either side of my empty bowl and pushed myself up before moving to stay beside Mina. "Are you sure you won't stay here, boss?"

"We've got this," Damon said, his worried gaze on Reuben.

"I'm coming," Reuben said simply, and that was that.

"Are you sure you don't need—" Enzo started.

"We've got this," Damon said again before unlocking and opening the door to the garage.

"If we don't come back in an hour, send help. And don't open the door to any strangers," I said.

"We won't," Caleb said as he hurried down the stairs. "Go." He actually looked concerned. Whether it was for his own safety, or for Reuben and the twins', I didn't know.

He might have even been worried about me, which

was sweet, but unnecessary. I had no intention of dying tonight.

No, my plans included Mina's pussy and Damon's cock.

I followed them and Reuben out the door and into the other SUV.

"Are you all right?" I asked Mina after she secured her seatbelt.

She glanced over at me and nodded. She was already in assassin mode. No smiles or laughs now, just stoic professionalism. She was never hotter than she was right then.

"I'll be better when this is done," she said.

"Everything is in place," Damon assured her, speaking over his shoulder. "It won't be much longer."

"I know," she said. "I've just been waiting a really long time for this."

I laced my fingers in hers. "You have. But everything ends tonight. By the time the sun rises again, Kurt Lasalle will either be dead or regretting every single one of his life choices."

"I can't fucking wait," she whispered.

"Neither can I," I agreed. "Neither can I."

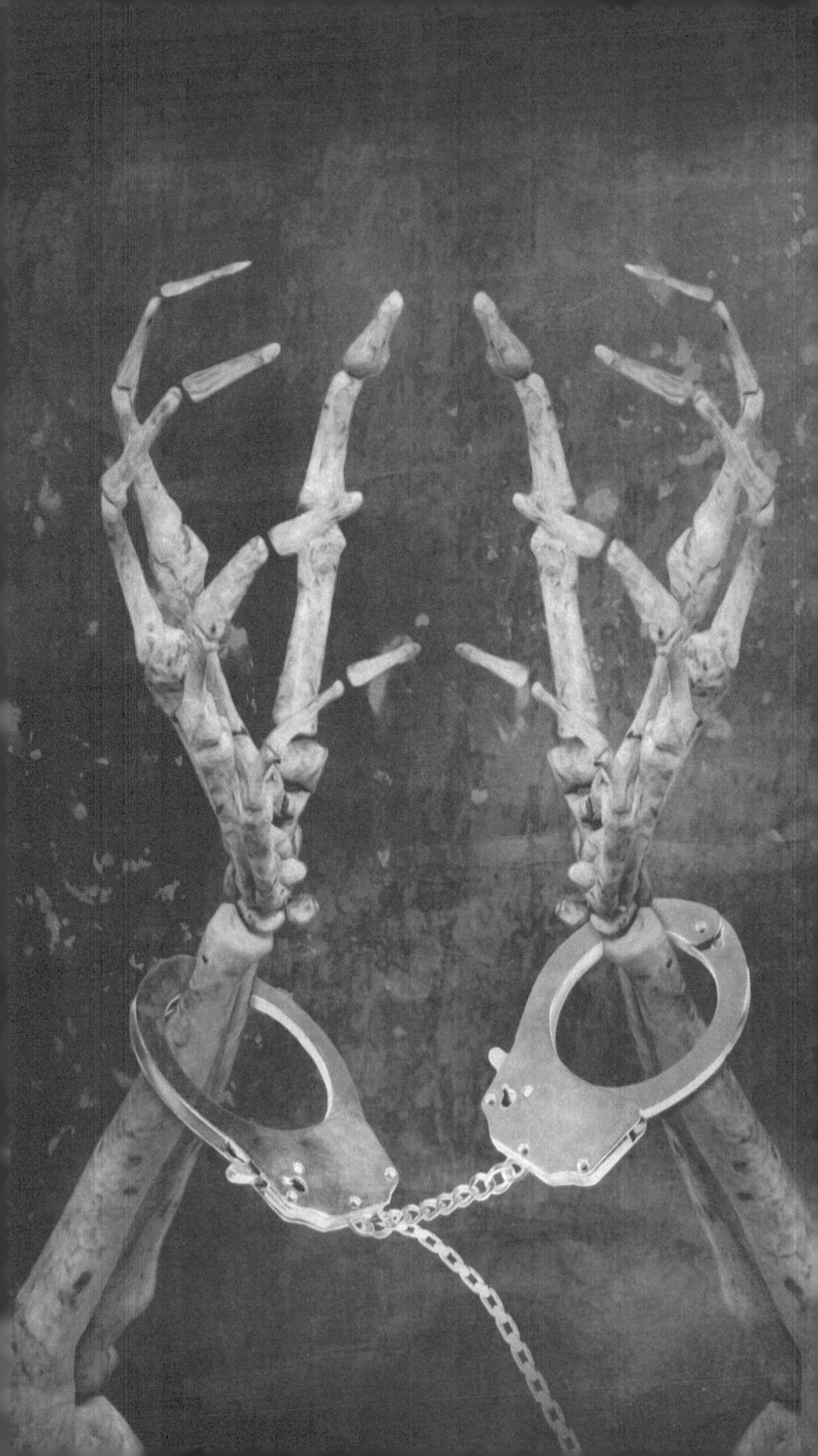

CHAPTER 16

MINA

"Where are they?" I leaned as far forward as the seat belt would let me and peered over the front seat. Damon had connected the tracker in his phone to the dashboard of the SUV, and glanced down at it every so often for directions.

"About another kilometre away," Damon said.

"Stop a hundred metres away," Reuben said. "We won't get any closer without being seen." He pointed at the map, and a street beside the flashing light that indicated the stopped SUV. A smaller flashing light showed the whereabouts of Leon Graves. One transposed over the other.

"Got it, boss," Damon said. He slowed the SUV a few moments later and pulled over to the side of the road.

I followed my three men out of the vehicle and down the otherwise empty suburban street. Shivers slid slowly up and down my spine.

I didn't need to, but I checked my knives and gun anyway. In the corner of my eye, I saw Gianni do the same. Then Damon. Only Reuben seemed calm in spite of everything.

I drew on that, using it to buoy my nerves. Anxiety wasn't useful. If I ever needed to be composed, it was now, tonight.

We reached the corner of an average looking street, lined with trees. On a normal day, nothing much exciting would happen here, not even in Dusk Bay.

A dog barked as we walked past one house. A TV was on in another. It sounded like they were watching some kind of game show. The kind where people answered trivia questions in return for cash prizes.

Gianni enjoyed one which involved a huge machine dropping discs like an arcade game, if the questions were answered correctly. He was good at pop culture questions and I was good at geography and history. Mostly, I think we were both mesmerised by the machine sliding back and forth, pushing the discs forward.

Through the trees, the lights of the first SUV were visible, along with three other vehicles, facing it. Three figures sat in ours, while several people surrounded it. They each had guns pointed at the windows.

"Good luck with that," Damon muttered.

I glanced over at him and nodded. All of Reuben's cars had bullet-proof glass. No one was shooting Leon or the twins, but they couldn't shoot out either.

"Can you make out Kurt?" Gianni whispered.

I squinted, but shook my head. "Not yet."

I wasn't sure if he'd come in person, but I hoped he would. Caleb had put out the word that Leon told us everything except Kurt's whereabouts. In addition to that, he'd put out the suggestion we were moving Leon to a different location. Somewhere likely to get more information from him.

It seemed Reuben had someone working for him, who had different torture techniques to force information out of people. When Gianni spoke of Ice Miller, he spoke with admiration. It took a lot to impress Gianni, so these techniques must be very efficient.

Shame Leon wouldn't end up there.

All of this, in the hope it drew Kurt out to save Leon or kill him.

Judging by the presence of the armed people around the SUV, that was exactly what we achieved.

"I'm going to go around behind the other vehicles," I said. "If he's here, he might be inside one of them."

Reuben nodded. "Gianni, go with her. Damon, signal the twins that we're ready." He pulled out a gun.

Shit was about to get very real.

———

Gianni and I circled back and slipped between two of the houses.

That meant climbing over fences and dodging a

very feisty dog. He looked like a cross between a Jack Russell terrier and a fox terrier, with a fan tail and a face that said, 'give me cheese,' rather than, 'I want to bite your face off.' He even let Gianni give him a pat, before rolling over onto his back and offering me his belly.

"You could use some work on your guard dog skills, buddy," I whispered. "But you're very cute."

The dog wagged his tail, got back up and ran off back inside when someone called his name.

"See, even dogs like you," Gianni said. "Dogs are very good judges of character."

"He liked you too," I pointed out. I gripped the top of the fence and pulled myself up, thankful for the strength I'd finally managed to regain.

"I rest my case." Gianni grinned and pulled himself up beside me. "When this is over, we should talk Reuben into letting us get a dog. We could train it to bite Caleb."

I managed a soft laugh, but we couldn't have done this without the help of Caleb. He was a prickly prick, but he knew how to get things done. That was exactly what we needed right now.

"It would probably bite Damon instead." I dropped down off the fence onto the grass.

"I see no problem here," Gianni said. "Damon would probably enjoy it."

"I suspect you'd enjoy it more," I said lightly.

Okay, thinking about biting Gianni was a distraction

I didn't need right now. I pushed it into the back of my mind for later.

We slipped across the next backyard and over another fence, before dropping down in the bushes beside the street. We were twenty metres behind the enemy vehicles.

"Can you see anyone inside?" Gianni asked.

I squinted. "I don't know. I need to get closer."

"*We* need to get closer," Gianni corrected.

"It'll be easier for one of us to go undetected," I said. It was a losing battle, but I was going to try to fight it anyway, to keep him safe.

"Maybe, but I'm not letting you go by yourself," he said firmly. He didn't put his foot down often, but when he did, there was as much chance of budging him as there was changing Reuben's mind, or Damon's. Or mine, for that matter.

I was about to rise, when the sound of gunshots rang out through the quiet of the evening.

The dog barked a couple of times, but that was the only indication anyone in any of the houses noticed. They must have assumed it was a backfiring car or someone else's TV.

A shout sounded close by, followed by another, then footsteps running toward our SUV.

"That's our cue," Gianni whispered.

I stayed in a crouch for a few moments longer.

Reuben, Damon and the twins were capable of taking care of themselves, and I was torn. I wanted to see if the person in the back of the vehicle was Kurt, but should we deal with his people first? If it was Kurt in there, we'd get another opportunity, sooner or later. But if my men died in the process… None of this would have been worth it.

"Reuben would want Kurt taken care of," Gianni whispered.

I shook my head. "Not at the expense of family. Killing him isn't worth losing them. We need to go back. We have to help them."

Another shot rang out, followed by a cry of pain. One that was cut short by another gunshot.

The blood froze in my veins.

For the first time in my life, I was unable to move.

It wasn't indecision, it was fear. This was my plan and so much could go wrong. It might already have gone to hell. If it had, it would be my fault. I could have let them kill Leon, or done it myself.

Instead, I'd come up with a plan to try to get Kurt's attention. To get him to come to us. My guys, the twins and Caleb had all filled in the blanks, but it was my idea.

If they died, their blood would be all over my hands. Seeping into my skin. Soaking my soul, like the blood of that little girl.

So much blood it would turn black and flow through the streets.

It threatened to wash over me and drown me, filling my lungs full until I couldn't breathe. My head spun.

"Mina." Gianni gripped my shoulders tight enough to bruise.

I wanted to flinch, but I couldn't even do that. My mind took me right back to the first moment when I woke up in that cage.

I was cold, bare. A tight strap around my ankle. I hurt all over. The insides of my thighs were sticky. I tried to sit up, but I bumped my head on the bars of the cage.

I winced and rubbed my head. What the hell was going on? Was this some kind of prank?

It was dark. My eyes took a while to become accustomed to the gloom. While they did, I felt around me, trying to figure out where I was and how I could get out.

A cage?

The cage was locked. It wasn't long enough to let me stretch out fully, or high enough to let me sit up. I had to curl up to get... Not comfortable. That wasn't happening here, there wasn't room. I couldn't lie flat. I was coiled like a spring instead.

There weren't bars underneath me, just concrete. The cage must have been bolted to the floor. The floor was cold and hard.

How had I gotten here? The last thing I remembered was my father bringing me a drink of... Was it lemonade? He had a strange look on his face, but talked to me about nothing in particular until I drank it all down.

I couldn't remember anything else. Nothing until I woke up alone.

Outside the cage, a door opened and someone stepped inside.

My blood turned cold.

"Mina," Gianni said insistently. "Come back to me. We need you right here, right now. You're not locked up in that cage anymore. No one will do that to you again. I promise. But we need to move. Come on, sweetheart. Come back to me."

I blinked a few times to clear my vision and my mind.

Where was I?

Still on a suburban street, an SUV parked nearby. Gunshots. Shouts.

Shit.

Could I have chosen a worse time to freak out and lose my mind in the shadows of the past? Anyone could have crept up behind me and I wouldn't have known. I tried to remind myself that wouldn't have happened, but I was so lost in the memory... There was no guarantee.

"I'm here," I whispered. "I'm sorry, I don't know what happened."

"What happened was, you're still human," he said gently. "But we need to decide what to do. Do we see if that's Kurt, or do we help the others?"

"I need to see if it's Kurt," I said finally. My guys were not going to let themselves get killed. They weren't. I had to have faith in that. But I needed to know. If we were this close to him and didn't even try, then we'd taken this risk for nothing.

"All right, let's go." Gianni dropped his hands from my shoulders, to wrap them around my fingers. "Unless you'd like me to go first."

"Not a chance," I said. Whatever happened to me, the flashback, it was gone now, replaced with efficient assassin mode.

I might let myself fall apart later, but for now I couldn't. I had to be Mina fucking DiMarco, the Sparrow, for a while longer.

We slipped through the darkness, moving slowly and silently towards the vehicle. A couple of metres away, I stopped again.

"What the hell?" I whispered.

In the back of the car was some kind of dummy. It was propped against the seat, high enough to look like a person. As far as I could tell, it had no face, but that wasn't what had me staring.

Sitting around where a person's chest would be, was a phone. The screen was on, showing a visual of our house here in Dusk Bay.

I couldn't tell who held the phone, but it was pointed at Kurt, who sat on the couch, a gun in his hand. Beside him was Enzo, Angelina and Caleb. They all looked pissed off. Their mouths were covered with duct tape.

Same with the fourth person on the couch with them.

Kurt's gun was pointed at the temple of my sister, Rose.

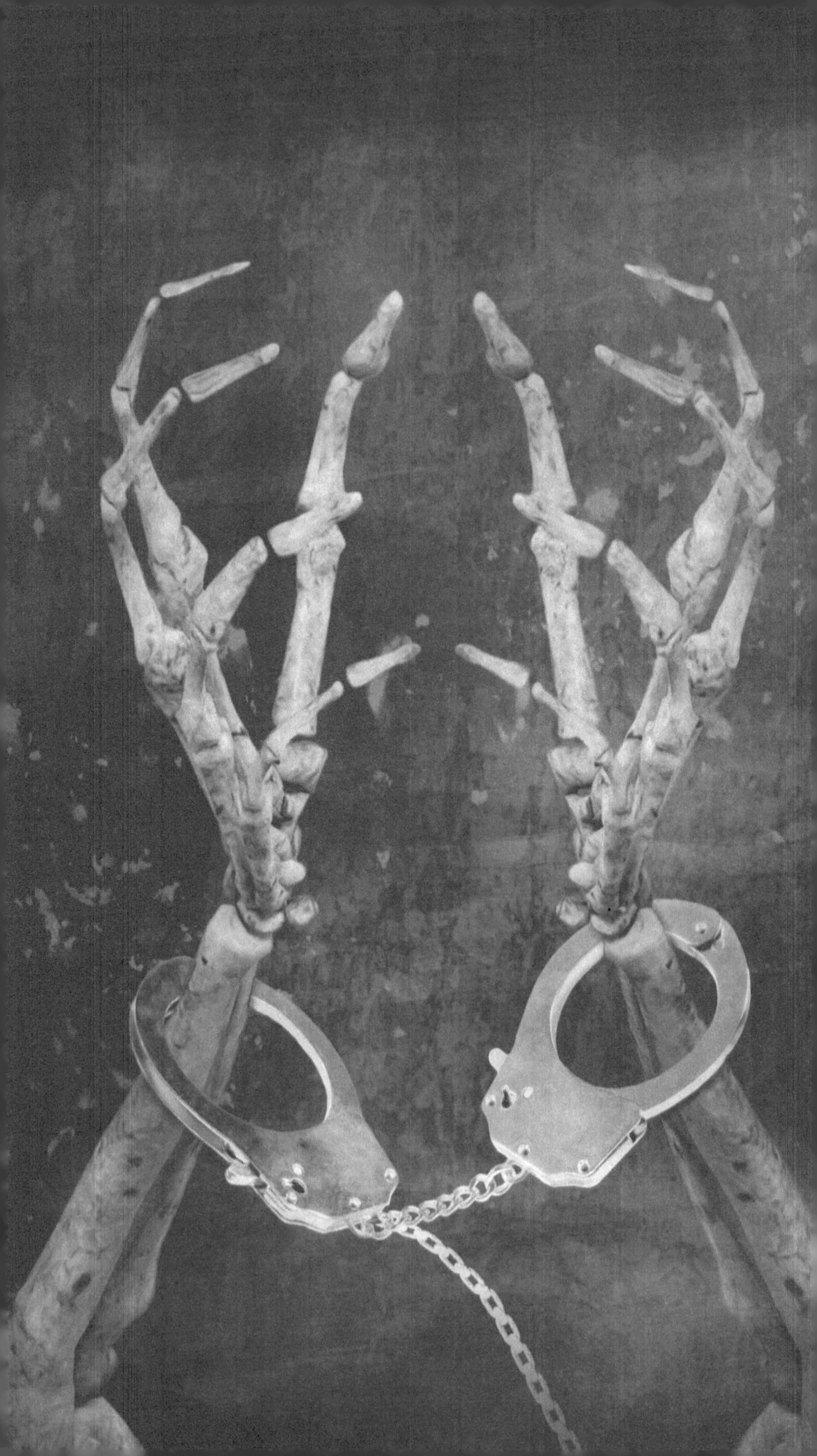

CHAPTER 17

MINA

"We need to get back," I said urgently. I darted away from the SUV, back to the shadows. "Now."

Gun in hand, I trotted in the direction of the gunshots, leaving Gianni to hurry to catch up.

Several of Kurt's minions still surrounded the SUV, their backs to the vehicle while they exchanged shots with Damon and Reuben. Two lay dead near the front tyres. The others were way too alive for my taste.

I preferred subtle and quiet, but when Kurt put a gun to my sister's head, all bets were fucking off.

I raised my gun and took out two of them with two shots before they even knew I was there. I ducked behind their second vehicle before they could turn and return the favour.

"We need to get away from these vehicles," Gianni said as he crouched beside me.

I glanced at him and nodded.

Another gunshot rang out. Another minion fell to the ground, Damon taking advantage of the distraction I provided.

That left ten. Too many for comfort.

I rose high enough to peek through the window at our vehicle. I caught a glimpse of the twins, both looking like they were waiting for an opportunity to push out of the vehicle and join in the gunfight. Both were frustrated they'd been designated with the task of keeping Leon inside the vehicle and stopping him from joining his 'friends.' If you could call them that.

I ducked back down, pulled out my phone and dialled a number. A couple of moments later, Daze's voice came down the line.

"Hey, Mina, what's up?"

"Just wondering if you're up to anything right now," I said lightly. "We could use a little help, if you're not busy."

Gianni rose and took a shot at one of the minions who'd turned his back at the wrong time. "Fuck." He dropped back down. "I missed."

"Are you having a party without me?" Daze sounded slightly miffed.

"You could say that." I peered around the side of the vehicle and took a shot at the closest set of ankles. "I know it's short notice, but if you'd like to hang out for a while, you're more than welcome. I've texted you the address."

She laughed. "We're on our way. That's only a couple

of minutes from here. Later, we might have words about you having a gunfight in my neighbourhood." She ended the call.

I smiled and pushed my phone back into my pocket.

"We just need to hold them off for a little while." I thought for a minute. "Are you ready to be a distraction?"

"If it involves you, I'm ready for anything," he replied. "Even a quickie while we wait."

I grinned at him and shook my head before scooting over to the other end of the SUV. "On the count of three?"

"Three works for me." He scooted up behind me, close enough to place a hand on the small of my back.

I whispered the words to count us down, before we rose and broke into a run. We swerved as we bolted to where, if I guessed correctly, Reuben and Damon were crouched behind a stand of trees.

Shots rang out behind us, but none connected. Somehow, we managed to make it to the trees and behind the thick trunks without being shot.

"Long time, no see," Gianni said to Reuben and Damon. He briefly filled them in on what we saw on the phone in the back of the car.

Predictably, they both looked pissed off as hell.

"We need to get the twins out of here," Reuben said.

Before I could tell him backup was on the way, two dark sedans pulled up behind our SUV. Both were packed with people.

The doors swung open. Daze was the first out. She ducked behind the door, a gun in her hand. Ric was right behind her. Followed by her two other boyfriends and six others, split between the vehicles.

"This really is a party," she called out.

I smiled. "That's what I thought."

One of Kurt's minions called out orders and several split off to approach the newcomers, a couple trying to get off shots before they were fully out of the sedans.

"Fuck off." I recognised my cousin, Phoenix DiMarco, who landed a bullet right between the eyes of one of the enemy.

"Good shot." One of his companions patted him on the shoulder.

I squinted. Was that... I'd have to wonder about that later.

In the corner of my eye, I caught a couple of the minions heading back to their SUV.

"It seems like not everyone wants to join the party," Gianni remarked.

I hummed my agreement. "Spoilsports."

They slid inside and turned on the ignition.

The SUV exploded with a burst of flame and a shower of metal and glass.

"That was meant for us," I said softly.

"As they say in the classics, suck shit." Gianni grinned.

"Seven left," Reuben said.

Apparently the twins had enough of sitting tight.

The front doors of the SUV swung open and they all but jumped out, taking out two of the men around them in the process.

"Five left," Damon said. "And they're outnumbered."

Evidently, the minions realised that too. They dropped back behind one of the remaining SUVs.

"I think they're reconsidering their life choices," Gianni said.

"I would be too," I said.

The other two vehicles might be rigged to explode. They had to decide if they could outrun us or not. Considering we had three vehicles which probably wouldn't explode, we had the advantage.

Reuben nodded to Damon and gestured for us to stand and join Daze and the small army she brought with her.

"There you are." She turned to me and grinned. "Thanks for the invitation."

"Thanks for coming," I said. I glanced back to see Reuben talking to a man around his age.

"Aidan Draeger, head coach of the Dusk Bay Demons," Gianni supplied. "Along with a bunch of the first line players."

That explained the presence of my cousin, and his friend, Coast Riggs, the team's centre. I should have suspected a team owned by Caleb would be made up of people like us.

Aidan gestured for his players to circle around and surround the remaining enemy. He didn't look impressed at being dragged out in the middle of the night.

I turned my attention back to where the minions still huddled. Every so often, one would rise and try to get off a shot, but they missed every time. None of our return shots connected either.

I chewed my lip. Something about this felt off. What would I do if I was—

"Tell everyone to come back," I said quickly. "Now."

Aidan looked at me, confused as to who the hell I was, and why I was giving orders, but Reuben nodded.

"Do it." He showed no sign of hesitation. He trusted my instincts completely.

Aidan shrugged, but called out the order for his players to trot back behind us.

"What's going on, Coach?" Phoenix asked.

"Hell if I know," Aidan said with a grunt. He glanced at me again.

I looked back, completely unflinching. I was right about this. Without a hint of doubt in my mind.

Phoenix squinted at me. "Are you—"

His words were interrupted when the other two SUVs simultaneously exploded.

Flames burst from the top of them and spread to either side, instantly incinerating anyone within a few metres. If any of our people were still there, they would have been killed along with Kurt's minions.

"Well, shit," Coast Riggs said. "I feel like we just won the playoffs."

"We might as well have." Aidan looked at me again, this time with grudging respect and a curt nod.

I nodded back and turned away from him, to Reuben. "We need to get home."

"Yes, we do," he agreed.

"I have so many questions," Phoenix said, staring at me.

"I have answers, but not right now," I told him. We had one more piece of unfinished business to take care of here. Then we needed to get home before Kurt could pull any more of his bullshit. Bullshit I was getting thoroughly tired of. We all were.

Whatever happened, this ended tonight.

My back straight, I marched over to our SUV and wrenched open the door.

Leon Graves was still inside, curled up around himself as though he hoped we'd forget about his existence. Or bracing himself in case this vehicle exploded too.

"Mina," he said when he saw me. "So good to see you're still alive. We were on our way to the city when those other vehicles stopped us. They told us to get out, but Hunter and Parker insisted we stay here."

"They saved your ass?" Gianni came up behind me and placed a hand on my shoulder.

"I... I guess they did," he said.

"Very heroic of them," I said dryly. "Maybe we should give them a trophy."

"I'll take a trophy," Parker said, appearing on the

other side of the SUV. "Can we have one each though? Having to figure out a way to share with Hunter would be a pain in the ass."

"I should be offended, but Parker is right," Hunter said. "We're good at sharing lots of things, but not a trophy. Remind me to tell you later about the time we played hockey as kids. Shit got ugly."

I snorted softly. "You don't need a trophy. Not from me anyway. I'm sure you're good at gathering your own."

Leon stared at me for a moment before realising I wasn't talking about a metal trophy. He let out an awkward laugh. "I'm sure there's still a few trophy heads attached to bodies out there. Can you believe Kurt sent all those people to get to me?"

"No, I can't," I said. Because he hadn't. Some of them were for Leon, but the rest were for me and my men.

"He doesn't get a trophy for world's best friend." World's worst would be more accurate. Kurt Lasalle was good at looking after his own ass while not giving a shit about anyone else's. He hadn't changed a bit in all the years I'd known him. He was a narcissistic psychopath who used people to get what he wanted. There was nothing and no one he wouldn't step on, kill or shove aside.

Leon laughed awkwardly again. "No, he won't. So... If you can't guarantee my safety from Kurt..."

"I don't give a shit about your safety, Leon," I said coldly. "I know you were the one who found out what my father was doing. I know you were the one who told Kurt. You gave him the ammunition to use against my father and me."

Leon's face paled. "I don't know who told you that—"

"You did," I said coldly. "Parker found your most encrypted files. Files you should have deleted. Messages between you and Kurt."

He looked genuinely confused. "I swear, I didn't have anything like that on the laptop."

"I saw it myself," I said with a slight edge of uncertainty. Either he was lying through his teeth, or this was another one of Kurt's setups.

"I wouldn't have left something like that on that," he insisted. His voice was high with panic. Clearly terrified we'd throw him back in the basement. Chain him up and leave him to rot.

"You're not denying that you were the one who told Kurt," Gianni pointed out.

Leon's hesitation was all I needed.

I raised my gun and shot him right in the centre of his forehead.

"We need to get home. Before he lays a hand on my sister."

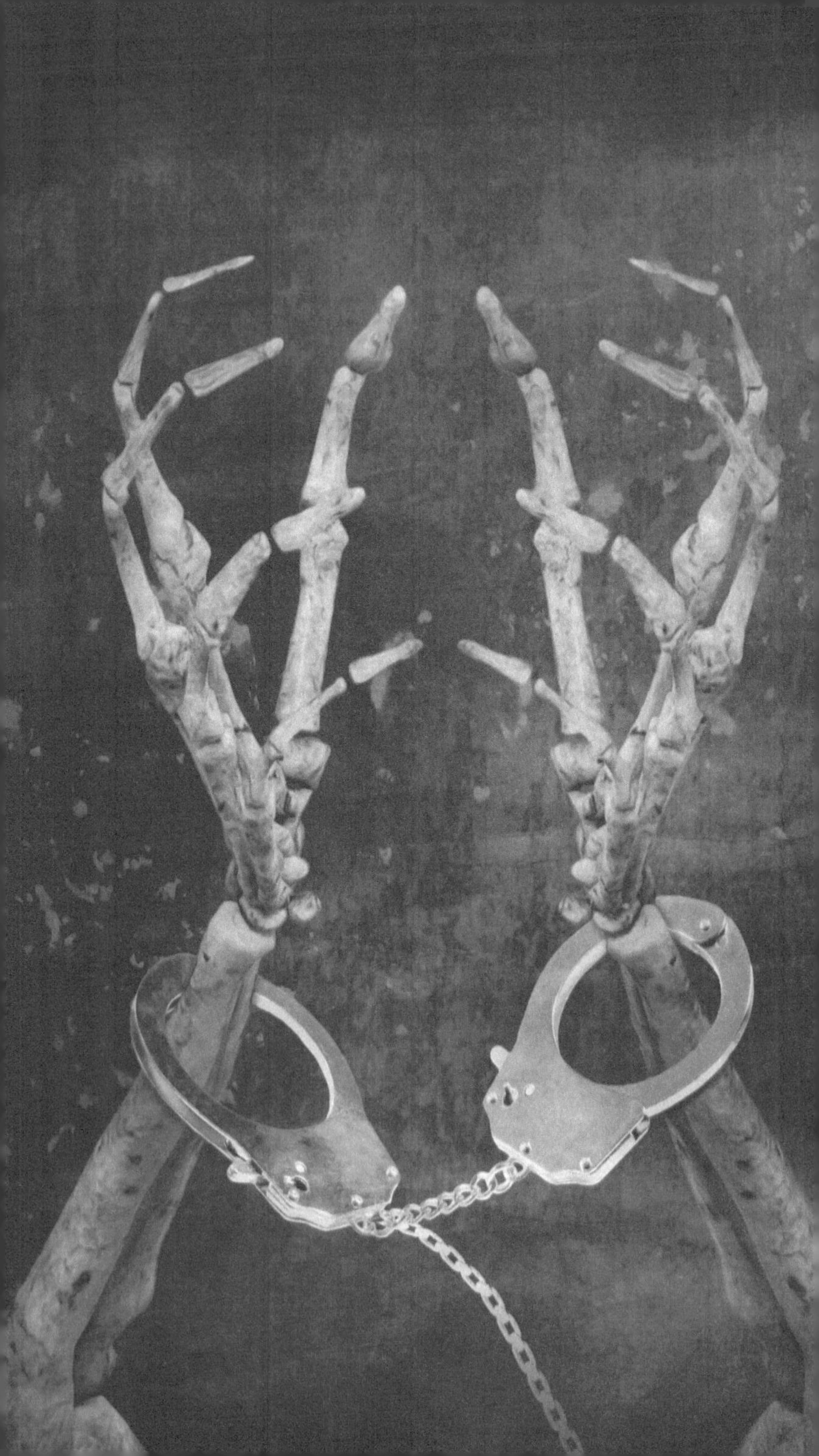

CHAPTER 18

MINA

The ride back was tense as fuck.

I sat in the back seat with Gianni, while Damon, as usual, drove. Reuben sat beside him, his back straight, shoulders stiff.

No one said a word. We were all thinking the same thing. How had Kurt managed to get inside, much less alive? How had he taken my sister? When? Had he…

I bit my lip. I didn't want to think about what he might have done to her.

"She'll be okay," Gianni said.

I nodded, but I wasn't so sure. Kurt was just as likely to kill her to get a reaction out of me. And kill Caleb to get a reaction out of Reuben. He'd probably be amused at provoking Carlos too.

I glanced back to the other two sedans behind us. The twins drove in front, in the other SUV, making a cavalcade of dark vehicles.

How many people did Kurt have with him?

Did we have enough? We had to. My sister's life might depend on it.

The twins slowed about half a kilometre from the house and pulled to a stop.

Damon stopped right behind them.

"What are you doing?" I insisted. "We don't have time to wait." The time it would take for us to walk, or even run, the extra kilometre could be time we needed to help Rose.

"We're not waiting," Damon said calmly. "There's more than one way into the house."

I should have anticipated that. The Brantley family wouldn't have a house here in Dusk Bay that didn't have a secret back door.

"But if Kurt knows where it is—" I started.

"He won't," Damon said. "The only ones who know about it are us and the twins. The rest of Dusk Bay is just about to find out."

Reuben let out a breath of annoyance at that, but he'd also do whatever was necessary to save my sister and get Kurt out of his house.

We all climbed out of the cars and, in quiet ranks, followed the twins onto a property beside the road. We swished through high grass to a massive water tank.

"No one ever suspects the water tank," Hunter said ominously.

I gave him a funny look, but followed him around to the rear of the tank.

It was Damon who pulled out his phone and tapped on the screen.

Without a sound, a door in the side of the tank started to rise. If I didn't see it with my own eyes, I never would have guessed it was there.

I tapped the side of the tank. "It doesn't sound hollow."

Damon smirked. "Of course not. That would be too obvious."

"The insides are lined with concrete," Reuben said. "Pipes take the water that lands on the rim of the tank down to our house. Simple but efficient."

I thought back to Clarissa and her hidden trapdoor. She'd love this, if she knew about it. Another secret door that didn't lead to Narnia.

"How many of these things do you have?" I asked. "Secret passageways and things like that."

"None we're going to discuss in front of anyone else." Damon jerked his head towards Daze, Ric and Aidan. And all the people they brought with them.

"I'll fill you in on all of them later," Gianni said. "You should know about all of them, just in case."

I nodded. We had to get through this first.

I let Gianni take my hand as we stepped through the door, into the tank.

Hunter and Parker both had the lights on their phone, showing the way.

The inside of the tank was massive, but like Damon said, lined with concrete. That made it seem a lot smaller. Small enough to make me anxious. This was exactly the kind of space that reminded me of Kurt's basement.

The same flashback that came over me while we were crouched in the bushes threatened to sneak back into my mind. Memories clawed back at me, trying to suck me back into the past.

That nightmare was my present for so long, putting it behind me was never going to be easy, but I couldn't let it get to me now. This was when I needed to be strong, for Rose's sake. And for mine.

"You've got this," Gianni said, his voice echoing. "I have to confess, this place gives me the creeps too, but we can do it. We can't let it get to us."

"I'm with Gianni," Hunter said. "This place is creepy as shit, and I know creepy as shit."

"Some people say you *are* as creepy as shit." Parker grinned.

"Some people can fuck off, and so can you," Hunter said to his twin. "I'm not creepy, I'm awesome."

"You pronounced 'awful' wrong," Gianni teased.

"The next time we need someone used as bait, the answer is no," Hunter said to no one in particular. "Gianni volunteers instead."

"Keep your voices down," Damon snapped.

I noticed he didn't tell us to be completely quiet. I suspected he was as creeped out by this place as the rest of us. Only Reuben looked unruffled. On the outside anyway. I doubted too many people would enjoy being in a place like this.

No one but spiders and people like Kurt, and Leon Graves.

And the cockroach that ran past my left shoe. I shuddered, but didn't flinch.

This time.

We fell into silence after that anyway. Lost in their own thoughts.

The ground dipped before the tunnel led to a set of steps. Two by two, we stepped down them, slowly and carefully.

After those, the tunnel widened, becoming slightly more comfortable before we headed up another set of stairs. If I had to guess, I'd say we must be close to the house.

It already felt like we'd been walking forever. Maybe forever and a day or two.

Enough time for a million thoughts to tumble through my mind. Chief amongst those was, how had any of this happened?

We were keeping tabs on Rose. The house should have been secure. So many questions and, like too many times before, there were no answers. Not yet.

We reached the top of the second set of stairs and stopped in a wide, rectangular room.

There, Damon gestured for us to halt.

Behind me, Aidan gestured for his players to do the same.

"Where do we go now?" I glanced around, but couldn't see a door leading out.

For half a heartbeat, I started to panic. Maybe there wasn't a way out. We might have come all this way only to end up stuck in the end of nowhere. This might have been someone's plan. To bring me here and—

I shook my head. Those thoughts were ridiculous. There was no way in the world that would happen. No one here would have allowed it, especially me. This was nothing but the past trying to get to me again.

I told it to fuck off, into a corner of my brain for now. I'd deal with one asshole at a time.

Parker turned off the light on his phone and tapped on the screen. "We could do with better connectivity in here, but this will have to do."

Damon nodded and pulled out his own phone.

I stared at them, confused until Parker said, "Got it."

He turned the screen to me, and showed camera footage of inside the house. "Now we just need to find where they are. And how many there are."

I nodded and waved for him to get on with it. Stopping to explain might be a waste of time. Time we couldn't afford to lose a moment of.

"He's still in the living room," Damon reported. "Rose, Angie and Enzo are still alive. Caleb too."

I peered over his shoulder.

Sure enough, they were still sitting on the couch, looking as though they hadn't moved since we saw them last. Kurt was pacing back and forth, gun still in his hand. He was surrounded by several other people.

I caught a glimpse of two of them and sucked in a breath. Sweat sprag out on my palms and under my arms. "That's Jason Andrews and Wade."

"Are you sure?" Gianni asked.

The angle wasn't good, and they were half turned away, but I was certain.

"It's them," I said softly.

"Good, then we can kill three birds with one stone," Gianni said. "Four, if you count Leon."

"There are people in the kitchen too," Parker said. "They don't seem to be anywhere else. None have shown themselves down to the basement."

"Yet," Hunter said. "I can see that place getting really full, really soon."

"Bring it on," Gianni said. "I've always wondered exactly how many people we could fit down there. Although, I was thinking about a party."

"Are you saying this isn't a party?" Daze asked. "Looks like one to me."

"It sounds like your boyfriends need to show you a good time more often," Hunter remarked.

"Don't even think about it," Ric growled. Hilton and Gunnar looked equally unimpressed.

Typically, Hunter just grinned. No one would have bought that he was interested in Daze anyway. He was just trying to lighten the mood.

That lasted approximately three or four seconds

before Reuben spoke.

"Where's Terry?"

Damon glanced up from his phone and shook his head. "I can't see any sign of him."

His expression was grim. They would have gotten past Terry over his dead body.

That was exactly what we were all afraid of. I'd become fond of the gentle, silent giant, not just for his cooking. He had a way of conveying his thoughts without words. He didn't put up with any shit from anyone and I admired that about him.

He was as much a part of my family as my men or my siblings. Or Daze and her boyfriends. Or anyone currently in this secret bunker, who'd come when I called. Every single one of them had dropped whatever they were doing and raced to help us.

For that, I'd always be grateful. Assuming I lived long enough to have much in the way of gratitude.

"It looks as though we have equal numbers," Parker said. "Approximately. There's still a handful out the front, along with their cars. The majority went inside with the asshole."

Reuben nodded. "Nothing we can't handle. They know we're coming, but they don't know where we're coming from."

"Chances are, they're expecting us to pull up out the front of the house and take on the people outside," Hunter reasoned. "They'll think we're complacent, after taking care of only a handful of assholes. They'll expect us to walk in through the door so they can ambush us."

I nodded my agreement at his assessment. Based on the placement of people, that was logical. It sounded like something Kurt would do. He'd make sure he was surrounded by a lot of people who would die while he made a run for it.

Fuck that.

"Maybe some of us should turn up out the front," Aidan suggested. "We can deal with them, and provide a distraction."

"A distraction is a good idea," I agreed. I met Damon's eyes and smiled.

He offered a faint smile in return. His version of a grin. Neither of us would hear or say that word again without thinking of each other.

Reuben nodded. "Four of you go. One for each car. Let them think we're all turning up at the front. Parker."

"On it," Parker said. He frowned in concentration and tapped at his phone screen. "There. The cameras out the front of the house are on a loop. Assuming they don't realise it too soon, anyone Kurt has monitoring will just see what's out there right now."

"Good job," Reuben said. His gaze followed Aidan, Phoenix, Coast and another one of the players back down the tunnel. "We'll give them five minutes, then we go inside."

Hunter rubbed his hands together. "Time to fuck some shit up."

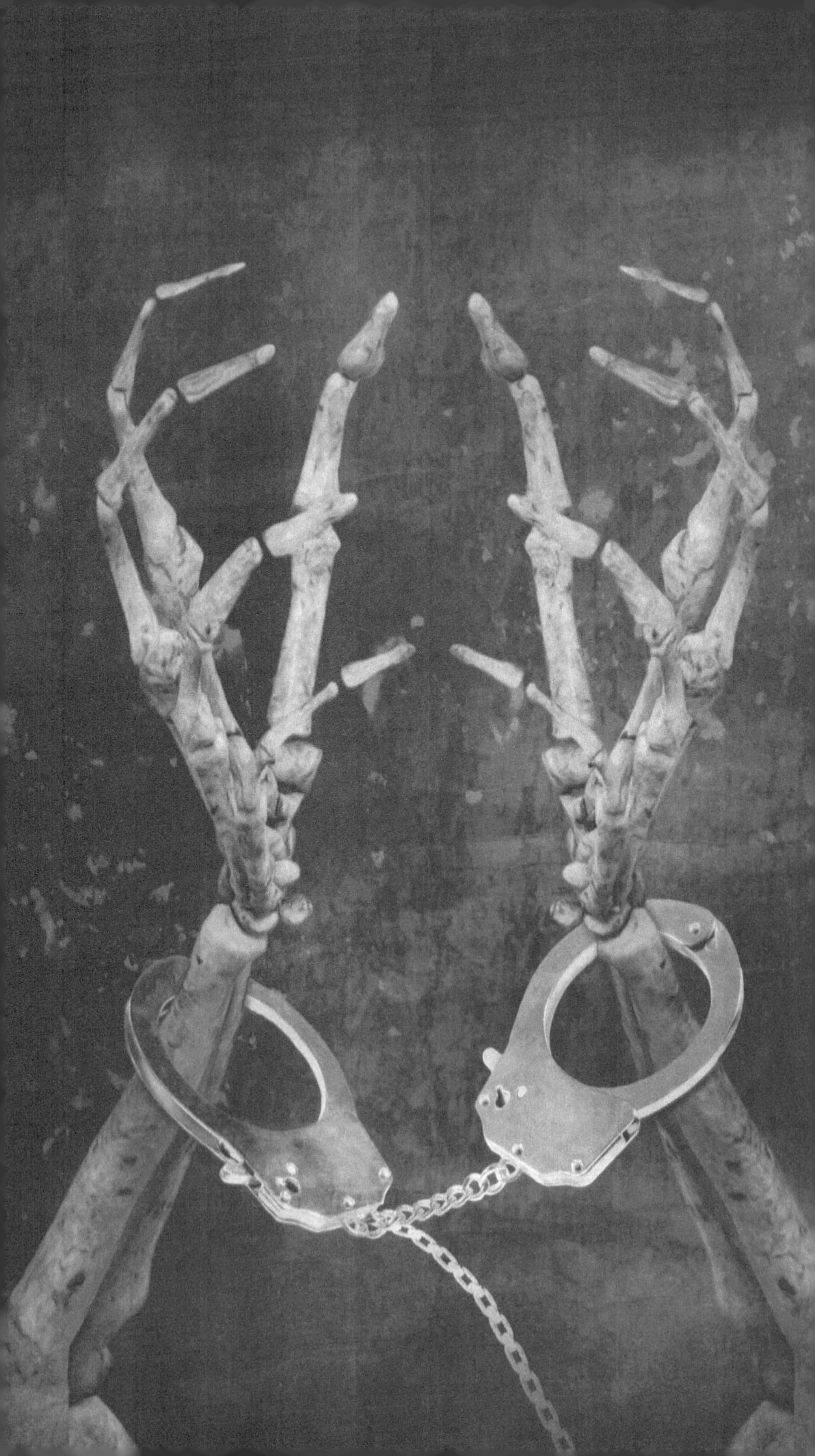

CHAPTER 19

GIANNI

"We need to split up," Reuben said before we unlocked the door leading into the house. "Hunter, Parker, Daze, you all go left, toward the kitchen. The rest of us will go right, around to the back of the living room. If we're careful, we can come up behind them. We'll try to surround them and take them all out."

Hunter raised his phone and pointed the light in the direction of a fuse box on the wall. "I'm ready to blow the lights."

"I'm ready with the knives." I squatted and opened a box that lay on the ground beside the door. Stored there for just this eventuality. It was full of blades and guns.

I handed out knives to anyone who didn't already have one. Mina, of course, was already armed with several. Could she get any hotter? She looked like some kind of angel, dressed in black and armed to the teeth. My kind of woman, through and through.

"No guns until you have to," Reuben added. "Once they know where we are, do whatever you have to do. Until then, be quiet. Let's not jump through the door and announce our presence."

I smiled.

I couldn't imagine Reuben jumping through the door and shouting out, "Heeeere's Reuben!" The twins, certainly, but not him.

"Got it, boss," I said. "Stealth mode. A trillion points to anyone who ends Kurt."

"Infinity points to anyone who helps us catch him alive," Mina said softly.

"What could we do with infinity points?" Hunter asked.

She gave him a bland look. "You can swap it for a Maserati."

"Fuck yeah." He offered Parker a fist bump. "I can't wait."

"You'll have to wait, that's my infinity points and my Maserati," I told them both.

I didn't give a shit about either of those things. What I really wanted was for us to get out of this alive. Preferably in one piece. A car, no matter how sexy, meant nothing in comparison.

I knew they agreed with that sentiment. They weren't shallow enough to really give a shit about an expensive vehicle. That wouldn't keep us from making jokes about it. Only our deaths would put a stop to that.

"Game on." Hunter grinned. "One Lasalle coming up."

Daze cleared her throat.

"One *male* Lasalle," Hunter corrected. "Have you ever thought about changing your name?"

"Have you?" I asked him.

Being a Brantley came with a lot of responsibility. And a metric fuck ton of expectations, especially from Reuben. Although, they were lighter than the ones Reuben put on himself.

"Can we focus?" Damon snapped. His expression was tighter than I'd ever seen on him before. I couldn't say I blamed him. In spite of the banter, I was tense myself. A shit ton of things could go wrong. We just had to make sure they didn't.

Somehow.

Reuben nodded at Hunter. "Kill the lights."

Hunter opened the fuse box and turned one switch at the same moment Damon opened the door.

For a split second, the house was illuminated, before it fell into complete darkness.

The curtains were closed, blocking out any moonlight and most of the starlight. The only illumination was the flashing of various electrical devices, like the front of the microwave oven, and the keypad for the air-conditioning system.

I hadn't realised how bright they both were. Even from here, I could make out the one in the microwave.

Voices muttered in surprise as we slipped off in the directions Reuben ordered us to go.

I stayed beside Mina, close enough for our arms to touch as we moved through the darkness.

We had the advantage that we knew this place better than the enemy, but I had no illusion this was going to be easy.

At this point, it had already stopped being fun. Trust Kurt Lasalle to suck the joy out of the people around him. I added that to the ever-growing list of reasons to hate him.

Another factor in our favour was that we'd stood in near total darkness for about twenty minutes. Our eyes didn't need time to adjust.

The same couldn't be said for the first two of our enemies we snuck up behind and dispatched silently. A quick slash to the throat and we lowered them to the floor.

I pictured the expression on Reuben's face at the idea of blood on the hardwood, but it couldn't be helped. Better their's than ours, anyway.

A low grunt sounded from the direction of the kitchen. That was quickly followed by another.

Mina grabbed hold of my wrist and pulled me to the side. Lucky she did, because I almost walked into another one of our enemies.

Instead, I grabbed them from behind, my hand over their mouth, my knife across their throat. They tried to cry out, but the sound was muted by my fingers and their quick death. Still, it was enough sound to inform others of our presence.

I lowered them to the ground and winced. I'd have to ask Reuben if we could put up speakers around the house. Music, when played loud enough, would mask anything and everything. We could have stomped through the house and never been heard.

That was an oversight. Something I hadn't considered before and I could kick myself for it now. In retrospect, it was obvious, but at least we could fix it later.

I hoped.

Light from a phone flashed out across the room in front of us. The living room.

"I know you're there, Mina," Kurt called out, taunting. "I know that you know I have your sister here. And Reuben's brother. And Damon's brother. How cosy all of this is. It's up to you whether they live or die."

I've always found it ironic when people said shit like that. The only one responsible for their deaths was him. It was past time he took responsibility for his own actions.

I made a note to tell him that later. Right before those actions led to his death.

"What do you want, Kurt?" Mina called back. Her fingers curled around my wrist, drawing me with her while she stepped forward. Reuben and Damon moved along slowly behind us.

"The same thing I've always wanted," Kurt said. "I

want all the power and influence the Brantley family has, and I want you."

Reuben snorted softly. An articulate expression of 'fuck that' if I ever heard it. He always did have a way of quietly conveying what he was thinking.

"Why?" Mina asked. "From the look of things, you have plenty of power and influence. There are women out there who are attracted to things like that. I'm sure you could find someone more than willing to be a part of your life. Why do you want me?"

"Because you belong to me," he stated, like nothing could be simpler. "I own you. Every millimetre of you."

"Why me?" she pressed harder. "Of all the women in the world, why do you want me?"

"We're wasting time here, Mina. And I'm running out of patience." The light flashed again, presumably Kurt turning around in a circle, trying to figure out what direction we might jump out from. "I'm going to start killing in a minute. How many die, depends on you."

A short grunt of pain came from the direction of the kitchen. My heart thudded in my chest. It sounded like one of the twins.

"Parker!" Hunter's harsh whisper was like the crack of a whip through the darkness.

Fucking hell.

Fucking hell.

Mina's fingers trembled. Her intake of breath was sharp, horrified.

"One of them is dead," Kurt sounded amused. "How many more are you going to allow to die? Hunter is surrounded, as is your sister. All I need to do is say the word. Or, you can hand yourself over to me. Reuben can step aside and give me the keys to his empire. That's all it takes for the rest of the people you care about to walk away."

Mina swallowed audibly.

"You can't," Damon whispered. "We're not—"

His words were interrupted by gunshots from outside the front of the house. Someone shouted and everything fell quiet again.

I pictured the scene outside in my mind, but couldn't draw any conclusions. Aidan and the Demons might be dead, or they might not.

I'd like to think they were more difficult to kill than that, but only time would tell. All I could do for them was to send good thoughts and hope like hell they made it through. The team needed them. The hockey team as well as us.

"What choice do I have?" she asked. "You can't all die for me."

"Enough of this bullshit," Kurt snapped. "Kill the other twin."

A shuffle sounded from the direction of the kitchen before silence fell once again.

Mina's breath was a soft sob. "I have to. It's the only way."

"I won't let you—" I started.

"You can't *stop* me," she said. "This is what I have to do. I need to do this for all of you. Forget about me."

There was conviction in her tone, but a heavy dose of fear. Yes, she would do this for us. She'd give up the rest of her life and spend it caged and chained so we wouldn't die, but the idea of going back to that life was the worst, most inconceivable nightmare possible. The fact she'd even consider subjecting herself to that again, just for us, made me love her even more.

She was, without a doubt, the most incredible woman I'd ever met.

I pulled her to me and brushed my lips over hers. "We will never forget you. Never." I held her tight like I might be able to change her mind if I held her for long enough.

"You have to let me go," she insisted.

"Who shall I kill next?" Kurt mused in a singsong voice. "I guess I could start with Angelina. She doesn't have any family here to stick up for her. Although…her death might be enough to convince you I'm serious."

Enzo let out a roar of protest from behind his duct tape.

"I think he's volunteering to go first," Kurt said. "How touching. Is that something Damon would do, too? Give up your life for the woman you think you love? Even while knowing she belongs to someone else? I bet Reuben would do the same thing, wouldn't you Reuben? And Gianni. So heroic for a bunch of criminals."

"Hey, everyone, I found the pot," I called out. "First of all, yes, we would die for Mina, because she belongs to us, not you. Secondly, you're the kind of person who gives the word 'criminal' a bad name. And coward. And asshole. And…" I could have gone on for hours.

"Sticks and stones," Kurt sneered.

"Breaking your bones would be my pleasure," Damon growled.

"Ah, there's Damon," Kurt said. "I changed my mind, I think your brother can die next. Then maybe Reuben's other brother. It was Caleb who helped to spread the rumour I was really the Sparrow, wasn't it? Do you realise that made it difficult for people to trust me? Some of them even thought they might turn on me. Instead, all you did was force my hand tonight. But don't worry. Before I came here, I put out word of who the real Sparrow is. Along with some damning evidence about something she once did. People were only too happy to believe the truth."

"I didn't kill her," Mina said softly.

"Yes, you did," Kurt contradicted. "The same way you just killed Hunter and Parker. The same way you're about to kill Enzo and Caleb if you don't hurry up and give yourself to me. I'm going to be generous and give you two more minutes. Then I'm done fucking around. Time starts… Right now."

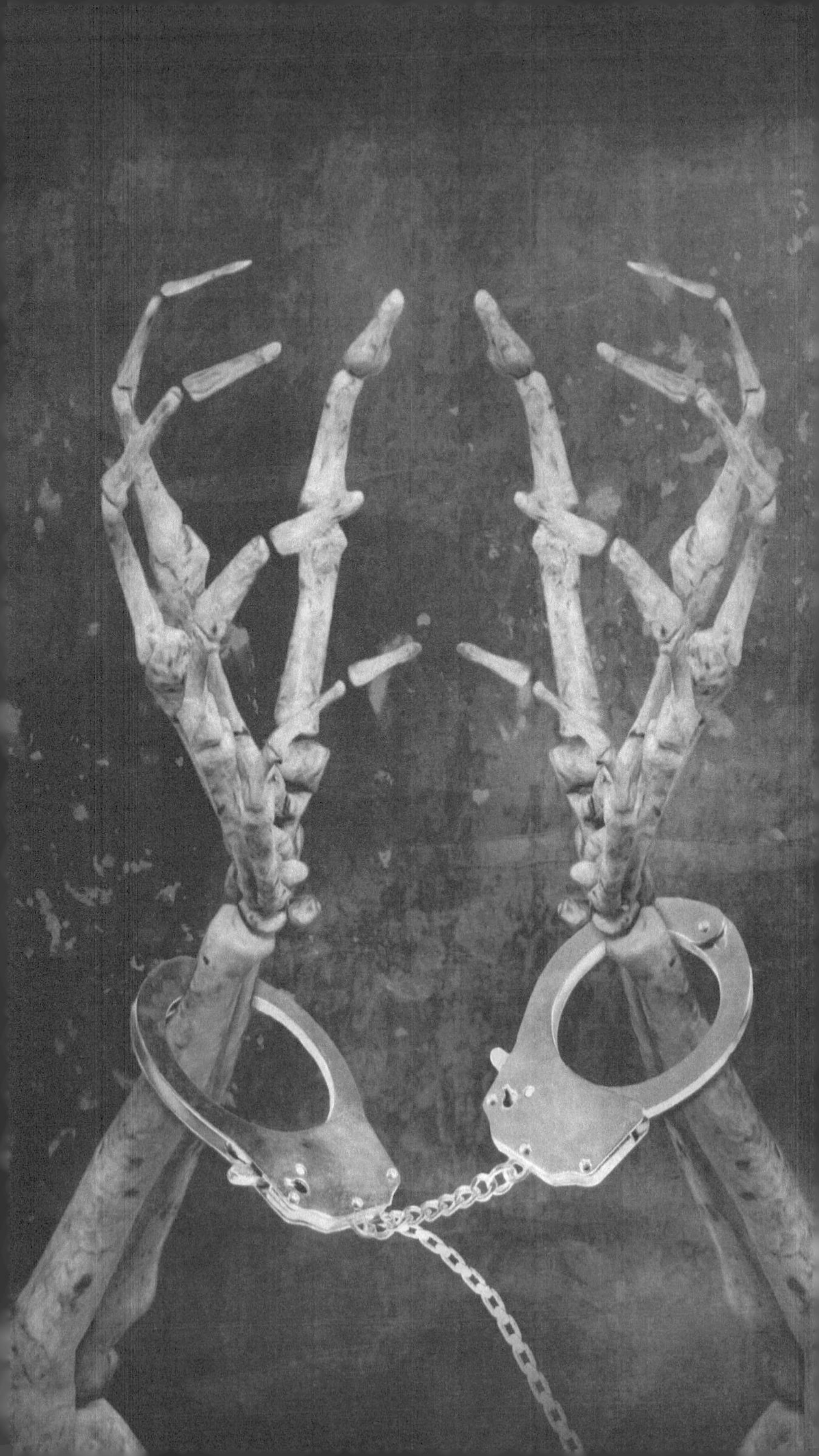

CHAPTER 20

MINA

I sank against Gianni for a few moments.

This could be the last time I got to see any of them. These few moments weren't enough. It never would be. All three of them had saved me in so many ways. They got me out of the basement and they gave me my life back. They gave me themselves and their hearts.

Now it was time for me to give back to them.

I could hardly believe that the twins were dead, they'd been so full of life.

They had to be the last. I couldn't let anyone else give up their lives for me. No matter how willing they were to sacrifice themselves. I knew all three of them would fall on their own swords for me. I loved them for it.

For so long, I hadn't thought myself capable of love, or worthy of being loved. They taught me how wrong I was. They showed me what it was to give everything and live every day to the fullest. For that, I'd always be grateful. Their love was what I'd hold on to when I was back where Kurt put me. For however much longer I lived, I'd hold on to that. It might be the only thing that kept me sane.

I pressed my ear against Gianni's chest and listened to his heart racing. I never knew anyone could have a heart as big as his. He'd contradict me, but I didn't deserve him. That was an argument we'd never get to have.

"I love you," I whispered. "All of you."

Before they could respond, I tore myself away from them and headed towards the living room.

"Mina." Reuben's whisper sounded devastated.

I had to force myself not to look back. If I did, I might change my mind.

I couldn't. People would die.

I stepped through the cased opening, into the living room.

At that moment, the lights came back on. I squinted against the glare.

Rose was in the same place she was sitting when I saw her on that phone.

How long ago was that? It felt like hours. Weeks.

It couldn't have been more than an hour.

She conveyed a dozen thoughts with her eyes. Frustration at having been taken. Anger at Kurt. Heartbreak that I'd consider giving myself up for her. Fear for me. And an insistence that she would also have offered herself in my place. She would have died for me.

All I could give her was conviction that I wouldn't let her. The world had lived without Mina DiMarco for five years. It could live without me again. It couldn't live without her.

My brothers would mourn her loss, while they went on thinking I was happily married, off in the suburbs somewhere.

They say ignorance is bliss. Never knowing what happened to me, could be theirs.

Caleb's eyes were also on me, his irritation clear. Not at me specifically, just in general. He tried so hard to be like his oldest brother, even now. He hated being bound and powerless. Just like Reuben would.

I hoped he'd find his own way at some point. He needed to step out of Reuben's shadow and be his own man. Maybe then, he'd be happy. Or at least, less unhappy.

Angelina and Enzo sat close together, their shoulders touching. Both looked as though they could shoot daggers out of their eyes if anyone touched either of them.

Angelina was as protective of Enzo as he was of her. If anyone doubted their feelings for each other, they wouldn't if they saw them like this. At least now they may get a chance at a happily ever after.

Finally, my gaze slid to Kurt. He'd lost weight since I saw him last, but he was still the same smug, hateful asshole I'd known for so long. He'd forced us to play his game and now we were at Checkmate.

Knight takes queen.

"You're looking well," he said smoothly. "Hand over all your knives." He nodded to one of his minions to step over and take them from me. "If she tries anything, kill her sister first."

Of course he'd plan for what would happen if I threw a knife and embedded it in his loathsome head. I considered doing it anyway, but several of his minions moved closer to Rose, ready to carry out his orders. I could kill him and a couple of them, but not before they got to her.

She growled in the back of her throat and gave Kurt a death glare, which he ignored. His gaze was fixed on me. Waiting for me to act.

I sighed and reached for my knives, handing them to the closest asshole, hilt end first.

I contemplated using one on myself, stabbing one into my own heart. Ending the pain before it began all over again.

If I did that, Kurt would kill everyone here. The only way they walked away from this was if I left with him. He knew I knew that. It increased his smugness level by at least double.

Asshole.

"That's all of them," I said finally.

"Make sure," Kurt ordered. He looked extremely amused at the idea of one of his men touching me, checking for any hidden weapons. I suspected he might be more amused at the thought of killing his man after he touched me, even though he'd done it on Kurt's orders. He was nothing if not fucked up.

His minion approached me carefully before quickly patting me down. "Nothing else there, sir." He stepped away from me quickly.

"Good," Kurt said. "Get a couple of cable ties and some duct tape and bind her."

The minion nodded. "Yes, boss." He hurried over to the couch to grab up both.

"In case you were wondering, Leon Graves is dead," I said. I glanced around, but saw no sign of Jase or Wade. I presumed they were in the kitchen. They might have been the ones who killed the twins. Grief flared inside me, white hot devastation, and burning hate for the hands that took their lives.

I hoped my men would catch up to them and return the favour. Long, slow and painful, preferably.

Kurt shrugged. "He outgrew his usefulness anyway. But he was helpful in bringing you back to me."

A couple of his assholes moved behind me to grab my arms and pull them behind my back. One of them held them, while the other fastened the cable tie around them.

Another tore off a long section of duct tape and raised it to my mouth. I pressed my lips together and let him stick it to my face.

"Much better," Kurt said. "I'm sure you'll agree we

have a lot to catch up on. Don't worry, I'll keep plenty of my people here, to make sure no one follows us. If they try, they'll be dead too. In a few hours, we might let them go, one by one."

He walked past Rose, close enough for her to kick him. She looked like she was about to, but I shot her a warning look. I hadn't done all of this only for her to provoke him into killing her. She had to understand that. This was my choice. My sacrifice. It would be for nothing if any of them got themselves killed for me.

His minions stepped back as Kurt approached me. "I like you like this," he said. "Bound and gagged is a good look for you." He took the second cable tie and held it in his hand. "We'll leave this until you get into the car. I could have you carried, but it's much more fun to see you walk voluntarily. Knowing your place."

He turned around, smiling at everyone in the room like he was about to receive his own trophy. When he turned back, his expression was darker.

"I only have two regrets in life. One is leaving you for Reuben to find. The other was not breaking you. I won't make either mistake again. When we're done, you'll never want to be away from me again. Your biggest regret will be going with them when you did. You should have stayed there and waited for your owner to come and get you. Like the bitch you are." He pinched my chin between his thumb and forefinger. "You. Should. Have. Waited."

I looked back at him, unflinching. Maybe he could

break me and maybe he'd kill me instead. I'd never give up until I provoked him to end my life. Whatever it took.

He released my chin and backhanded me across the face so hard I staggered back against his minions. Two of them grabbed me at the last moment before I fell.

Rose growled.

I shot her another warning look. I knew she was trying to be the big sister I needed, but right now I needed her to be inconspicuous. I needed her to hold her peace, for both our sakes. If Kurt killed her, it would be one step closer to him breaking me. I couldn't allow that to happen.

"We've wasted enough time here," Kurt snapped. "Let's get out of this dump. You, stay behind and kill them if they try anything." He waved a hand at several of his assholes.

They nodded and moved to stand around the couch, and the corridor where my men still stood.

"The rest of you come with me," he ordered. He grabbed my arm and pulled me towards the front door of the house.

I glanced back at my sister, giving her a silent apology and trying to tell her I loved her.

Her eyes widened slightly.

Before I could turn back, a loud clang echoed through the room.

Kurt's grip on my arm loosened before his hand fell

away. His eyes rolled back in his head and he started to fall to the floor.

He landed with a thud heavy enough to make me wince.

Eyes wide, I looked up from where he lay.

Terry stood with his hands around the handle of a heavy frying pan, a satisfied look on his face. He nodded to me and then actually grinned.

He must have lain in wait for Kurt before smashing him over the head with the pan.

The front door burst open and Aidan and his players poured inside. A couple of them were bleeding from what appeared to be bullet wounds in their shoulders, but they only appeared to be grazes. Not enough to slow them down or stop them from playing.

Coast Riggs was grinning like he'd never had so much fun in his life.

My guys appeared from the corridor, heading towards me at a trot. All three of them were frowning, but relieved to see me still standing. They were at least as relieved as I was to see them.

They were the most beautiful sight I'd ever seen in my life. So much so, my heart might burst out of my chest.

On the other side of the room, Daze and her guys appeared followed by—

I blinked a couple of times to make sure I wasn't seeing things.

Hunter and Parker were right behind Ric. They were

both covered in blood, but didn't seem to be badly hurt. Like the Demons centre, they were smiling like they were having the time of their lives.

Thank fuck.

I couldn't have been more grateful they were both still alive. I was so sure…

For half a second, I thought maybe I was dead and this was some kind of afterlife. But the tear that trickled down my cheek felt real enough. That was followed by another one.

"Take them all," Reuben ordered. He gestured towards Kurt's men, who were stepping back away from the couch and looking as though they were trying to find somewhere to run to. They had nowhere. One by one, they started to toss their weapons to the floor.

In moments, all of the minions were surrounded and I found myself in Reuben's arms, where I sagged and silently wept.

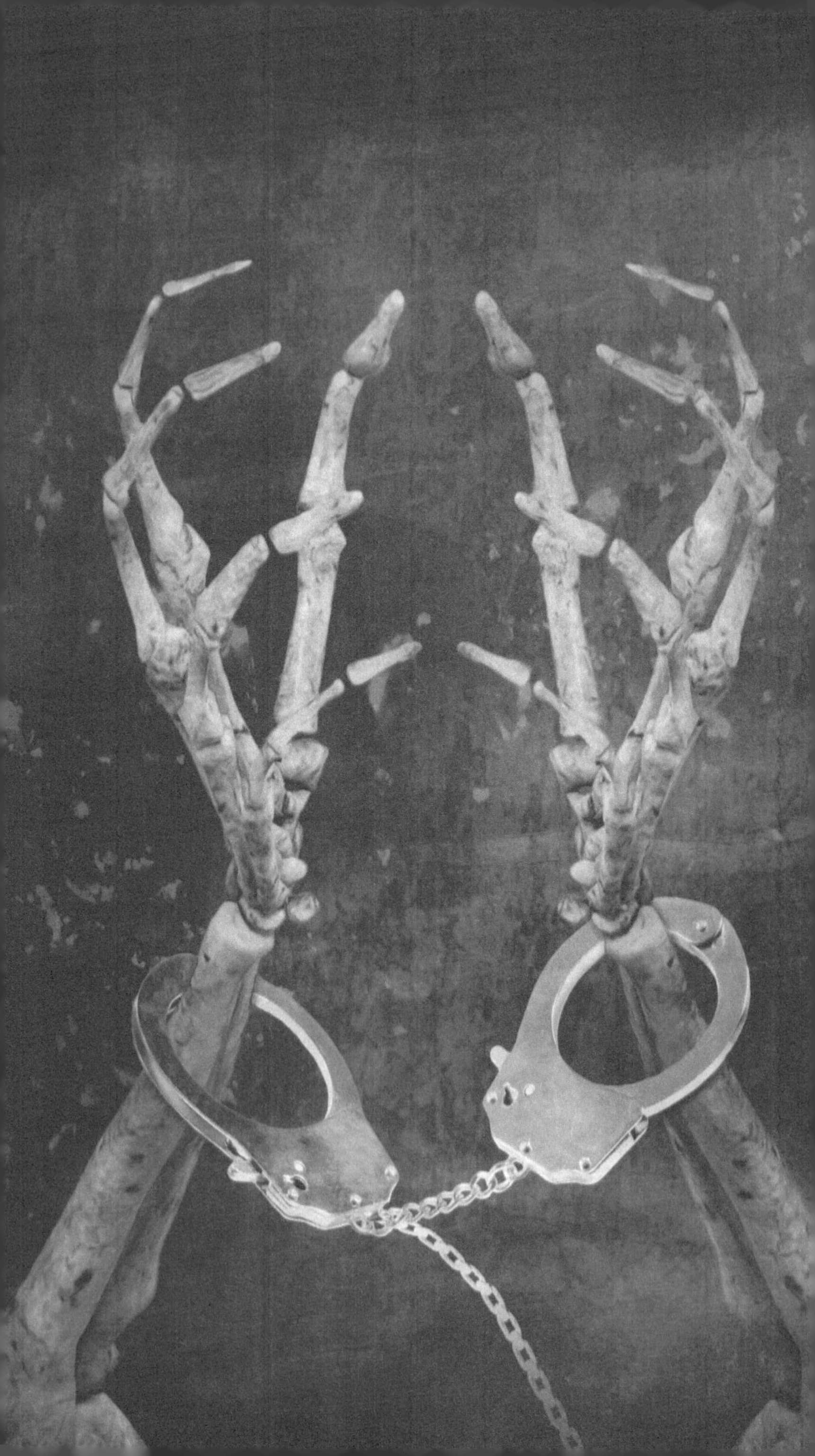

CHAPTER 21

MINA

I handed Rose a cup of steaming tea Gianni made and lowered myself down beside her. "Are you okay?"

She offered me a smile. "I should be asking you that."

I shrugged. "I'm fine." After a moment I added, "More or less."

I sipped my own tea and winced at how hot it still was. "How did he—"

"I got a frantic phone call from a friend, asking for help," Rose said. "Turns out she had a gun to her head. When I got there, I was overpowered. He brought me here and convinced one of the staff to open the door. That's everything I know until you showed up."

Damon sat down on the other side of me. In his hand, he held what looked like a triple whiskey. He and Gianni, with help from the twins, had taken Kurt down to the basement. "He's still alive. For now. Terry and his frying pan knew just the right place to connect."

I managed a small smile for the gentle giant. If it wasn't for him, things might have worked out very differently.

"According to the twins, he hid out when the asshole showed up." Gianni sat on the floor beside my feet and placed his own cup of tea on the table.

"Are you talking about us?" The twins approached before squeezing onto one of the chairs together.

"I'm glad you're both alive," I told them.

"Us too," Hunter agreed. "We found Jase and Wade in the kitchen. One of them went for Parker."

"Hunter warned me just in time for me to turn around so he could fall on my knife," Parker said cheerfully. He leaned into his twin and grinned.

"And Parker gave me the opportunity to dispose of the other one," Hunter said. "We were going to come and help, but that's when we saw Terry. He was waiting for the right moment, so we waited with him. If anyone deserves a trophy, it's him."

Gianni grinned. "Terry is the real MVP here." He waved over at Terry, who was in the kitchen making sandwiches with Daze and a couple of the Demons. "He deserves a raise, right, boss?"

We all turned to Reuben, who was standing off to the side of the room, talking to Caleb. I couldn't hear what they were saying, but Reuben was clearly worried about his younger brothers. All of them. And as relieved they were alive as I was.

Reuben nodded. "He does. Double." After a moment he amended that to, "Triple."

"And a Maserati," Hunter said.

Terry raised his eyebrows, but didn't look like he'd decline if a fancy car turned up at the door with his name on it. Personally, I'd give him just about anything he wanted right now. I had a suspicion he wouldn't ask for much anyway. He seemed to enjoy a simple life.

"Aidan and his boys took care of everyone at the front," Gianni said. "A couple of them gave them trouble, but they won't give anyone any trouble anymore."

"Neither will any of the ones inside the house," Damon said darkly. "Some of them were quick enough to turn on Kurt. The rest will be dealt with in the morning."

Reuben patted Caleb on the shoulder and came over to join us. "We have some work to do to seize the rest of Kurt's assets, but Caleb is going to get a start on that tomorrow. You two can help." He nodded to the twins.

They responded with identical grimaces, but ultimately shrugged and nodded in return.

"Whatever it takes to tear him down the rest of the way," Hunter said.

"And make an example for anyone else." Reuben sank into a chair and rubbed his forehead. "We also need to destroy the access from the water tank. Too many people know about it."

"I'll put that on the to do list for tomorrow," Damon said. "I've already ordered a cleanup on all of those exploded SUVs. People will start asking questions if we leave them as they are."

"Let them ask questions," Gianni said. "We can give them honest answers. It was all Kurt Lasalle's fault. He got too big for his boots and decided to come after us. But, because we're awesome, we won."

"We did, didn't we?" I asked. "It's over." I couldn't begin to get my head around it. After everything we'd all been through in the last few months, we finally had Kurt. He'd never touch any of us again.

Rose put her arm around me and held me carefully. "Yes it is. You're finally free to live your best life. Just like you always were supposed to."

I placed what was left of my tea down on the table in front of me and hugged her back. "I'm sorry you got dragged into this. You deserve better."

"We both do," she said firmly. "I saw the expression on your face. You would have gone through with it. You would have gone back with him to save all of us. You must have a uterus of steel. Like balls of steel, but a lot stronger."

"I would have," I agreed. "I couldn't see any other way out. He would have killed all of you without a second thought. He would have laughed at the expression on my face while he did it. He would have reminded me of it, over and over again until I broke."

"Just like he did with that girl?" Rose asked gently.

I was too tired to hide my surprise, or pretend to be confused. "Just like that."

"Her name was Jana," Rose said. "I heard the rumour about Kurt being the Sparrow, and did some digging. According to my sources, the Sparrow was on a job, and Jana died. The thing is, my sources confirmed that Kurt Lasalle was there that night, to do something else. I figured the Sparrow must be someone else."

"I guess that's possible," I said evasively. Most of the people in the room knew the truth, but not all of them. Those who didn't know didn't need to. I was relieved that my sister did though. I didn't want to keep any more secrets. Not from her.

"Who the hell are your contacts that you can find out something like that?" Caleb asked. He'd moved to stand behind the couch.

She glanced back at him and smiled. "I'll tell you mine if you tell me yours."

He grunted and moved away. Apparently not everything was smoothed over yet.

Hunter whispered something to Parker, which made him laugh.

"You think?" Parker looked at Rose, then over to Caleb.

I snorted and looked at Rose myself.

She looked amused. "I don't know who'd kill who first, me or him."

"You'd be adorable together," Hunter told her.

"How much did you bet that my sister would get together with your brother?" I asked bluntly.

Both twins grinned.

"We'll never tell," Parker said. "Twin privilege."

"I don't think that's a thing," Damon said.

"If you two don't have anything better to do than speculate on other people's love lives, then I better give you more work to do," Reuben said dryly.

"We have plenty to do," Hunter said. "We can multi-task. Right, Park?"

"Right," Parker said. "In fact, we have to go and do some of those things right now." He managed to ease himself out of the chair without tipping it over and sending Hunter sprawling.

I stood too and gave them both a hug each. "Thank you."

"For what?" Hunter asked. "We were just doing our jobs."

"You were being the best younger brothers I ever had," I said. "The only ones, but still the best."

"I guess that makes Rose our big sister too," Parker said. "Which means she can't get together with Caleb. That would be weird."

"It totally wouldn't," Hunter argued. They headed away up the stairs, friendly banter following them the whole way.

Rose shook her head. "Those two are a pair."

"Pair of clowns," Gianni said, but in an affectionate way.

"A pair we thought were dead," I said softly. My heart had broken for a little while. Seeing them alive... I couldn't put it into words.

If they'd died, they would have left a huge hole in my wonderful, found family. A hole no one would have been able to fill. No one I ever met was quite like the Brantley twins.

The younger brothers I never had. The younger brothers who'd always have my back and I'd have theirs.

"Pair of cockroaches then," Gianni said jokingly. "Always underfoot, but virtually impossible to kill."

Damon grunted a laugh. "That sounds about right. Just don't tell them that, they might start to think they're invincible." He didn't need to remind us that none of us actually were.

I suspected we all felt very mortal right now. I certainly did.

If not for Terry...

I'd have to try to think of a way to thank him for what he did. Him and his frying pan. He'd succeeded where guns, knives and technology had failed. Sometimes the simple, old-fashioned methods worked the best. I, for one, would never look at a frying pan the same way again.

Thinking about the kitchen brought my mind back to something I'd tried hard not to think about. Something I had to face, whether I liked it or not. There were still a couple more demons I had to put to rest.

I licked my lips. "I need to see Jase and Wade. I need to be sure it's them and that they're really dead."

If I didn't see with my own eyes, I'd never fully believe it. I'd never put them behind me. In the back of my mind, I'd always wonder if they were still out there, coming for me.

Fuck that. I wasn't going to live my life in fear of them. Not when there was no need.

"Are you sure, sweetheart?" Gianni asked gently. "I know you're not scared of death, but…"

"I'm sure," I said. "I need to do this now." I'd hesitated long enough, drinking tea and talking instead. Filling in the moments before I faced those ghosts.

I left Rose on the couch and walked with my three men, to the side of the kitchen, where a row of bodies lay. Mostly faces I didn't recognise. Several men and a couple of women. None whose deaths I'd mourn. They made up their minds when they worked for Kurt. They wouldn't get any sympathy from me.

I walked down to the end of the line and saw two faces I did know. Both already pale, and splattered with blood.

Jase had a gaping wound in his chest. His clothes were soaked with his blood. His eyes were half open, staring like he wanted to give me nightmare fuel even after he was gone.

Wade lay beside him, a smaller wound in the side of his neck. His clothes were also soaked with his blood, but his eyes closed, making him look almost peaceful.

He might have fooled me, if I didn't remember the way he looked when he was alive. Not to mention the things he'd done.

"That's them," I said. "That's all of them. Leon, Jase, Wade and Kurt. And my father."

"Kurt isn't dead yet," Gianni reminded me. "But that's just a formality we can rectify any time you're ready." He looked like he was looking forward to doing just that.

Of course he was; so was I. We all were.

I had no doubt they'd give me first choice, otherwise they might resort to rock, paper, scissors to decide who ultimately took his life. Even Reuben looked keen to get his hands dirty himself, just this once.

"You might want to hold off for a little while," Damon said. "I have a surprise for you. Something I think you'll like."

"It can wait until morning," Reuben said. "We all need rest first."

No one bothered to argue with him. What I needed right now was a quick shower and a long nap.

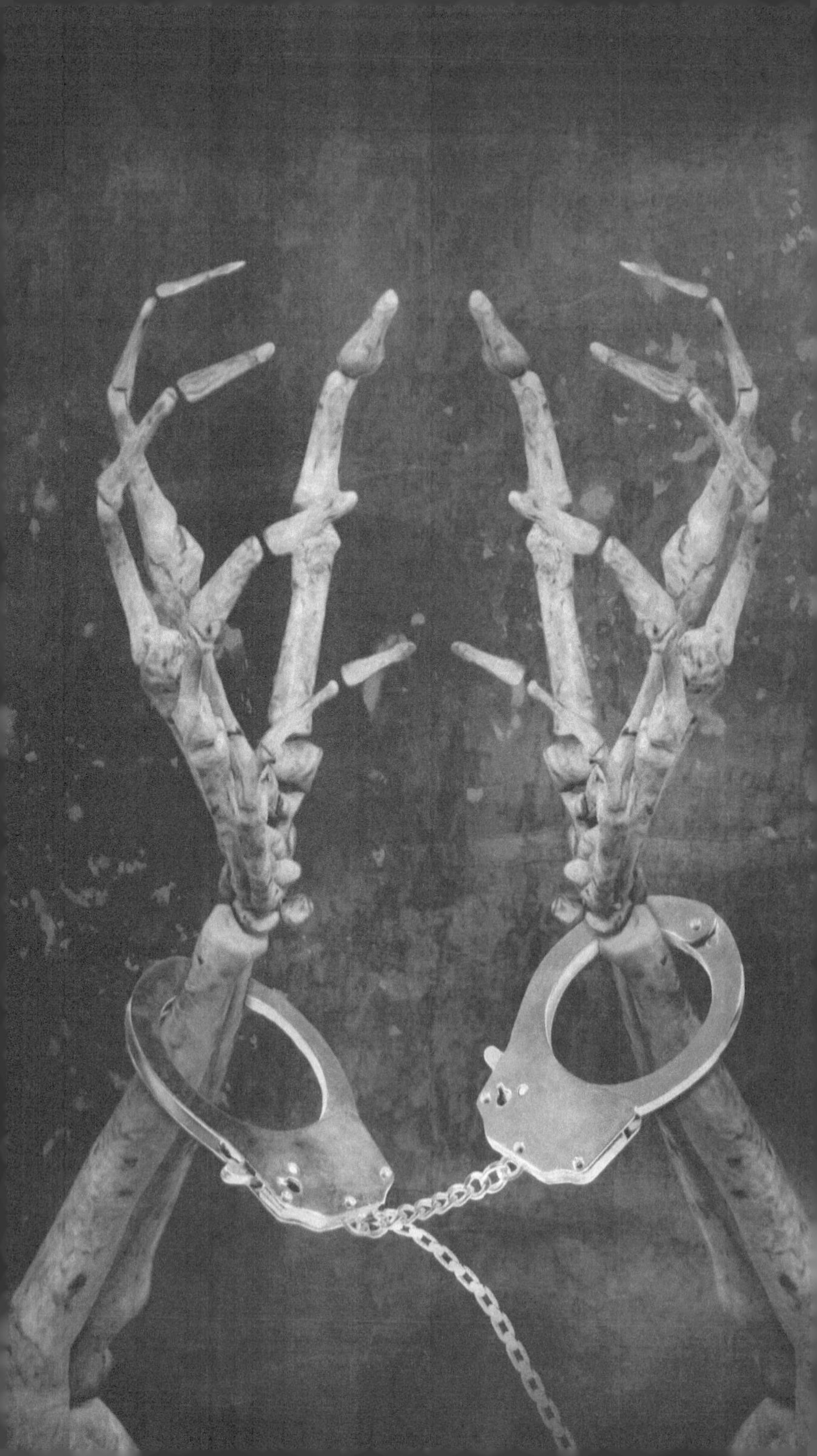

CHAPTER 22

MINA

"Don't ask if I'm all right," I told my men as they followed me into Reuben's bedroom.

"Were we going to do that?" Gianni asked. He turned back around to face the other two, his hands spread to either side.

"Yes." Damon stepped around him, into the room. "That's exactly what we were going to do." He looked at me questioningly.

"I'm fine," I said with a sigh.

I touched my mouth, where the duct tape was adhered. Taking it off had sucked like a bitch, but it was better than having it on there. The cable tie only needed a snip with a decent pair of scissors. Being restrained by that was worse than the tape over my mouth.

If anything was going to give me nightmares, it was that.

All three of them looked at me sceptically.

"I'm *fine*," I insisted. "Tired, relieved and okay. And in need of some hot water."

"I'll turn it on." Gianni hurried to the ensuite to turn on the shower.

"I'll help you in." Damon nodded for me to raise my hands, before gripping the hem of my T-shirt and pulling it over my head.

Reuben undid the clasp of my bra. I dropped my arms to let it fall to the floor.

Damon undid the front of my jeans and they both worked them down my legs and off my feet.

"Thank you," I said graciously before stepping towards the shower. Gianni was already naked, and ready with the body wash. All I had to do was step under the delicious warmth and let it wash the night away.

"Turn around," Gianni said.

I turned to face the water and let him rub body wash all over my back before massaging it into a lather. I closed my eyes and enjoyed the way his hands felt on me, and the occasional brush of his erection against me.

"You're so tense," he said. He worked out the knot in one of my shoulders while Damon and Reuben stripped off and joined us, using the shower head on the opposite wall.

They moved around each other carefully, not quite touching while they washed, but both with erect cocks.

"It's been a long night," I pointed out.

"Very long." He pressed the head of his cock against me deliberately.

I reached around behind me to grip his length and run my hand up and down from his head to his balls. "Very long and very hard."

He moaned softly. "Accurate." He rinsed the last of the body wash off me and his hands, before shampooing my hair and turning me around to rinse that off too.

While I washed it away, he slipped his hand between my legs and rubbed it back and forth over my pussy.

It was my turn to moan.

After all we'd been through for the last handful of hours, he still got me going. His touch and the sight of the other two men, virtually dancing around each other.

Finally, Damon grabbed a bar of soap and started to wash Reuben's back. That was all he did, but the intimacy was both endearing and arousing.

If I ever doubted the way they felt about each other, I didn't anymore. They went way beyond being boss and employee or even brothers. I wasn't sure when they'd crossed that line, but they had. They'd become something much more. Something deeper.

"Cute, aren't they?" Gianni asked. He let his feelings for Damon show on his face. He cared about him, wanted to be physical with him, but I wasn't sure if they'd ever have a deeper relationship. His heart was with me.

Reuben and Damon, their hearts were with me, and with each other.

"Very cute," I said breathlessly.

Cuter still when Reuben turned around and kissed Damon, while Damon slowly pumped Reuben's cock. Okay, maybe cute wasn't the word. Smoking hot might be more accurate.

Gianni sank to his knees in front of me and gently parted my legs, just far enough to be able to tease my pussy with his tongue.

"Why are you always so delicious?" he asked.

I assumed that was a rhetorical question, because I couldn't respond with words. Just a groan as he slid a finger inside me, then another.

I kept my eyes half open, watching Reuben and Damon become more bold with touching each other. They both had their hands curled around each other's cocks. Reuben's touch was more tentative than Damon's. Like he'd imagined doing this, but never thought the moment would come.

I was the next to come, my head back under the hot water as I rolled my hips, increasing the friction as Gianni fucked me with his tongue and hand.

The world exploded in fireworks, and something I'd never experienced before. A true and absolute sensation of letting go. I held absolutely nothing back, not one drop of blood, not one beat of my heart. Heat roared through my body like an inferno, engulfing me, burning me down to my core before I was reborn from the ashes.

In that moment, my past was finally behind me. I could be the woman I was always meant to be. Fully, totally free, belonging only to these three men, and to myself.

Finally, I drifted back down to reality, panting lightly.

I waited until Gianni pulled his fingers out of me to pull him to his feet and wrap my leg around his waist. I positioned the entrance of my pussy against his cock and nudged him with my heel on his ass.

He obliged by sliding slowly and carefully into me, my back pressed against the side of the shower.

"Why do you always feel incredible?" he said breathlessly. Another rhetorical question, because after that we only communicated with thrusts, rolls of our hips and moans.

His piercings massaged my insides and drove me all the way back to the edge, holding me there for the longest time while he thrust into me with slow, deliberate, savouring strokes.

I sensed he felt my epiphany. Maybe he experienced it too.

Where before we felt like time was limited, now we knew it wasn't. We won, and now we got to enjoy that wonderful, beautiful victory.

The only sound in my ears was the roar of blood and the delicious sound of three men close to coming. Was

Gianni waiting for Damon and Reuben? If he did, he timed it to perfection.

Almost simultaneously, all three men reached their orgasm, grunting, groaning and thrusting hard and fast.

Reuben and Damon spilled themselves into each other's hands and Gianni into my body. The hot water from the other shower head quickly washed away the pearly cum, from their fingers, but the sight of it was something none of us would ever forget.

It wasn't just release, it was acceptance.

Love.

It meant everything and it was arousing as hell.

I tipped my head back and closed my eyes, letting Gianni's piercings hit me at exactly the right angle. The friction from them was fucking incredible. The gift he gave me by having them was next level.

I came for a second time, along with them. The shower was awash with steam and bliss. My whole body was alight with pleasure, even more intense and powerful than the first time.

It was like nothing I had ever experienced before. A rush of moisture gushed from me, drenching Gianni's cock even more.

"Good girl," he managed to say, his words strained as he was still coming down from his own orgasm. "You fuck so beautifully. Not like anyone else I've ever met. So perfect. So fucking ours."

"So yours," I agreed when I was finally able to speak again. "So yours. You're all so mine."

I was the luckiest girl in the world.

Maybe I had to go through what I went through in order to end up here. In which case, maybe it was worth it. If this was the light at the end of a long, pitch black tunnel, then I was happy to bask in every bit of that glow.

Reuben and Damon exchanged soft looks. They didn't say the words out loud, but we heard and understood. They were so each other's too.

"Let's get out of here," Reuben said finally. "It's past time for us to get some rest." He didn't look as though he regretted taking the time to shower first. Partly because he would have been as dirty as the rest of us and partly because he'd taken this next, huge step.

"Good idea, boss," Gianni said.

"Yeah, good idea." Damon looked like he didn't know if should address Reuben as boss or something else. Evidently, that was a conversation for later. He stepped out of the shower and started to dry himself before tossing a towel to each of us as we stepped out with him.

"This feels like it was always meant to be this way." Gianni dried himself and wrapped his towel around his waist. He grabbed another to start drying my hair. "All four of us. We all had dysfunctional families, to some extent, but we all found each other and now we're family."

"We are," Reuben agreed. He too finished drying and wrapped his own towel around his waist. He seemed lighter as well. Like he'd spent years carrying the weight of the world on his shoulders and now he was sharing that weight. With us and with his brothers.

In spite of his stoic exterior, I suspected this was a relief for him. He had been raised to take over the family, but that was an enormous job for one person. His pride had stopped him from delegating as much as he should have. Maybe now he'd do more of that. After all, the twins did need to be kept busy. And I suspected Caleb would appreciate more responsibility.

I wondered if I could convince Reuben to step down as head of the family and hand it over to one of his brothers. Probably not, but I'd do what I could to lighten his load.

"And family looks after family," Gianni said. He put the towel aside and picked up a brush to start on my hair. "Especially when they're the family you choose. That's the best kind of family."

"They certainly make more sense than people we're related to by blood," Damon said dryly. It seemed as though he and Enzo still had some work to do. Hopefully they'd sort things out. I had a feeling they both needed each other more than they realised.

Which reminded me, there were some conversations I needed to have. Asher was at the top of that list. But that list could wait until tomorrow. For now, I want to snuggle up with my incredible men, and get some rest.

I didn't bother with a towel. Once I was dry and

brushed, I padded over to the bed and climbed in, laying in the centre.

Gianni crept under the covers on one side and Reuben and Damon on the other. They all shuffled over closer to me and each other, close enough that I felt their presence, warm and solid.

After so much death tonight, I felt very much alive.

So loved.

The next day wouldn't be easy, but we'd get through it. Together.

I closed my eyes and listened as one by one, they drifted off to sleep. Gianni started to snore slightly.

A smile on my lips, I drifted off as well. Into a sleep full of dreams, which bordered on nightmares. None as terrifying as the ones I used to have. Those gradually retreated to the back of my mind, ready to be forgotten.

Finally.

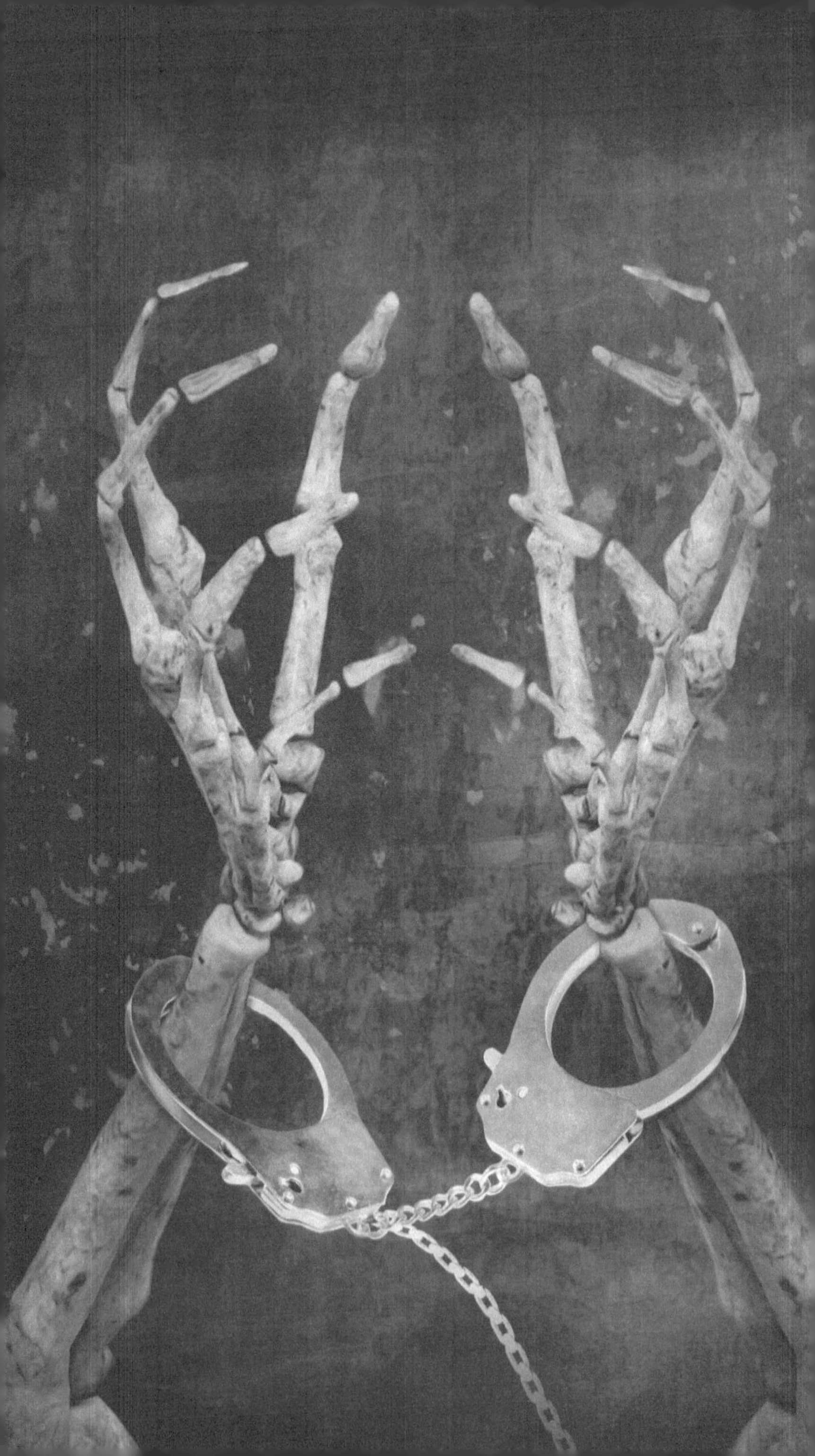

CHAPTER 23

MINA

"Are you going to make me close my eyes?" I asked.

They hadn't suggested blindfolding me, but Damon and Gianni looked cagey as fuck. Even Reuben was watching me for my reaction as they led me down the stairs to the basement.

After a long night, we all got a few hours of sleep. Fitful and full of dreams, but much-needed sleep.

"You could," Gianni said. "You trust us not to let you fall or walk into anything, right?"

"Of course I do," I said. "I'm just curious what's going on. You didn't kill him yet, did you?"

"Absolutely not," Gianni said. "We wouldn't kill him without you knowing about it. No, we've gone to great lengths to ensure he enjoys his time with us for as long as we want him to. And when I say enjoy, I mean… Why don't we show you?"

Gianni stood behind me and placed his hands on my shoulders.

Damon nodded at me to close my eyes, and put his hand on the door handle.

I exhaled playfully, as though annoyed with them, but closed my eyes and let Gianni steer me forward, one step at a time.

The first thing I noticed was the tang of blood, mingled with sweat. The rattle of something all-too-familiar. A soft, pained groan.

"Okay, open your eyes," Damon said.

I hesitated for a moment, before opening them and staring at the sight in front of me.

On the floor, in the corner of the basement was a cage. It was big enough to fit a large dog, but not big enough to comfortably fit a large human.

Kurt was hunched up inside, both ankles circled with manacles attached to chains on the wall behind the cage. His hands were free, gripping the bars of the cage as he stared at us.

"Surprise," Damon said blandly. "I figured he could use a taste of his own, sour medicine."

"You did this?" I looked up at him.

"It's been in the works for a while." He shrugged. "But yes, I did this."

I wrapped my arms around his neck and pulled him down for a kiss. "I love you. This is the perfect surprise. You knew exactly what I wanted, when I didn't."

It hadn't occurred to me to do to Kurt what he did to

me. Although, in retrospect, it should have. He deserved exactly this.

"Damon is so thoughtful," Gianni enthused. "I have to admit, I was just thinking chains. The cage is…" He mimed a chef's kiss.

"It was inspired," Reuben agreed. "We should have had one of these down here already."

"No one else has quite fitted one as well as he does," Damon said modestly. "I'd suggest it's because he's a dog, but that would be an insult to dogs."

"It certainly would." I stepped closer to the cage. So, this was how it felt to look at someone the same way he looked at me for so long. He looked sad and pathetic. Scared, but still with a hint of defiance. Somewhere, in the back of his mind, he was still convinced he was in the right. That maybe I came to let him out and we could live our lives together.

He must have been out of his fucking mind.

"Mina," he said softly. "I was hoping you'd come to me. I know you missed me as much as I missed you. You and I, we belong together."

I crouched down in front of him. "You must be delusional. You have been for a long time. I'm sorry you never got the help you clearly needed. If you had, we might not be here now."

"You can help me to get help," he said. "I can get better and we can be together."

They were just words, he seriously didn't think anything was wrong with him. He didn't seem to grasp the concept of what he did to me was fucked up. Had Terry hit him so hard he'd broken something in his brain? He was always a little unhinged, but this was new, even for him.

"I don't want to be with you, Kurt," I said bluntly. "I never have. That was why you had to cage me, remember?"

He frowned. "Cage you? I would never do that to you, Mina. I love you." He reached his hand out towards me.

I shifted away and glanced back at my guys. They all looked as doubtful as I felt.

I turned back to Kurt. "What was the last thing you remember?"

He looked even more confused. "I remember… We practised this morning. You're getting so good at throwing me over your shoulder." He actually looked proud. "Then we went to… You had a job. I waited outside. I shouldn't have been there, I know that. I just like watching you sneak in and sneak back out. You're incredible to watch. Oh, I was thinking about this the other day. I think Fiori is the perfect name for you."

I stood and stepped away, my blood cold. "I remember that conversation. My father was trying to encourage me to choose something else." I shook my head as I thought back. "Fiori. It's Italian for flower. My mother was obsessed with flowers."

"Right," Kurt said. "Fiori. But he didn't like it. He said it was the name of a car."

"It was," I said. "A Subaru. He didn't want me to have the same name as a car." This whole conversation was surreal. I hadn't thought about any of this for years. At least seven or eight.

Kurt chuckled. "I'm sorry I teased you about that. You're right, flower would be perfect. You always were a beautiful flower." He cocked his head at me.

I swallowed down the small breakfast I'd managed to eat before the guys brought me down here. I glanced at them again. I didn't know what to think. In his mind, it was like the last few years never happened. Like he never laid a hand on me.

"What are they doing here?" Kurt asked. "Why am I in this cage?" He kicked his feet, rattling the chains. "Is this some kind of prank your brothers are pulling on me? No offence, but it's not funny." He was starting to become agitated.

"It's not a prank," I said quietly. "You held me in a cage for five years. Just like this one."

"I would never—" he started.

"You raped me. So many times I lost count." I leaned back against Reuben as he stood behind me, his hands on my upper arms.

Kurt's eyes widened. "Mina! I would never do that to you. I know it's going to take some time for you to turn to me, but you will. When you do, you'll willingly give yourself to me. Why would I force myself on you?"

He looked horrified. Not as horrified as I felt. Those moments ran over and over in my head on repeat, hard as I tried to ignore them and push them away. I could still feel him on top of me, pinning me down, pushing himself into me. Thrusting.

I swallowed hard. "It was what you did. You even had one of your friends video you raping me. I saw it. They saw it." I jerked my head towards my guys.

"Yes, we did," Damon said coldly.

Kurt gaped before sinking back to the back of the cage. "I wouldn't do that. I wouldn't do that. I wouldn't do that." He said it over and over at least a dozen times, while shaking his head.

"What the fuck do we do now?" Gianni asked. "He's still the same asshole."

My tongue swept over my bottom lip. He was, but at the same time, he wasn't. Terry must have hit him extremely hard.

In Kurt's mind, he hadn't harmed a hair on my head. Maybe, like this, he was harmless. Defenceless. Could we actually kill him like this? If we didn't, then I had no idea what we'd do with him.

"You could let me out of here," Kurt said pitifully. "Whatever I did, I'll make it up to you. I swear. Whatever you need me to do, I'll do it. If you think I need help, I'll get help. Just please..." He crawled back to the front of the cage and gripped the bars again.

"Please, let me out of here." He looked like he was going to burst into tears.

Something I'd never seen him do. Something I never would have thought he was capable of.

Reuben stepped forward, crouched down right in front of Kurt. "No," he said simply. There was an air of absolute finality in his tone. It didn't matter what I said, Reuben was absolutely not letting him walk away. Never.

Kurt's expression changed like a switch was flipped. He snarled at Reuben and tried to take a swing at him. He couldn't reach through the bars, Reuben was just out of reach.

"Reuben motherfucking Brantley," Kurt growled. "You think you're so fucking better than everyone else. You and your asshole sidekicks and your slut." He glared at me, teeth bared.

"It was all an act," I said softly.

Of course it was, he'd always been a good actor. He must have figured this was his only chance. If he appealed to my humanity, maybe, just maybe, I'd go soft on him. At least I had some humanity left. He had none, not even a tiny bit.

The grin he gave me was brutal and nasty. "You almost bought it, stupid bitch." He raised his voice to a high-pitch. "Mina, Mina, I never touched a hair on your fucking body. I *sweeeear.*"

He closed his mouth and smirked. "You would have let me out, wouldn't you? You would have let me walk out of here. I would have come straight back for you. You would have been the one in the cage again. Like the stupid bitch you are. Fucking slut. You spread your legs for the first man that came along. Didn't you? *Didn't you?*"

"At least we know what to do next," Gianni said. "Let's see how long he lasts in that cage. I'll tell Terry to save some scraps to feed him every few days. Maybe some water here or there. What about some country music thrown in for shits and giggles?"

Kurt jerked his legs against the chains. "Fuck off. Get it over with and kill me. You know you all want to."

He lifted his chin, as though daring me to grab another length of chain and wrap it around his throat. Tempting, but that would be far too easy.

"All the more reason to leave you alive," I said. "Because you want to die, just like I did. And it gives us something else to look forward to, when we get bored."

I yawned playfully, my hand in front of my mouth. It was past time I had some fun with this asshole. He'd had the upper hand for long enough. Now it was my turn.

"Fucking bitch!" he snarled.

"Sticks and stones, Kurt," I said. "Sticks and stones." I turned around to leave, but then turned back. "Gianni, do you think Terry will let me borrow his blowtorch later? I have a favour to repay."

Kurt glanced down at his chest and shook his head. He started to plead and went on pleading as we left the basement, closing the door behind us.

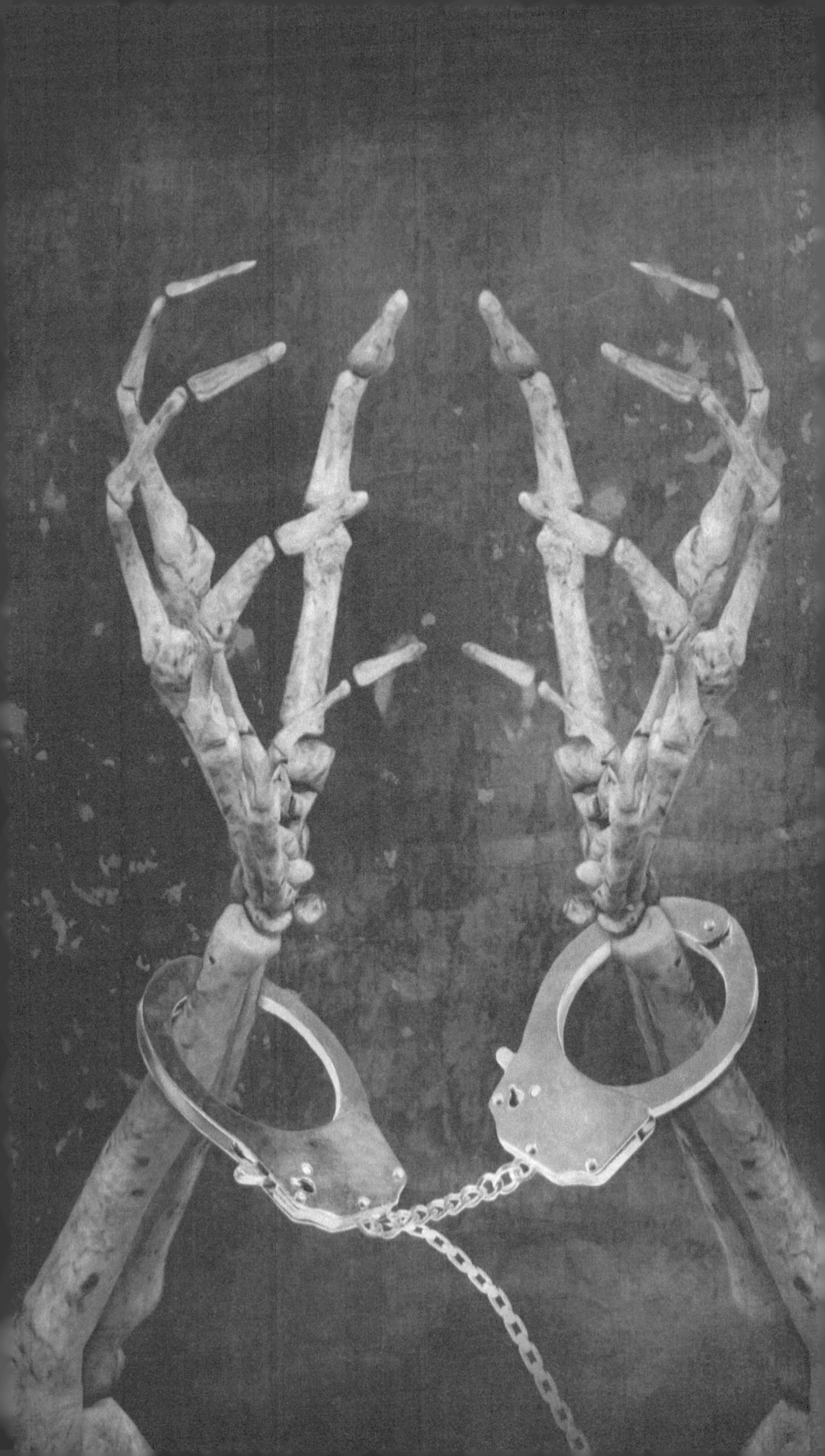

CHAPTER 24

GIANNI

"This is the life." I laced my fingers together and placed my hands behind my head. I leaned against the back of the outdoor lounge and gazed out at the view.

"It could be worse," Damon agreed. He sat down beside me and copied my pose.

"It has been worse." Mina sat on the other side of me, her legs crossed. She wore black leggings and a dark purple T-shirt with the logo of Bobby Starlight, her childhood favourite pop star, on the front. She wore her brown hair tied back in a ponytail.

For the first time since I saw her in that cage, she looked like a woman who was almost twenty-four, not so tired and world-weary. Not quite carefree, but we'd work on that.

Reuben sat on the edge of the lounge, lost in thought. His polo necked shirt looked new. It might have been hanging in his wardrobe for years, but he hadn't let himself relax enough to wear it. It wouldn't last long, but it was good to see him take a rare day off.

Mina uncurled and walked on her knees to place her hands on his shoulders. She started to massage them lightly, her upper body pressed against his back. "You should get a professional masseuse."

He dropped his chin down to his chest. "Why would I need one when I have you?"

She laughed, soft and husky. "Because I'm not a professional. Although, maybe now I could be. I could go back to school and get myself a day job. Something to keep me busy between contracts."

"If you need the money—" Reuben started.

"I don't," she said quickly. "I just want to do something interesting with my life. Maybe not masseuse. I wouldn't mind learning about technology and how to use it the way the twins do. Then you wouldn't have to call on them all the time for things like that."

Reuben grunted. "It keeps them busy, but if you want to study, you can. Any university would be lucky to have you. Brutham Academy has an excellent computer science department. The campus is a long way from here or Sydney. For a number of reasons, they don't do external study."

"You're on the board of Brutham," I pointed out. "They'd open a campus here in Dusk Bay if you insisted on it. And funded it. We could live here during term time and back in Sydney when Mina isn't studying."

"You could go back to school too," Damon said. "Learn how to do something useful."

I flipped him off. "Ha fucking ha. I'm very useful." I rolled onto my side to face him. "If I went back to school, it would be to teach. Psychological torture one-oh-one."

He turned his face until his nose was almost touching mine. "You're an expert at that. I feel psychologically tortured right now." His eyes shone with humour, his equivalent of laughing.

"The only thing you're suffering from right now is the suppressed desire to fuck me," I said. "An issue I'm happy to rectify any time."

His eyes were immediately darker.

Nail, meet head.

I lay perfectly still. He'd either make the first move, or he'd shift back away from me. Whatever he'd do was fine with me. I wouldn't put any pressure on him to…

The thoughts flew out of my head when he moved closer, brushing his lips over mine.

Then I was kissing him back, deepening the kiss before rolling onto my back and pulling him with me. His upper body lay across mine, growing erection pressing into me.

I slipped my hands up the back of his shirt and over his firm, scarred skin. Every centimetre of him was warm under my palms. With every caress, I wanted to feel more of him.

He groaned and pushed his tongue between my lips, like he was thrusting into me.

I was so hard by now, I'd be lucky if I didn't lose my load in my track pants. I managed to whisper his name right before I undid the front of his pants and pushed them down so I could palm his cock.

I raised my hips so he could pull down my track pants and do the same to me. His hand was hot and firm around my length. His fingers explored my piercings with fascination.

"Did they hurt?" He broke off our kiss to look down at my cock.

I glanced down too, marvelling at the way his hand fit around me. "A little, but it's completely worth it."

"It definitely is," Mina agreed. She and Reuben were watching us with heated expressions. He gripped her hips and pulled her over to straddle his lap. His hands slipped up the front of her T-shirt so he could palm her breasts. She pulled her T-shirt off over her head and threw it aside. She wasn't wearing a bra.

"So fucking gorgeous," Damon whispered.

"I know I am." I pulled him back in for another kiss. He grunt-laughed against my mouth, but kissed me back.

I grabbed the back of his T-shirt and pulled it up over his head. He did the same for me before we both shimmied the rest of the way out of our pants.

Mina discarded hers, before helping Reuben out of

his. She placed her hands on his shoulders and lowered herself down onto his length.

"If you want to…" I raised my eyebrows at Damon.

He swallowed visibly and nodded before pushing himself up off the lounge and heading inside. He returned a minute or two later with a tube of lube in his hand. He gestured for me to lie on my side and opened the tube to squirt some lube onto his fingers.

Eagerly, I lay still while he applied the cool lube to my rear hole. Tentatively, he pressed a slippery finger inside and worked it around to spread the lube and relax my muscles. He added a second finger, which made me quiver with pleasure and anticipation.

"Have you ever been fucked here?" he asked.

"Not recently," I said. "But yes. Please… I need you inside me."

He lay down behind me and pressed the tip of his cock to my entrance. "I don't want to hurt you."

"Yes, you do," I said teasingly.

He hesitated for a moment before bringing his hand down hard against my ass cheek.

My eyes widened and I almost came on the spot. I groaned. "More of that. Please."

He slapped my ass a couple more times, harder each time. Stinging, but perfect. After the third slap, he pushed himself inside me. Slowly at first, stopping to let me stretch and get used to having him inside me.

"That feels so good," I said.

"You're so fucking tight," he groaned. He pushed himself all the way inside me and lay still for a while.

I savoured the way he felt inside me, while watching Mina bouncing on Reuben's lap, her breasts bouncing with her.

"Good girl," I told her. "You're making him feel so good, with your perfect pussy."

Reuben's hand was between her legs, massaging her clit while she rode him. "She's a very good girl," he agreed. "The best." His voice was strained, attention split between looking at her in front of him, and watching Damon fuck my ass. Not with any jealousy, just with fascination and approval that I was making Damon feel good.

Damon snaked a hand over my hip to grip my cock. He pumped it at the same time as he thrust into me.

I moaned. "Fucking hell, I'm going to come."

"Me too," he said. "Can I…"

"Come inside me," I said. "Please. Fill me with your cum." That threw us both over the edge, coming hard and fast with each other. My balls clenched tight before exploding in his hand, covering his fingers with pearly, warm cum. At the same time, he filled my ass with his.

Reuben and Mina came moments later, him grunting while she tipped her head back and screamed out his name. I'd never get enough of watching her come. Him either. They were both hotter than hell. Sexy, smart and incredible. And mine.

Damon slumped down behind me, puffing lightly. "That was amazing."

"I told you you liked me," I teased.

He actually laughed softly. "Maybe I do. Don't tell anyone, or I'll have to kill you."

"My lips are sealed," I said. "Until the next time they're on your cock."

He groaned. "You're going to make me hard again." He carefully slid out of me.

I rolled over to face him and grinned. "Sorry, not sorry. Making people hard is part of my job description. It's on Mina's as well." She'd been doing that since we met. "See, I do have useful skills."

"Possibly." He lightly kissed my mouth before rolling onto his back and exhaling.

I propped myself up on my elbow and looked out at the view. "I know we have to get back to Sydney tomorrow and back to work, but we can enjoy this for a while longer, can't we?"

"This is why I bought the place," Reuben said. "So my family could enjoy the peace of the ocean." His arms were around Mina, her face pressed against his chest. He was running his hand up and down her bare back, just lightly, lovingly. Like she was cherished. Like he could sit with her like that forever and never need another thing.

I couldn't remember having ever seen him look content before. He did now. Holding her like that, he looked as though he'd come home to someplace he'd wanted to be all his life.

I knew he'd loved her for a long, long time. Now he had her, he wasn't letting her go. Neither were Damon and I.

She was the piece of the puzzle that completed all of us. The sun the rest of us circled around. The centre of our universe. Our beautiful, badass assassin.

"And we do," I said. "I love my job, but it's nice to stop and smell the sea air once in a while."

Not for too long though. I'd get bored if I wasn't running around getting shot at, shooting people and slitting throats. Those were the things that made life worth living. Especially doing them with the people I loved.

"That reminds me." Mina raised her face reluctantly. "I've come to the conclusion that the Sparrow is too burnt. After the rumours we spread and whatever Kurt said about me, the Sparrow needs to die. Figuratively," she added quickly.

"What are you saying, sweetheart?" I asked gently. "You're going to give up being an assassin and become a hacker instead?" That would also be hot. Whatever she did, would be.

"No," she said. "I want to keep working as an assassin. But I want to build a new name. I want to use the one I would have chosen for myself if my father hadn't insisted. Fiori."

She looked shy, as though she thought we might

laugh, but if we did she was ready to deal with us. She wasn't taking shit from anyone, not anymore. She was so fucking strong, so beautiful it almost hurt. So incredible.

I'd never laugh at anything she ever wanted to do. Whatever she did, we'd support her, every single moment. The same way she'd support all of us.

"Flower." I smiled. "That's absolutely perfect. Just like you."

She smiled back and my heart never felt so full. I couldn't have been more proud of her. This new name was going to be even more successful and feared than the Sparrow. I couldn't wait to be on the sidelines, cheering her on. Maybe she'd even teach me some of her assassin skills.

She was so fucking perfect.

So fucking ours.

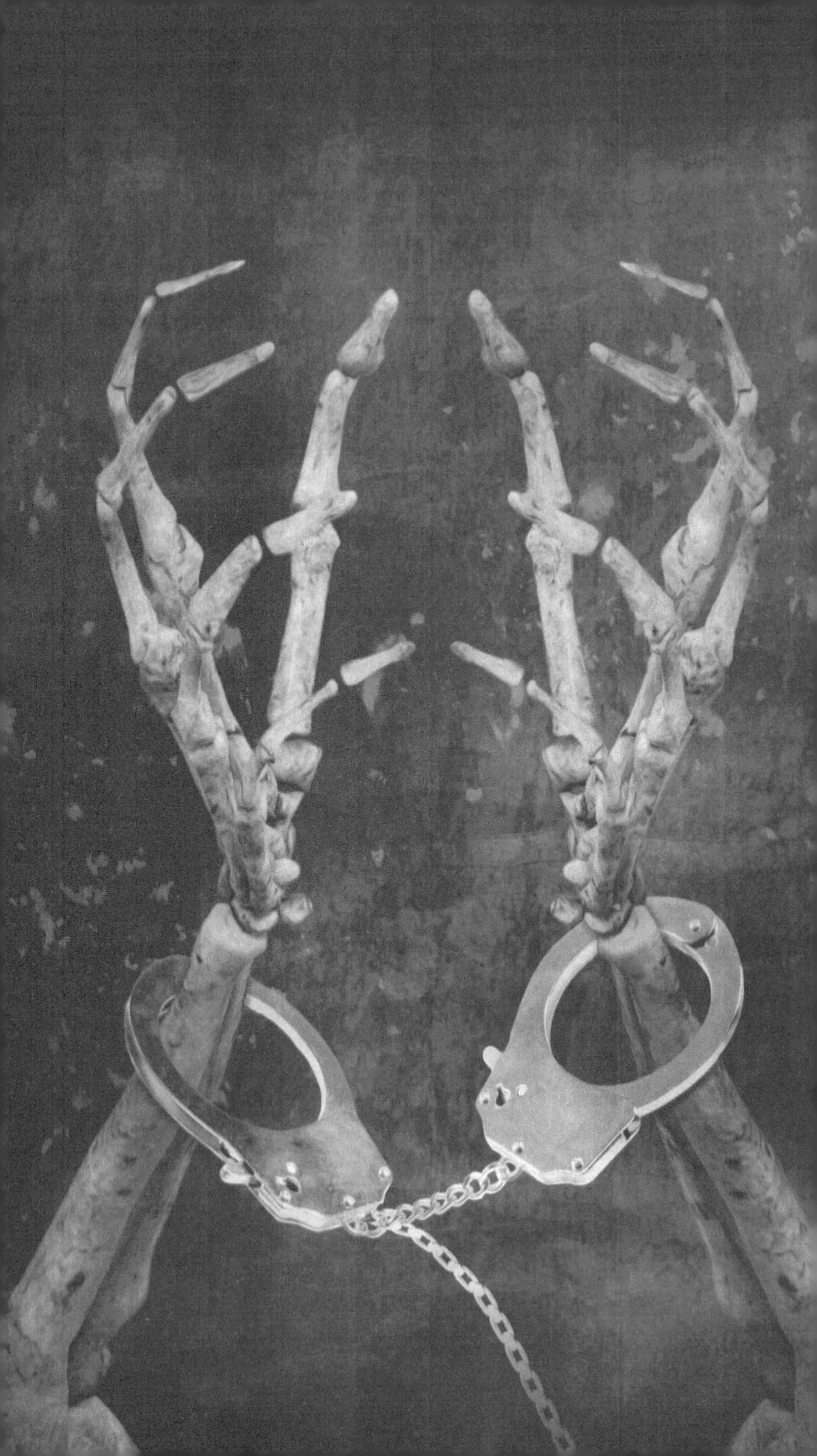

EPILOGUE

MINA

Voices came from Reuben's library.

I knew they were here, and why, but knowing that and stepping into the room, were two different things. I'd waited so long for this, but now I was paralysed.

I could let Asher go on living in his happy bubble, without ever seeing me. The selfless part of me wanted to do that. The realistic part of me knew he'd find out about me sooner or later. The longer I waited, the more hurt he'd be, knowing I was here all along.

I stopped outside the library door to listen to him and Zeke talking to Reuben. They'd brought their girl-friend, Abbie. Them and the twins were discussing something that took place at the end of Wolf Venom's world tour.

I knew the details, but was more interested in listening to my brother's voice than what they were talking about.

The twins were currently defending themselves to Zeke. I liked Zeke, but I couldn't help bristling slightly at his accusing tone. The twins could take care of themselves though, so there was no need for me to stab Reuben's rock star brother. If Reuben wanted him stabbed, he could have the twins do it.

I placed a hand on my swollen belly and held my breath.

At a break in the conversation, I took a few heavier steps forward, so everyone in the room would know I was there.

"You can come in," Reuben called out to me.

The nerves almost got the better of me, but I forced myself to step inside.

Asher's eyes widened the moment he saw me. He pushed himself out of his chair and gaped. His gaze slid to my pregnant belly. The first thing out of his mouth was, "Whose baby is that?"

I swallowed hard and tried to conjure the words. When they wouldn't come, it was Reuben who filled the heavy silence.

"Mine," he said. "And Gianni's, and Damon's.

Asher blinked a couple of times before putting his arms around me and giving me a careful hug. "I missed you. I'm super confused right now, but I missed you."

I hugged him back and laughed softly. "I missed you too."

I hugged Zeke when he also rose to embrace me. I

smiled at Abbie, who was looking at me and Reuben like she was wondering what I saw in him.

I tried not to bristle at that too, but I knew Reuben hadn't made their lives easier for the last little while. Hopefully we could start to change that today.

I sat down beside Reuben, my hand on his. "It's a long story." I took a deep breath and started.

"Six years ago…"

Thank you for reading. Please leave a review before you go!

If you want to read more about Mina's brother, Asher, you can find him in Saving Abbie.

For Daisy Lasalle's story, you'll find that in Dark Daze.

Hunter and Parker, and their girlfriend, have their own story, Brutal Academy.

If you'd like a light-hearted scene of Gianni and Mina, stealing a pop star's underwear, read the bonus scene here.

Next up is a rugby RH series, Ruck Boys. It starts with Filthy Ruck.

ABOUT THE AUTHOR

Maggie Alabaster writes reverse harem romance.

She lives in NSW, Australia with one spouse, two daughters, one dog, and countless birds.

Sign up for Maggie's newsletter! Sign Up!

Join Maggie's reader group! Join here!

Follow Maggie on Bookbub! Click here to follow me!

Check out Maggie's website- www.maggiealabaster.com

ALSO BY MAGGIE ALABASTER

Ruck Boys

Filthy Ruck

Sparrow and the Mafia Kings

Possessive

Ruined

Corrupted

Pucking Dark Hearts

Pucking Hearts Collide

Pucking Forbidden Hearts

Pucking Hardened Hearts

Dusk Bay Demons

Puck Drop

Breakaway

Power Play

Brutal Academy

Book 1 Heartless

Book 2 Cruel

Book 3 Vengeful

Court of Blood and Binding

Book 1 Song of Scent and Magic

Book 2 Crown of Mist and Heat

Book 3 Sword of Balm and Shadow

Book 4 Whisper of Frost and Flame

Dark Masque

Book 1 Bait

Book 2 Prey

Book 3 Trap

Saving Abbie

Book 1 Pitch

Book 2 Pound

Book 3 Session

Book 4 Muse

Book 5 Rhythm

Book 6 Encore

Novella Venomous

Saving Abbie books 1-4

Saving Abbie books 4-6 + Venomous

Ruthless Claws

Book 1 Ivory

Book 2 Crimson

Book 3 Elodie

Harmony's Magic

Book 1 Summoned by Fire

Book 2 Summoned by Fate

Book 3 Summoned by Desire

Shifter's Vault

Book 1 Discarded

Book 2 Deceived

Book 3 Disgraced

My Alien Mates

Book 1 Star Warriors

Book 2 Star Defenders

Book 3 Star Protectors

Academy of Modern Magic

Book 1 Digital Magic

Book 2 Virtual Magic

Book 3 Logical Magic

Complete Collection

Summer's Harem

Book 1: Shimmer

Book 2: Glimmer

Book 3: Flicker

Complete collection

Short reads

Taken by the Snowmen

Jingle All the Way

Also by Maggie Alabaster and Erin Yoshikawa

Caught by the Tide

Book 1–Pursued by Shadows

Book 2 Pursued by Darkness

Book 3 Pursued by Monsters